The Hous

Colvil tapped his cane as a golfer might to annoy a greenkeeper.

'We have a smidgen of a problem.'

'Then it shouldn't be too difficult to resolve. Mm?'

'Charles, please. So uncharitable.'

Bannister fidgeted. He had to be at Prime Minister's Questions, that twice a week, fifteen minute parliamentary gameshow played out to bolster the illusion of political leadership. As Party Chairman, Charles Bannister preferred to be at his master's elbow. Once when he attempted to reassure the Premier that he was right behind him, his leader had said he felt safer with his Chairman not behind him, but at his side. In these difficult times, a broad back was more vulnerable than a broad front. Now Bannister eyed Colvil with suspicion. Both knew it to be justified.

Christopher Lee

THE HOUSE

Mandarin

A Mandarin Paperback
THE HOUSE

First published in Great Britain 1994
by Mandarin Paperbacks
an imprint of Reed Consumer Books Ltd
Michelin House, 81 Fulham Road, London SW3 6RB
and Auckland, Melbourne, Singapore and Toronto

Reprinted 1994

A CIP catalogue record for this title
is available from the British Library
ISBN 0 7493 1631 4

Printed and bound in Great Britain
by Cox & Wyman Ltd, Reading, Berkshire

In Praise
of
Radio Four

One

George Cameron shuffled uncertainly across the room and leaned against the mullioned window arch. The November sun, almost gone from the cobbled courtyard below, caught the wisps that topped his small ears. For a moment he stared into the perfect square as if expecting the cloisters of the Wren chapel to give up some comforting ghost. For the tenth, perhaps the twentieth time that hour, he didn't know, Cameron peered at the letter that had arrived by the afternoon post. He bent his head and drew the single page closer to his tired eyes and again scanned the few lines. The tap at the door startled him and it took a while to bid his caller enter. He blinked at the door and when he called, the bidding was croaky, unfinished, from an ancient's throat, a throat needing to be cleared more often than before, one that now carried that odour of rotting time.

The young girl, he supposed she was a woman really, smiled and asked after his health. He said 'Yes, Yes,' a few times and waved her to a leather sofa, not deep, buttoned and shiny, but flat, cracked and dull, yet made welcoming by an old tartan travelling rug thrown across its misshapen back. He paused, stared again, wondering why she sat there, young long legs crossed, patterned felt-tip poised above large notepad. She watched his uncertainty with no alarm. He was an eccentric. Everyone in college knew that. These days he saw few undergraduates. She thought herself lucky. There was a silence which held no embarrassment and he turned, one white and mottled hand on the back of his favourite chair, and still holding the letter, nodded towards an oak table and its sherry decanter. She shook her head. It was a ritual. He glanced down once more at the paper, stuffed it into his sagging cardigan pocket and slumped into the chair. Polishing his glasses on his tie, Cameron smiled, then using both hands slipped their wire arms over his ears, wriggled further into the patchwork cushion and opened *Pamela*. The girl relaxed. For a moment, just for a moment, she had thought there was something wrong.

Two

It was cold. Bannister's sober scarf was loosely tied, his furled umbrella in the crook of his arm, his hands deep in his heavy overcoat, his step military, reliable. As Bannister was tall, still slim, elegant, his companion was short, stout, dapper. Henry Colvil's hands were grey-gloved, his soft leather shoes precise among the fallen leaves of the London park, his Malacca cane held neatly just as it had been before him by an Edwardian great uncle. From across the roof tops, Big Ben chimed the quarter hour and as it did, the two paused. They had lunched well. They usually did.

'Always get a recent bit of fish at your club, dear heart. Much obliged. Much obliged.'

'A pleasure old man.'

It was indeed a pleasure. To Bannister, his brother-in-law was usually amusing, often infuriating, and as now, as Colvil turned his round face to squint from beneath his green bowler, never boring.

'I must away, my dear, but there was a small matter I wished to raise over lunch, but it, ah, it ah . . .'

'Slipped your mind?'

'So it did.' He looked again at Bannister. 'Well not really.'

'Is it small enough to wait? I must be in the House for PMQs. Mm?'

Two passing Scandawegians, tourists by their guide books and bold video-camera, eyed the two men, caught Henry Colvil's look and made quick and hopeless reference to the A-Z, as if expecting to find marked these monuments to a just gone age.

Colvil tapped his cane as a golfer might to annoy a greenkeeper.

'We have a smidgen of a problem.'

'Then it shouldn't be difficult to resolve. Mm?'

'Charles, please. So uncharitable.'

Bannister fidgeted. He had to be at Prime Minister's Questions, that twice a week, fifteen minute parliamentary game-show played out to bolster the illusion of political leadership. As Party Chairman, Charles Bannister preferred to be at his master's elbow. Once when he attempted to reassure the Premier that he was right behind him, his leader had said he felt safer with his Chairman not behind him, but at his side. In these difficult times, a broad back was more vulnerable than a broad front. Now Bannister eyed Colvil with suspicion. Both knew it to be justified.

'Henry, I am not at all uncharitable. I simply refuse any more to be involved in our skirmishes. I sometimes wonder if Intelligence is the right job description for your people.'

'Charles, please!'

Colvil looked about him as if suspecting a long range microphone to be recording every damning phrase.

'This is not skirmishing. It is a matter of considerable importance. And, it is one which is quite likely to come to your Herod's attention. I thought it best you knew in advance.'

'The PM?'

'Naturally, Charles, naturally.'

He was gazing at the tap holes made by his cane in the damp ground. He looked up.

'You see, Charles, we have a little difficulty with a visitor.'

'You mean your ghastly defector fellow. Viktor whatever his name might be.'

'It might be Grishin. Ah, I imagine I do. Ghastly? I suspect one of your more perceptive understatements, Charles. A famous name, but one worn with little distinction by our friend. He is unspeakably lacking in any known charm.'

'Henry, I'm extremely late.'

'He wants to write a book.'

Bannister's look was sharp. Viktor Grishin was one

of the last defectors. He had come in while Gorbachev was still trying to give life to his dream of glasnost and perestroika. The Cold War was on its last legs even though the hawks on both sides attempted to keep it going. They had their personal reasons, many of which were to do with position, privilege, careers, while others were unshakeable in their ideology and the more perceptive concerned that while the Kremlin could manage the Cold War it might not be able to manage the revolution peace would bring.

Grishin had come over before it was too late. He guessed that he was under suspicion in the new building outside Moscow which had replaced his section's home in the Lubyanka. There had been many double agents. But he had been more senior than most. Valuable to the British, especially when he defected and the Secret Intelligence Service, the SIS, had been able to brag of his role to their American cousins in Langley, Virginia.

Most important to Viktor Grishin was his perfect understanding of his future. He had no future in the KGB. But he had a past and so the British owed him more than protection. They owed him not just the hope but the reality of a future. He wanted money, luxury and his appetite satisfied by young, soft boys. He knew the British would look after him. They had promised. He knew also that in these so-called enlightened and easier times, neither of which he believed would last, their interest would wane. He knew also that the KGB's would not. And so he had jumped. He had been brought out black under a prearranged plan. It had been easy.

The KGB, at anything but the highest echelons, was never as efficient as the British and Americans had thought. Grishin had come out with his insurance in his mind. He had never told the SIS everything. They had never dreamed he would. Bit by bit he had dribbled. Now he wanted to make the last shift in direction. He wanted a more public, and therefore to him, more lucrative venture. He wanted to write a book. The first of many. He saw a list stretching over ten years which would make him so rich and the British happy that they would not have to support him – not entirely anyway.

Bannister had been looking at his toe-caps. Pondering. His head bowed in question not reverence, he squinted sideways at Colvil.

'What sort of book?'

'Oh you know . . .'

'No. I don't. I'm a politician not a publisher. What sort of book? Mm?'

'The usual thing.'

'There is one?'

'Most certainly Charles. Most certainly. My life as a KGB agent and other so often turgid nonsense.'

'Is this wise?'

'I would say so. After all, the Cold War is won and anyway, others have already said much of what has to be said.'

Bannister knew there had to be more to his brother-

6

in-law's aside. He regarded Henry's asides as being as innocent as Talleyrand's.

'He has no surprises I take it.'

Colvil rather hoped that even former KGB agents held surprises. He didn't say so.

'To some.'

'What does that mean?'

'It means, Charles, that surprise is a reflection of knowledge, so yes, I suppose he may surprise a few people.'

'But you would make sure the right people were not surprised.'

'Part of one's function, my dear. Naturally we would never allow him to commit anything to manuscript unless we approved.'

'Then I really don't see the problem.'

'My Herod says no.'

Colvil puffed his cheeks and his annoyance at the pale afternoon.

'You're saying that C does not want Grishin to write this book. How curious.'

The other man puffed once more and shook his head in agreement. He looked up.

'Nor any other book. He has doubts.'

'Good. That's what we pay him for.'

Bannister was terse. He had too often fallen in with Henry Colvil's plans to extend the M.I.6 in-fighting to the corridors of Westminster. That was bad enough, but now Bannister smelled more than the sort of jealousies within Colvil's department. Bannister didn't care to be involved in the internecine war that raged between the Security Service and Colvil's SIS. He could once again sense that the attitude of C – Controller, Secret Intelligence Service – had more to do with those internal politics than Intelligence judgements. Bannister said as much. Colvil shook his head once more, this time in disagreement.

'His doubts are unfounded. They will come to your Herod's attention. I simply wish you to make sure he is not surprised.'

'Is that all?'

'Well not really. There is one aspect of great urgency. A matter of some principle.'

Bannister shivered. Cold, not alarmed. He would not enter arcane debate on the principle and way of Intelligence in modern political administration. Colvil would. It was his favourite subject. Bannister looked at his watch, anticipating Big Ben's half hour chimes. For the moment he had been told all he needed to know. He anticipated more to come. Now was not the time.

'Good. Lovely to see you old man. By the way, Mary sends love. Tomorrow about eightish? Mm?'

'Might we not have time for some tea tomorrow? Four. It is Wednesday you know.'

Bannister was on the move.

'Yes. Why not. The Rag. Four o'clock. There should be some cake. You'll like that. Bye.'

Henry Colvil watched the retreating figure. Upright. Black toe-capped shoes treading a firm line for the House of Commons in which Bannister encouraged a form of tyranny far removed from the inordinate beliefs he held in the principles of democracy. With a small shrug of his plump shoulders, Colvil brushed away a speck which may have settled on his brown velvet collar and made off in a busy foxtrot towards the south side of Jermyn Street where he expected to buy two eggs. His Man would stand over them while they boiled for two and one half minutes. Then he would serve them with brown bread when it was time for tea.

Colvil did not look back in the direction Bannister had taken across St James's Park. If he had, he would have seen his brother-in-law fall into step with a tall, slim young woman whose stride was more at home on the moors than the corridors of Whitehall and Westminster.

Three

Juliet Cameron had been an MP for just two years. In that time she had become something of a celebrity. From the Opposition Benches, she was for ever sniping at the Government and on most occasions she drew blood. Juliet Cameron did not bother with political point scoring. She left that to her own Front Bench, partly because it was prudent to do so but mainly because she considered set piece exchanges in the House were a complete waste of time. She shuddered every time her Party leaders, the men in their ventless, double-breasted suits and incongruously coloured ties, the women in up-market, off the peg, mix and match, called for resignations which would never come and did nothing more than tell everyone that they had little point to make that would make any point at all. Instead, Juliet Cameron researched her subjects, read and reread previous ministerial statements, culled Hansard for Government responses which could now usefully be held in evidence against them and above all, brought her own incisive intelligence to bear on the often little brains of the Party Opposite. Her own people were suspicious of her. They liked good minds as long as they weren't intellectuals. Senior politicians in the two main Parties distrusted intellectuals. They saw them as dangerous ideologues. They were 'those people' who could confuse issues by their infuriating habit of intellectual argument and seemingly ignoring the gulf between structured debate and *realpolitik*. When Stalin had been advised to respect the Roman Catholics, he had enquired, derisively, how many divisions had the Pope. When Front Benches were urged to humour Party intellectuals, they asked how many seats would Descartes win. Party leaders never let ideology get in the way of politics. That's why they were on the Front Benches and that was why the others jumped up and down from the cheap seats.

The relatively new MP brightened the Chamber and the Economics Select Committee with her humour, intelligence and of course her exceptionally good looks. Long legs which appeared even longer when crossed, and tousled red hair which looked ready for bed, plus a brain, had, in two short years, made Juliet Cameron the darling of every television political chat-show producer. And she was single. The Shadow Cabinet couldn't make up its mind about her. Worse still, although she treated senior Members with courtesy, there was for ever a slight hint that she regarded them not as Yesterday's Men, but as Never Weres – a phrase of hers picked up by a gossip writer at her first Party Conference, published with a tongue firmly out of cheek and resulting in a good talking to from a senior Party manager who went away feeling that he may have just been patted on the head. It had not helped that a carefully arranged early morning photo opportunity for the leader of the Opposition yomping along Blackpool's sands had been upstaged by Juliet Cameron's arrival from London on her high-powered Kawasaki and dressed in racing leathers apparently cut from lime green cling-film.

Juliet Cameron, in spite of her popular image, was a loner. Newspapers had tried to link her with any number of celebrities and to be fair to the tabloid editors, any number of celebrities had tried to link themselves to the red-head MP. Bannister's friendship was a natural relationship that comes in the Commons and in most cases remains an innocent meeting of political moment. In spite of both being in the House, Charles Bannister and Juliet Cameron had met for the first time when they were together on the radio programme, *Any Questions*. Or rather they thought they had. Afterwards he had given her a lift back to the centre of London in his official car. She'd thought that funny.

'Opposition coolies are not supposed to be travelling in the great mandarin's rickshaw you know. The rice paddies will be full of talk.'

Bannister had chuckled. A relaxed chuckle, which had surprised her. She'd said so and Bannister had wondered why few events and even fewer people relaxed him enough to make him chuckle. Laughing was easy. Every politician learned to do that by his or her second constituency wine and cheese party. Laughing came in three degrees and had nothing to do with humour, only with votes. Chuckling was a genuine reaction and therefore, in Charles Bannister's make-up, something to be controlled and best still, avoided outside the immediate family. Juliet Cameron had made him chuckle on that first proper meeting. She still did.

They appeared to have little in common. Indeed Mary Bannister, with the deep instincts of a politician's wife, believed anyone who did have common interests with Juliet Cameron would be very common indeed. On most counts, Mary Bannister was correct. On most.

Politically, Juliet Cameron and Charles Bannister were complete opposites. He, a senior parliamentarian, she, just starting. Their senses of priorities were almost incompatible. Yet, time and time again, they found themselves agreeing on aims even though they could never agree on the way towards them.

And so it was an easygoing relationship, which had risen to first name terms because they had wanted it to and not because of the assumed friendliness affected by so many Members. It remained an unusual friendship in a House of Commons not known for bringing many of its members together once they were politically divided. But there was something more. During that first car ride back to London, Bannister had joked with her that many, many years before they had met. Bannister had been one of her father's undergraduates at Cambridge. Juliet Cameron had been hardly more than a toddler.

And now, as he fell into step towards Birdcage Walk and Parliament Square, the banter was not forced, the assumptions about each other's personality quite natural. They had become friends because they were far enough apart to be nothing less nor more than friends.

'Hello Jules, what are you doing here?'

From a distance, she had seen him talking to a man she did not know and was only mildly curious because of the other's appearance. Bowler hats were now uncommon, green ones even more so. She smiled.

'Oh, I hadn't realized the Keep the Proletariat Out of the Royal Parks Bill had got its Third Reading.'

He returned her smile.

'Where've you lunched. Anywhere nice?'

'Lunch? You must be joking. I'll have you know I've been working.'

'So you have.'

'What?'

'Have me know. But then I would never expect you

to do anything else. Let me guess, a smart lunch with some City brokers. Mm?'

She shook her head. She had been looking at figures on Commonwealth aid. Bannister made a mental note to mention this to the buxom Overseas Development Minister. There was a debate the following week. She might need to know that the Member for Norwich Central was laying in stocks of statistics. They paused to cross the main street. A car with the name of a Cambridge Volvo dealer went by.

'By the way, how's your father?'

She looked at him. Still smiling.

'That's amazing. I was just about to mention him. What made you ask?'

'I'm naturally interested.'

He did not bother to mention the political Pelmanism triggered by the car sticker.

'I often think of him you know.'

He didn't. Political ways slipped so easily off the tongue. Even between friends.

Juliet's smile had gone. Her face was quiet. As they moved across the road, along the side of the Treasury, into the square, he waited for her to speak. He knew she would. Knew again it would be wrong to prompt her.

'He's not at all well. I'm worried. It's not just his eyesight. The new glasses worked, I think.'

'What then?'

Bannister was concerned. He had only seen George Cameron half a dozen times or so since Cambridge.

Bannister had returned for the occasional feast and had found himself involved in fund raising and those sometimes puzzling dinners in the Master's Lodge when it was never clear if they had purpose other than proving to others in the university that the college was still providing a good share of the Cabinet and that he, the Master, counted them among his circle.

When they had seen each other, Cameron had always been friendly enough. He had, as dons do, followed the careers of his promising and then rising graduates, basking in their success as if it were his own. It was a common vanity among Fellows, and a reflection on a collection of even modest careers could usually be stretched through the long winters of quiet Sunday dining among the dwindling band of resident and bachelor dons. Bannister asked again, uncertain of her silence.

'What's the matter with him?'

'I'm not sure. He seems very agitated.'

Bannister was relieved. He hated illness in anyone.

'Well he's always been absent-minded. Even when I was up he was something out of Central Casting. The perfect absent-minded professor.'

She shook her head.

'It's not age, at least not that sort of age. It's almost as if he were getting too old. Running out of time. D'you understand?'

They paused. Her eyes were full of worry for someone she loved. This was a Juliet Cameron far removed from the scathing Back-bencher who in a few minutes would be pointing to the veneer of the fifteen minute parliamentary side show.

'Look Jules, even fathers grow old. The Christmas vac will be here shortly. It'll do him good. Does he still go down to Umbria?'

She shook her head once more.

'Not this year. I asked him. He said there was no time.'

'I see.'

She recognized the sign. She already knew him well enough to know that when Bannister said that he saw, then for the moment at least, he did not. Mentally she straightened. The smile returned. A little too readily.

Bannister did not notice that. He was relieved. He detested human problems being discussed as if he were expected to know what to say. He never did. He never tried. In the constituency, they were happy with 'All well? Jolly good,' and his speeding on before they could tell him. He couldn't do that with Juliet Cameron. She sensed his fear. She glanced up at Big Ben's clock. Not long to go before the Chamber would be filling. She started to move off and across a gap in the traffic. It was still best for the coolie to pass through the Members' Entrance without the mandarin. He called after her.

'Give him my regards won't you.'

She was avoiding a late swerving taxi. She waved an arm in salute. She had heard. And she would.

Four

Questions had been predictable. The Prime Minister had, as was usual, answered none. Instead, as was usual, he had made a series of statements which varied from accusing the leader of the Opposition of being the least qualified to give lessons in economic management to praising the diligence of some Right Honourable or Honourable friend and gladly wasting time by referring Right Honourable and Honourable friends to the answer he had given 'a moment ago'.

After a brief word in the Prime Minister's room, Charles was now back in his own office scratching his signature to letters which he had not written nor read but which were designed to soothe, satisfy, praise, admonish, congratulate, commiserate, thank, or even bless the recipient for his or her efforts.

The labour saving device which created the gems of personally written correspondence was called Rose. She now stood at his elbow collecting the unfolded sheets as he topped and tailed them at her bidding. Her wheezing, inspired by the golden shreds of Virginia tobacco she rolled herself and smoked when she could, set a tempo for his long signature and not for the first time she wondered how it was that such a tall, elegant man as Bannister could have such small straggly handwriting. He finished and Rose rewarded him with a wheeze which was part fanfare, part raucous sigh.

'That's the main lot. I'll pp the others.'

Bannister grunted his thanks. He meant it. He didn't know how he would ever cope without Rose. She had been with him since the day he became the Member for South Hampshire. Rose was an anomaly.

Most of the secretaries-cum-personal assistants could trace their pedigrees to common design. They looked the part, they sounded the part, they had been bred for the part. In his Party they knew their different ways around Oxbridge secretarial colleges, Liberty prints and *Country Life*, especially if they lived, as most of them did, in London or its more socially acceptable suburbs.

Rose had been born in one of the less acceptable London suburbs where her father had been a tram conductor between Abbey Wood and New Cross and then on the trolley buses until they too were scrapped. They gave him a job as something in one of the depots until one morning he dropped down dead. It had been three days before his retirement and Rose's mother and father had planned a fortnight in a caravan near Herne Bay. That's where her mother now lived. Not in a caravan but in a tidy nursing home run by a couple who were in it for the money. Yet they made their twenty money-spinners comfortable and did everything but ease the conscience of people like Rose who knew in her heart that she wished she'd made a life for them both together. She had not.

Rose had never married. She knew why. She had never been attractive to men. She had always worn thick glasses, her legs were storky and no matter how expensively she dressed she would always appear to be wearing a crumpled woolly cardigan. She also had a tongue that could lash the arrogance from any courtier. Minister or cabbie. It had not helped the two or three occasions when Rose had come near to romance.

The day Rose met Charles Bannister had been something of a mistake. Rose had been to secretarial school, flashed through shorthand and typing and then after one look at an insurance office and another in the personnel department of a motor spares factory had gone back to college to learn about legal office work. She had arrived as a holiday relief in Charles Bannister's chambers where he was still relatively junior. Even being taken on in chambers was an unusual arrangement because the clerk normally managed work to coincide with staff holidays. An overload had meant a call to the legal secretarial agency run by the clerk's sister and three weeks temping for Rose, which stretched into three months which stretched to a year.

When Bannister had been elected to Parliament, she went with him, on a temporary basis, to help him get started and until he found someone more suitable. He had never got around to finding anyone more suitable. After more than twenty years Rose was till on a temporary basis.

She gathered up a couple of spare files with the letters and started for the door. Then paused.

'By the by. Mr Baxter was looking for you again. I said you were with the PM. He said he'd be back.'

She smiled her fixed smile and the eyes closed to

a crease behind the heavy brown-framed spectacles. Bannister nodded. He was hardly listening. He was remembering a small moment in the Chamber just twenty minutes earlier. Juliet Cameron had been called. But she had not been as sharp. She had not cast the barb she might have done. She had allowed herself to be mocked. For one second she had lost her edge. No one particularly noticed. But Charles had and when, looking across and up to the right of the Chamber, he had caught her eye, it had been dull. She had, as she would always do, quickly looked away. But he was worried for her. He swung in his high-backed chair and for a moment stared at Rose.

'Sorry. Miles away. What was that?'

'Mr Baxter he was . . .'

'Oh right. Dougal. Did he say what he wanted?'

As Rose was about to tell him no, the door swung open and a man entered with the gusto of a bombastic 1930s magician coming on to a booing first house. The conjurer was short, slightly built. His dark hair was firmly brushed flat rather than combed and ran parallel to his heavy, though not bushy, eyebrows. He paused, as the magician would have done.

'Ah, Charles, there you are.'

Bannister sighed. Dougal Baxter's ability to annoy him was simple. He had done so since their first day together at school. The same dormitory, then cubicles, then rooms next to each other. Although different colleges, they had been at Cambridge together, even won their seats at the same election. The only time they had been apart was when Bannister had been called to the Bar and Baxter had gone into the family publishing firm. They had married within six months of each other. Baxter was godfather to the Bannisters' only child, Polly.

The Baxters had no children. In fact Ros, Dougal's wife, was also a barrister and spent much of her time away, out of London. They had what he called an understanding and what she called nothing. Ros was discreet. Baxter was obvious. He was a too long time friend. Bannister sometimes wished that he would be long lost, especially when he barged in as he did every day with the assertion in his words and tone that, at last, there was Charles and that he, Dougal Baxter, had been searching high and low. He never had. It was simply Dougal's sense of importance. He could never see how ridiculous he always appeared. He was flopped into the leather captain's chair in front of Charles Bannister's desk and was about to speak. Rose got in first.

'Tea?'

Bannister opened half a hand to Baxter. It was a question. Baxter, straightening his tie as if he were about to be interviewed for a job, shook his head.

'I don't have time for tea. Anyway, I've decided to restrict my intake. Filthy stuff.'

'Strewth. Found somewhere else to put it have we?'

With that she was gone. The door closed softly without any commotion behind her.

'Charles, I have to say, that woman is very rude.'

Here was another ritual. Dougal and Rose were continuously hostile towards each other. Charles of course, hardly noticed. Now he just nodded.

'That's right old man. Now, what was it? Mm?'

Dougal shifted and rested his right ankle across his left knee.

'This. Of course.'

Baxter waved the evening paper at him like an angry shareholder confronting the board at a noisy AGM. Charles had seen it. It made less than flattering reading for the Government and in particular the Prime Minister. It had been the point of discussion in the PM's room after Questions. The Prime Minister, sometimes over-sensitive to polls and the headlines they inspired, had asked Charles what he intended to do about it. Bannister had pointed out that the weakness in the newspaper articles was that they centred on personal attacks rather than criticisms of policies and that there was, for the moment, little to worry about. He did not mean that at all, but the PM appeared partly satisfied, which was as much as Bannister could hope.

One headline writer had picked up the PM's nickname used by only the closest members of the Cabinet. 'Bombardier Could Get Marching Orders' screamed the tabloid. Dougal had a copy. He tapped it with the backs of his fingers.

'I take it you've read the details. We're two points from being in third place. They're fourteen points ahead, for the third month Charles. The third month.'

The tone was indignant, but then Dougal Baxter had

honed indignation until it was the blade of his vanity. As Home Secretary, he held little regard for budgetary detail as he had been forced to do during his time at the Defence Department.

It was there that Baxter had impressed the Prime Minister and frustrated the Chiefs of Staff with his uncompromising attitude towards hallowed institutions. He had never allowed the Army to overwhelm him with their gins and tonics, invigorating rides in tanks and then scarlet and gold guest nights. He had swept aside the cunning of the air marshals who dressed him in macho overalls and photographed him in the cockpit of a fighter bomber. He had never forgiven the stupidity of the admirals for taking him to sea in their latest frigate and making him seasick – nor had the Navy forgiven its leaders.

So with a successful trail of post Cold War defence cuts, Baxter had left the stricken Whitehall battlefield for the more senior Cabinet post as Home Secretary. Dougal Baxter understood law and order. He understood the need for prison reform. He understood the fight against drug barons. Most of all, Baxter understood the real possibility of using the Home Department as a stepping stone to his ultimate goal, 10 Downing Street.

As he waved once again the damning opinion poll, Baxter's instincts were beyond the sorrow of the Party. He regarded himself as standing in the Party's wings. The more depressing the poll, the greater the chance of Dougal Baxter being called centre stage. He saw himself as the only alternative when the Downing Street show came to be re-cast. Bannister was hardly unaware of his unlikely friend's ambition. He leaned back in his chair, hands clasped behind his head.

'I've spoken to the Prime Minister. He plans a policy review weekend at Chequers. You'll hear about it this evening.'

'Charles, you and I both know that these figures having nothing to do with policy. They're all to do with leadership. The people who matter don't believe the Bombardier.'

Bannister's gaze was hard. He, better than most people, understood Dougal Baxter. He knew his motives. He knew also that, ulterior motives or not, Baxter was right. The voters liked the Prime Minister. They saw him as a very likeable person. A good family man who would never betray his office, who sought no honour and only glory for his Government. Sadly for the Government, when there was a major issue in the offing, the voters had got used to the idea of not bothering to turn on the news to see or hear what their Prime Minister had to say about it; he was one of the most forgettable people in politics. Not one person in a recent poll conducted by the department of politics at a regional university could remember a single phrase or speech made by the nation's leader during the previous twelve months. Baxter was not letting go.

'You know the most telling factor?'

'Go on Dougal, you're obviously going to tell me.'

Dougal Baxter nodded furiously.

'I shouldn't have to. The most telling factor is that they don't even dislike him. There isn't any emotion at all. They are indifferent Charles, utterly indifferent.'

'I feel you're being carried away old man. This country does rather well when there's quiet government. After all, we even pray that we may be quietly governed. Mm?'

Baxter dropped the paper onto Bannister's desk. His reply was triumphant.

'You Anglicans may. We don't. No Charles, there is a difference between quiet government and a total political siesta. That's what we have. If we don't get up quickly, we'll be out next time. He can have all the meetings at Chequers he likes. It won't do any good unless he gets the bells ringing.'

'I feel you're being carried away with your metaphors Dougal. But,' he sighed the sigh of an understanding housemaster, 'I understand and hear what you're saying. But if this is an early attempt to lay down a marker for the leadership, I'd rather you didn't discuss it with me. I disapprove of plotting.'

'Of course you don't. You disapprove of being involved in the plot. You, Charles, would have made a bad Guy Fawkes, but you'd have been excellent as the man who put the idea into his head in the first place.'

Bannister laughed. Not quite a wine and cheese laugh. Almost.

'Come on. What are you up to?'

Baxter was satisfied.

'Nothing yet. But you should know that I'm not alone in this. There are some of our colleagues who are having to think to the future. They want a clean job.'

'If it were anything else then it might go to a confidence vote.'

'You think that would save him? Or us?'

Bannister thought exactly that. 'If it goes to a confidence vote the Party will support the Government. It has to. Anyone who did not would be deselected overnight. Anyway, in the present climate, an election would mean too many of our colleagues would lose their seats. No they'll go into the right Lobby. Your time has not yet come Dougal. For the moment at least, we shall make do with the Prime Minister we have.'

Baxter smiled.

'I like that Charles. I like it. For the moment at least. You're right of course. You see, you do agree with me. It's for the time being.'

'And then you plan to make your move.'

In an instant, Baxter dressed himself overall in his brightest flags of indignation. 'That is very crudely put. I would never dream of putting myself forward.'

'Really?'

'Really.' He paused, the smile became almost a leer. 'Of course, if asked . . .'

'You would consider.'

'In the interests of the Party you understand.'

Five

Bannister was in the empty Committee Corridor. It was much later in the evening. The long carpet stretched comfortably into the distance and the corridor had the same warmth and insulated reliability that it gave out at all times, on all days, in all weathers, in all seasons. The light oak doors to the Committee Rooms were long closed and only the occasional soft clanging of the Chamber monitor high on the wall gave a reminder that another Member had risen to his or her feet, to speak in what was now an adjournment debate, a device which would, by the morning, be forgotten by all but the local Press eager for news of its MP. The Division five minutes earlier had been innocuous enough and the Government had won easily, in spite of its small majority and really because the Opposition had not felt moved enough for more than a handful of them to turn out to vote. There would be long and acrimonious nights when the usual channels would fail and the Whips would be out in force threatening vengeance on any sceptic, rebel and lazybones who fancied it hardly worthwhile returning to the House in time to pass the tellers before the Lobbies were locked.

Bannister was doing what he often did in the quiet moments of the late evening. Before him was, to him, one of the more intriguing portraits in the Palace of Westminster. Not a politician. Not a statesman. But a hero. Admiral Beatty. There he was with his half-smile, half-sneer, the dark blue naval officer's cap of the day at a cocky angle which would never have been tolerated by the gunnery instructors at Dartmouth, nor by the Jimmys and commanders in the ships Beatty had served as a young man. Cocky angle? Jaunty angle? A bow-tied civilian lecturer at the naval college had once told Bannister that if he wished to understand leadership then he should understand Admiral Fisher and later, Admiral Beatty.

Beatty had become Bannister's obsession. This portrait was a shrine. A curious subliminal belief in the past. Bannister would never have dreamt of talking to a portrait of his father. But then he had never sought his father's advice, even when he had lived. He had rarely seen him. So Beatty was a confidant. Silently he wondered what the great man would have done. He was deep in the silent thoughts of the admiral and was surprised by the quiet voice in his ear. He had not seen Juliet Cameron approach.

'I suppose it's better than talking to trees, Chang.'

He turned. Smiled. He was pleased to see her. He looked up and down the corridor, hoping she had not been overheard. He wagged a finger under her nose.

'You must not call me Chang.'

'But you're a perfect Chang. The absolute mandarin. Don't worry, don't worry. I wouldn't in public.'

Her laugh was soft, slightly mocking, but not offensively. She looked at the admiral, then at Bannister.

'Are you related?'

'My God Father James, whatever made you think that?'

'There's a similarity. Anyway, I've heard that between you, you and your wife are related to almost everyone who's anyone in Britain.'

'Never believe all you hear.'

They turned and walked slowly along the continuous pattern towards the central stone staircase.

'But I do. Then I wait until someone says no. That way I'm never surprised.'

'Your father would disapprove. He taught me to question everything and never to believe the explanation. But then that was many years ago. You were in nappies.'

She laughed again, perhaps to hide the blush.

'You were,' he said. 'I saw you.'

It was Bannister's turn to blush. His recovery was a little too quick.

'How is he this evening?'

'I was about to call him. I don't know.'

'Isn't it a little late?'

'He hardly goes to bed.'

'He's not living in college?'

'No. He kept on the old house. I've told him he should move to something smaller. But guess what he says?'

'What would I do with my books. I know. The last time I saw him, it must have been ten, twelve years ago, shortly after your mother died, he was already saying that.'

'He'd love to see you, you know.'

They paused, the corridor silent, still.

'Whatever for?'

'He likes you.'

'He hardly knows me.'

'You were one of his favourites. He once showed me a diary. You must have been a second year. He thought you should go into the church.'

Bannister laughed.

'Me? Are you sure?'

'Course I am. He said that you'd become a bishop. I read it. He said "Bannister will not seek preferment, it will however, be thrust upon him".'

Her eyes were full of amusement at his embarrassment.

'There, how about that?'

Bannister wagged a temporal finger.

'You know my brother did. Become a bishop, I mean.'

She nodded. Bannister's twin had become an Anglican monk and then was tucked away as a foil to a most conservative diocesan bishop.

'I heard him preach. He's not at all like you. Doesn't even look like you.'

'You've never seen me in a brown habit. Come to think of it, you've never seen him in a suit.'

'So the uniform matters.'

'Of course it does. It's much easier to be taken seriously in a habit if you want people to pray.'

'And in a pin-stripe if you want them to vote for you.'

'Or a frock if you think they might not.'

She aimed a punch at him. 'Cheap.'

He nodded playfully. 'Sorry. There are exceptions of course. So, your father thought I'd go into the church. Then I must be a great disappointment to him.'

'Pa? Not at all. He's an atheist. He's rather pleased.'

'Your father a what? He can't be. I'd have known.'

'Like Saul it came to him later in life. Only the other way round. There's a lot you don't know Chang, in spite of your waistcoats and stiff collars.'

Bannister tugged, self-consciously at the bottom of his waistcoat. He didn't understand why this slip of a girl, as his father would have called her, should touch him this way. He couldn't hear himself saying what he said next.

'You fancy a nightcap?'

She shook her head, not quickly, but as gently as she smiled.

'That's very sweet of you Chang. But that would not be wise.'

He nodded as if he agreed. But he did not. There were times when Charles Halifax Bannister was quite fed up with wisdom and its impositions. But he understood. They said nothing else other than good-night and Bannister continued his way towards the main staircase and she returned to the back stairway. She was still in the corridor when Denis Wigton appeared.

Wigton had become something of a political minder since the day Juliet Cameron had first entered the House through a by-election. She liked him. He was rough tongued to the Front Benches, including his own, and he believed passionately in the hopes of the miners who supported him through his union and the collective vote from the neighbouring pit villages he represented.

'Consorting with the enemy then Jules?'

The voice was gruff, but then it was never anything else. He scratched then tugged at his right ear, a sign she had long picked up as a prelude to some Wigtonism. She clasped the files and papers in her arms, and waited.

'All right Denis. Snooping were we?'

'Was I heck. But you want to watch yourself my girl. This place has eyes and ears in the back of its head.'

'You're not seriously suggesting that anyone would find a whisper of gossip in anything I do? You silly old fool.'

'Listen Jules, don't play silly buggers. There isn't a newspaper that doesn't follow everything you do. Look at those pictures last week.'

'Stupid tabloids. No one takes them seriously.'

'Those stupid tabloids must employ midgets to take pictures like those. What was the headline?'

Juliet Cameron started to blush. She'd been photographed getting out of a friend's mini, never the easiest of tasks with legs as long and skirts as short as hers.

'There's no need to remind me.'

'But you know what I mean love. You're public property, Just be careful. And another thing, don't forget the people who vote for you read what you call stupid tabloids. So watch yourself.'

'You won't find too many cameramen in the Committee Corridor, now will you?'

Wigton looked up through his bushy eyebrows and
ran a thinking hand across his thinning hair.

'I've been around a bit Jules. I've seen most of it
and I've seen it a few times. You and me have been
pals since the first day you came through that door.'

'I know all this Denis, but really, I'm quite grown
up.'

'Not in this place you're not. Happen you're learning
fast, but you've got "Not Yet" written right across your
c.v. I've watched you. You're too easygoing. You're too
trusting. One bit of advice . . .'

She started to interrupt but he held up his hand.

'Hear me out and then you can tell me to piss off.
One bit of advice. When you've been around as long
as I have you'll spend most of your time listening to
people laughing at you and the rest of it watching the
weather. That way folk don't see you as a threat and
you see the little black clouds coming before anyone
else does.'

'You've lost me.'

'No I haven't. You've got ears and a bit of a brain
to back it up.'

'Then trust me to use it.'

'Just watch yourself. You're a good-looking lass and
you've got more than a pretty red head on your
shoulders. There's them who don't like that. Jealousy
they call it. They're just waiting for you to take a
tumble.'

Juliet laughed and switched the folders to the crook of her arm and linked the other through Wigton's and started to walk him towards the end of the corridor.

'My, you do have a way with words. Listen to me Uncle Denis, there's nothing to worry about because there is nothing. And instead of pissing off, why don't we have that wee dram you're always promising me but very conveniently, Mr Wigton sir, you somehow avoid buying. Okay?'

As they walked arm in arm, George Sharpe came out of the Committee Room over which Beatty kept a weather eye, and quietly secured the door which, until then, had been ajar.

Six

The late porter watched anxiously as the old man negotiated the step up to Fellows' Lawn. It had rained earlier, but the stone had long dried. An undergraduate in the porters' lodge seeking the squash court keys for a late work out after a night in the Junior Common Room bar, tossed his head knowingly in the direction of the unsteady don. The porter gave him the hard look the lodge reserved for young gentlemen stepping out of line and the student hastily scribbled his name in the key book and stepped lightly and athletically into the cloisters. He watched the old man carefully picking his way across the lawn. He knew him, but sent no greeting. Undergraduates did not speak to

Fellows unless asked to. He never understood why. Perhaps they were deep in some thought about the origin of the species or, he thought more likely, smashed out of their minds.

The porter raised the counter, came to the doorway and was ready to spring to old Cameron's help as he teetered to the edge of the grass and the cobbled path. He was not needed. Cameron paused, put one foot toe first as if testing the pool and then half turning, made it to the path and shambled beneath the arch and out into the Cambridge night. The porter sighed, shook his head and went back to his sports page. Nice old boy Cameron, he thought to himself. Nice old boy. Always asked after the family. Made it sound as if he were interested. He'd sent a card when the grandson had been born, not to the parents, but to the porter and his wife. Nice touch. Nice man.

Across the street, a very ordinary figure in a very ordinary suit, with very ordinary soft-soled shoes, watched the departing academic, let him get fifty yards on and then casually, so as not to catch up, strolled after him keeping to the other side of the street. He hung back as Cameron turned, paused at the kerb and waved at a chance taxi heading for the station. After a little help, the old man settled into the back seat. The cab pulled out and the watcher strolled to where he had left his car. He passed the taxi on its way back and pulled over two or three houses along from the ramshackle Edwardian home behind the overgrown privet hedge. A light was on in the front of the house.

The watcher knew it was the study. The hour was late, but it glowed all night until it disappeared not with a flick of a switch but with the rising of the morning sun. It had been a long night for both of them.

Seven

Henry Colvil finished rubbing his corpulent figure with the pale fluffy blue bath towel and lightly dusted himself with a gentleman's powder supplied to him from Floris. Apart from an occasional visit to his hatter and bootmaker in St James's, Colvil only shopped in Jermyn Street and then only on the south side. Dusted, he took a deep breath and, teeth clenched, worked his mouth outwards and inwards in a ooh and smile motion. The exercise was the only one he permitted himself. He wrapped his round figure in his grey, heavy cotton robe (he regarded silk as ostentatious) and stepped into soft monogrammed purple slippers, the gift of an admirer. He made another tuck in the robe's ties and went to the small dining-room where His Man had set his place at the head of the table. Colvil glanced approvingly at the half pink grapefruit, sprinkled a little white pepper over it and said nothing as the Nepalese poured him the first small espresso of the morning. After the first sip, he leaned forward to *The Times* ready for him on the mahogany reading stand. He scanned the main headline and then read quickly through the second lead. He thought his brother-in-law had done rather well. Responsible. Reliable. A splendid man. He heard the telephone, heard it silenced by His Man. A few seconds later, the glass-panelled door opened and His Man stood there, silently. Colvil never spoke in the mornings unless it were immensely urgent. He felt it so unnecessary. He would not have been disturbed, particularly at his breakfast, unless it were important. Colvil patted his lips with the crisp napkin and gently pushed back his chair and waddled quietly to the other room. He took the receiver handed to him and made a small coughing sound to signify his presence and the voice at the other end made his report, clearly, precisely and briefly. Colvil returned the receiver to His Man who whispered his master's thanks to the caller and without waiting for an acknowledgement, replaced the ebony and ivory instrument on its rest. Colvil went to his dressing-room where his clothes were laid out and wondered if it might just be an interesting day and if the Chinese were always right in their curse of interesting times.

Eight

Dougal Baxter was wearing a towel and looking carefully at his shoulders and at what he could see of his back in the bathroom mirrors. He rubbed at a red mark on his upper arm. Beyond his reflection he could see Kay in the bedroom. She was sleepy still, slightly swaying then stretching. She was tall with black straight hair that fell nearly to her waist and which one day would be too long. But thirty was far from one day and her proud breasts and taut tummy were testimony to the evening visits to the Commons gym, the thirty lengths in the apartment block pool every morning, a careful if sometimes exotic diet and her belief that when the looks went, so would she. With a small yawn she stretched for the ceiling, the movement feline, her olive nakedness scented and erotic. Baxter carried on probing his flabby torso. When he spoke to her it was over his shoulder and without looking.

'Can't you put some clothes on Kay?'

She stopped. The smile disappeared. For a moment she watched his reflection and then moved from his sight. When she reappeared she was shrugging into a light silk wrap which had been designed to please. He'd stopped his searching but still looked carefully at his jaw and neck line. Kay raised one still pencilled eyebrow.

'What you looking for?'

She knew, but she wanted to hear it from Dougal.

'You were quite brutal you know.'

'I didn't bite you, if that's what you mean.'

'You scratched me.'

'Where?'

She looked. There were a few red marks where Dougal had tugged at his skin. She shook her head.

'Nonsense. You'll live.'

He wasn't satisfied and arched his head trying to see the quarter of his neck.

'I bruise very easily you know.'

There was no reply. She was trying not to laugh.

'I do.'

He caught the corner of her smile.

'It's no joke. If I go home to Ros with scratches and bites all over me, well, she's not daft you know. You do know that don't you?'

He was quite agitated. There were times when she almost hated him. This was one.

'You could have tried going home in the first place.'

Kay turned, went back into the bedroom and flopped back on the rumpled and giant pillowed bed. The robe fell open to the top of her thigh. Dougal walked past the bed without looking at her and opened the wardrobe. He scanned the dresses and blouses.

'Have I got a clean shirt here?'

Kay stared at the ceiling and sighed an infuriated sigh.

'I said you could have gone home.'

Dougal was running the hangers to one end in search of a shirt.

'I heard what you said.'

'Well?'

She was looking at him. But Dougal Baxter knew the look. For a moment he toyed with the idea of destroying her. He could. He knew it. He only had to tell her it was all off. He knew what would happen. The same thing that always happened. She would say 'Okay' and then later in the morning turn up for work and apologise and want to make up. But not this morning. He would rather have no more hassle. It was gone nine and he had a meeting in the Commons at ten. He smiled.

'I don't because we're good together. Right?'

Kay said nothing. She knew what he was doing. She knew also that she would have backed down. But next time. That's what she wanted to tell him. Next time. She didn't.

'There are two in the top drawer. I had them laundered. Socks and underwear are where they always are.'

Baxter smiled. He opened the drawer and started to strip the clear wrapping from a green and white striped shirt.

'That's nice.'

His voice was silky. With a hint of Morningside forgiveness. Kay turned away on her side, pulled the discarded duvet over her head and said nothing.

Nine

Bannister was successfully hidden behind *The Times* when his daughter arrived in the large kitchen. Polly was noisy at the quietest of times. Now she was whistling. Bannister hated whistling. She knew he did. Mary Bannister was scraping toast into the sink and the Radio Four continuity announcer was describing the minor chaos caused by a lorry having shed its load on the A303. Polly poked at the paper. It annoyed him. She knew it did.

'Morning!'

From Polly, the first greeting of the day was an animal instinct intended to warn the family of the evening before or welcome them with the thoughts of her day ahead. Bannister rustled his paper, grunted and bent his barbered head slightly to one side waiting for the morning kiss she insisted on giving both parents. Mary, wrestling with the charcoaled bread, glanced across at their bedwarm only daughter.

'You obviously had a good time last night.'

'Why "obviously".'

'Because that's what you're being. Obvious.'

Polly, still in her dressing-gown, a howling wolf outlined on its silk back, reached for the tall pot and splashed, rather than poured, hot coffee into a china mug. It was decorated with a smaller version of the dressing-gown wolf.

'I was being happy. I suppose that's not allowed.'

Mary counted to ten and then said it anyway. 'Not at this time of the morning it isn't.'

Polly put on what she called her grumpy face and swilled coffee into her mouth. Mary closed her eyes and said to the ceiling.

'Polly! That's disgusting.'

'So's the coffee.'

She clattered the mug on her empty plate and glanced towards the broadsheet wall.

'Morning Daddy.'

Charles Bannister appeared slowly from behind the centre spread.

'What? Oh. Morning darling. Sleep well?'

'You must be joking.'

He stared for a moment.

'Yes. I suppose I must. Never mind. Try again another time.'

He went back to his paper. Mary sat down with the rescued toast and started to read the front page of her husband's newspaper.

'Did you really say that darling.'

There was no response. Polly caught the headline and paragraph beneath.

'Course he didn't. He never does. And every time he does, he never does. You ask him. Do you Daddy?'

Bannister half closed the paper and looked around as might a landlord having heard a late tenant.

'Did I say what?'

Mary was munching and trying not to make a noise.

'Did you actually say that one opinion poll doesn't make a summer?'

Bannister paused, blinked above his tortoiseshell half-frames.

'Not exactly.'

Polly sensed fun.

'I thought *The Times* got things exactly. Isn't that the whole point of it?'

Bannister folded the paper and laid it by his plate. Outnumbered in his own kitchen, he had given up.

'*The Times* is like any other paper. It tries to get things right, but sometimes things are taken out of context.'

Polly went for the kill. 'So you did say it.'

'Well yes, but I said a lot of other things, which of course they did not report.' His sense of fair play intervened. 'Well actually they did, but not at the same time. If you read on, well, the whole thing's in context.'

Mary was spreading more toast. In the Second World War it would have required a whole ration book to have got the huge amount of butter. Bannister watched fascinated as she then ladled thick-cut marmalade from the side of her plate.

'I thought you were on a diet.'

'She is.'

'I am.'

Bannister's humour was not quite up.

'Doesn't look like it.'

Mary paused, the laden toast halfway to her mouth. 'Darling we've been married twenty-three years and at least once a week in each of those years you have had a go at me about my diet.' She bit deeply and the marmalade spread dangerously to the edges. Polly was now wide awake.

'Tell me, Daddy. why do you always have a boiled egg and a half-slice of brown toast for breakfast?'

Bannister sighed and reached over his cup and saucer to his daughter. 'Pour me another cup would you darling? Then I must go.'

Polly was smug. 'Exactly. So we'll keep quiet about the egg if you keep quiet about the toast and marmalade. Right?'

She poured his coffee. Polly loved her father and she

even liked him most of the time. The telephone on the tiled wall burbled and Polly was smiling fondly to herself as she got up and answered. She listened and handed out the phone. She had hoped it would be someone interesting. Perhaps a party. At the very least a concert. It was not. Bannister looked expectantly across his spectacle tops.

'For me?'

As he took it, Polly was already wandering languidly in the direction of the shower. She called over her shoulder.

'It's your boring old Prime Minister friend. Tell him he might at least say good-morning as if he meant it.'

Ten

The meeting was in the Cabinet Room. Bannister didn't understand why. The Prime Minister had once told him that it was the only secure room in the building. Bannister had not said anything. Henry would have smiled. In fact he did when Bannister repeated the conversation. There was no secure room in Number 10.

The Bombardier was in his middle seat, Bannister across from him and four places to the right. The Prime Minister insisted that when what he called bilateral conversations took place, Cabinet ministers should assume their regular seats even if no one else were in the room. He had lost weight since Christmas and instead of looking trim, was haggard, teeth exaggerated as if he were seriously ill. Charles wondered if his leader might be ill. Couldn't be, he thought, he'd have been told. His second cousin was the PM's doctor. He told him everything. A sachet diet apparently, nothing to worry about. Pity, it would have solved one or two immediate problems. The Bombardier, his jacket buttoned, was rolling a yellow pencil up and down the memo pad. He never doodled. Too tidy, thought Charles. The pencil play stopped. He could not see any problem with Grishin's book.

'I can't really see what harm there'd be. I mean, we don't have to worry about them now. They need us more that we need them. You should have seen him when he was here last week. Almost begging me to make some announcement about export credits.'

Charles Bannister nodded. He had been to one of the receptions for the visiting President of the Russian Federation. It wasn't so much the money they needed as the public declaration that they would get some. It was a toss up between being seen at home as in the West's pocket and bringing home the bacon, or in Russia's case, the sausage. Bannister imagined the diplomatic tensions if the Grishin book blew away anything of the diplomatic cobweb which at times and conveniently hid the private deals and promises of international relations. Given that the KGB were always privy to those private negotiations, or had been until they were restructured and given their new and meaningless title, Grishin might after all have something to say. Bannister smiled what Juliet Cameron would have called his mandarin smarm.

'I'm advised that Controller SIS has doubts for other reasons.'

The Bombardier sniffed, took out a white handkerchief and made inconclusive blowing sounds. He never had quite got used to blowing his nose in public.

'C is too cautious. Frankly he never tells me anything he doesn't want me to know.' He sniffed again and wiped the end of his pointed nose. 'Tell you the truth Charles, I never really know what to ask him. I know that sounds daft but nothing they do nowadays seems relevant. I know everyone says they are important, but it's difficult to get too interested. In fact you know, I think we should be taking a look at what they're supposed to be doing.'

Bannister's instinct was to come to the corner of the SIS.

'We're still getting good stuff from Moscow surely?'

The PM shook his head. 'Not really. I get a better idea of what's going on from newspapers. Our people are good when it comes to deep background, but frankly when do I get a chance to read that stuff? If it weren't for Harold I don't think I'd bother at all.'

Harold was Harold Pawle, the Prime Minister's Private Secretary-cum-adviser seconded from the Foreign Office. Given a good run with a successful Prime Minister, few if any of the secondments ever intended to go near the FCO again. Instead they used their contacts made at Number 10 and their undoubted inside knowledge of the system to get lucrative directorships once the political connection came to an end.

Pawle had already lined up a series of offers, any one of which would make him rich once the Government fell and most of which he would juggle so that he could take on more than one role when he left Number 10. The suggestion from the PUS that he would be considered for an embassy when he returned to the FCO was laughable. That was the last place Harold would be seen dead in. He spent much of his time carefully feeding the PM with foreign affairs briefs and Intelligence, most of which he, Harold had subbed to three or four paragraphs. He put in front of the PM, or in his night box, only those things he believed his master really needed to know and then only at the last minute. Both Pawle and the Cabinet Secretary tended to monitor carefully the information available to the PM. After all, they ran things, he did not. One consequence of this grip of the two chamberlains was that the PM was often well briefed on those things he needed to know and totally out of his depth on matters others wished him to know.

The Cabinet Secretary and Pawle had long decided that Intelligence was one of these areas in which the Prime Minister should dabble as little as feasible. The PM had got over his schoolboy delight in coming face to face with the head of the Secret Intelligence Service. He had actually asked if C would like his coffee stirred but not shaken. C did not mind the arrangement especially since the PM had been quietly side-tracked from the JIC. The Joint Intelligence Committee had received a boost during the latter months of 1982 after the Intelligence debacle which led to the Falklands War, but under the latest tenant of Number 10 the Committee had rather gone into what the Cabinet Secretary described as that glorious limbo of an intellectual sewing circle. No wonder the PM felt out of it, and he said so to Bannister.

'Good Lord Charles, when I asked him what was going on in Baghdad he looked at me as if I were daft. I asked what Saddam was up to and he gave me some old shit about the man being unpopular among the people. Well, Christ, I said, we're all that.'

Bannister laughed. It really was one of the PM's funnier remarks. Unfortunately the Bombardier's smile was his standard fixed grin. Charles was about to don his trusted adviser disguise when the PM continued.

'You see Charles, the Establishment screws up far more often that it produces.'

This was a danger area. The Prime Minister had a tendency to lash out suddenly at the Establishment. It was a reckless tendency. He needed reminding that it was the Establishment and not the voters that had made him Party leader and therefore Prime Minister. For some reason Bannister had yet to fathom, the Bombardier had held on to the curious belief that political preferment was all about the triumph of meritocracy. Charles Bannister would only concede this on some occasions, and most recently, it had been not a triumph of meritocracy but a failure of the Party aristocracy.

Bannister was of the school which believed it better to have absolute control of the Party leader. Bannister had once offered the thought that the role of the Prime Minister should be similar to that of a Master of an Oxbridge college. He (Bannister, in spite of experience, could never think of a Prime Minister as being a woman) should be more than a figurehead if the college were to prosper but, like a Master, should never forget that he needed to have the vast majority of the governing body on board for even minor policy changes. There were moments when a Master needed reminding that rather than cause a confrontation it was best to take and act on the advice of the most senior dons.

Now as the Prime Minister talked, Bannister sensed one of those moments and he switched on the understanding adviser smile.

'What you're saying is that since the wall came down, the spying business hasn't been so, ah, dramatic. Mm?'

The Prime Minister nodded. He meant much more than that, but for the moment it would do. Charles too nodded and continued.

'But there's still an awful lot we don't know about what's going on there. The whole empire's been far more unstable since the old guard went. Personally, I think we probably need the SIS more than we ever did. What's going on in our theatres of interest is far more difficult to predict. Mm.'

'I suppose you're right but nothing we get from them, well nothing which reaches me anyway, makes a blind bit of difference to what we can do.'

Bannister was often aware that the Prime Minister suffered from occasional feelings of diplomatic inadequacy. He had come to office knowing little about international issues, but like all his predecessors it had taken only one summit meeting for him to taste power, and like those who had gone before him, he preferred the feeling of importance on the world, rather than the domestic, stage. One was West End and Broadway the other was local dramatic society. But as Charles often reminded him, when it came to a general election there were never any votes in foreign policy.

'As I say, they've been jolly good about the French. We seem to be getting a lot on them.'

'But they're on our side Charles.'

'I wouldn't have gone so far as that, but I do understand your feelings. Yet if I remember rightly, you were quite pleased to know what they were doing behind your back during the Brussels summit.'

The Bombardier looked down. He found it all silly.

'I suppose I did. Mind you, they were probably doing the same. They probably had us bugged as well.'

Of course they had. Bannister was quite certain that the French and many of the other allies kept a covert eye on each other. As long as they were not found out, no one really minded, especially as the Americans were bugging everyone, or trying to.

The Americans had the advantage of having satellite electronic intelligence on most of their allies if they really wanted it. LIM, the monthly London Intelligence Meeting, often produced titbits from the Americans about other nations including the Germans and French, but as the PM observed, that had not stopped the French ripping off the British in the Council of Europe nor had it told the Chancellor which way the Germans were going to jump on the exchange markets.

'Well before you call in the removal men, just remember where all those foreign policy briefings come from. Look at the Paris meeting last month. You know yourself that the SIS had the French delegation bugged within twenty-four hours. You knew everything they were going to say by the time you walked into the Elysée.'

The other man looked back at his notepad and started rolling his pencil. Perhaps he had been embarrassed. Bugging an ally was something he found difficult to go along with. It was only when his own security people had diverted the French efforts to listen into his conversations that the Prime Minister had relaxed. Henry had concluded that like many of his type, the PM wasn't so much bothered about the monitoring as what would happen if the operation were publicly exposed. It was also Henry's hypothesis that if that happened, then the PM's popularity ratings would rise dramatically. Now Bannister stuck in the final SIS flag.

'I believe you're right when you suggest we should take a look at the Intelligence services. But frankly, they're the best in the world. We'd only have to put something else in their place.'

'That may not be a bad idea.'

'But in these days, what we were doing would get

out. The Press would demand to know what had gone so badly wrong that we had to change the system.'

The Prime Minister nodded again. But he had thought of that. 'We would simply say it was part of our review to make the Intelligence services more accountable.'

'Fine. But then we would have to. I don't believe either of us wants that. It certainly wouldn't be in our interests to do so. Not at the moment anyway. Mm?'

The sigh from the other side of the table was long and said all this was very well but it didn't solve the immediate problem.

'So what do we do about this Grishin thing?'

'I suspect there's nothing we need to do for the moment. My guess is that CSIS is laying down a marker. Like any good department head he's got in early. The next thing will be the backstair approach, probably through the Cabinet Secretary. Weren't they at school together?'

The PM nodded. 'Probably. Everyone round here tends to have been at school with everyone else.'

Charles smiled, pausing as a chaplain might while his bishop's smile warmed the chapter. He was starting to think that the conversation had ended when there was a discreet tap at the Cabinet Room door and a stubby, pinstriped figure appeared. The Cabinet Secretary was one of the few people who could intimidate the Prime Minister and the way in which he bustled into the room suggested that nanny wanted to know exactly what her charge was doing in this part of the house. He did not sit. His short, sharp throat clearance was enough to make the PM smile across at Charles as if, or in the hope that, they shared some secret joke. The Cabinet Secretary placed a single sheet of white paper with double spaced typing in front of the Bombardier.

'CSIS has sent this across. On this occasion Prime Minister, it would appear that he does have a point.' He looked across at Charles, almost daring him to challenge his judgement.

The Prime Minister scanned the paper and skimmed it across the table. 'What you make of that?'

Charles took out his half-frames and deliberately took his time. He rather cared to annoy the Cabinet Secretary, a man Charles had never trusted except in the most difficult crisis. The paper was marked Top Secret and was a memo from the Controller, Secret Intelligence Service, from whom all memos were at least Top Secret, to the Cabinet Secretary for whom no secrets existed. The message was simple and uncompromising.

After due consideration, in my judgement it would be unwise at this juncture for the memoir of V. G. to be published. There would be a real chance of national security being jeopardized and questions stemming from what he might have to say would possibly have to be answered in Parliament to such a degree that further questions on security matters would be raised. Thus, I see no purpose to be served in publication.

Bannister re-read the memo. V. G. was obviously Viktor Grishin but there were no hints to what further questions might emerge. He passed it back. The Prime Minister did not pick it up. He blinked at Charles. He needed support in front of the Cabinet Secretary. Charles nodded. The PM waited.

'Well Charles? What d'you think?'

Charles shrugged. He would string this out. 'It's one of C's usual clever memos. He says that national security could be jeopardized. But he doesn't say in what way.'

The Cabinet Secretary interrupted. 'With respect, a memorandum such as this is not the place for detail.'

Charles agreed. 'True. But it immediately puts the Prime Minister on the spot. To ignore the Controller's advice when he says national security may be compromised would be, at this stage, difficult, to say the least, especially if we went ahead and then somehow it was leaked that we had ignored his recommendation.'

The PM looked alarmed. 'You think that likely?'

Charles shrugged. He did. He didn't say so, not directly. 'It is something which we must guard against, Prime Minister.'

Bannister was always very formal when the matter itself was formal, particularly in front of the Cabinet Secretary. It helped remind the bureaucratic knight of his place in the Cabinet Room. The Bombardier wanted not only guidance, he wanted the decision lifted from him. Charles moved his gaze to the window as if considering a response.

Both Charles Bannister and the Cabinet Secretary knew exactly what he was about to say. Bannister looked back at the PM. Smiled, almost reassuringly.

'I think that at this stage there is no urgency. Agreed?'

The PM nodded. The Cabinet Secretary smiled. Charles put both hands on the table as if it were his meeting and he were about to call it to a halt.

'In that case Prime Minister I think the matter might be referred to the JIC and that perhaps, if I may suggest, should there be an opportunity to do so, you might get from C his private thoughts on the matter.'

The Bombardier nodded slowly as if it had all along been his preferred solution. He had thought of the Joint Intelligence Committee, but could not quite see that it came under that group's terms of reference. Never mind, it did mean the whole matter was off the agenda for, he flipped through his mental calendar, another three weeks. He stood and smiled sincerely and downwardly at the dumpy Cabinet Secretary. From the other side of the table, Charles noted with some satisfaction the Secretary's discomfort. In fact, he thought, the PM was much taller than the public thought him to be. His problem was not one of height but of stature.

Eleven

The Central Lobby was crowded. Charles Bannister was having a brief word with a peer friend who seemed to have got lost on his way to the Lords bar. The title was Irish and ancient and its bearer rarely had reason to come to the Palace of Westminster although on one occasion that year he had made a useful speech on the future of the British merchant shipping industry. Today he thought he would listen for a while and so be entitled to his appearance money, as Dougal called the daily rate paid to peers who attended and remembered to sign in. Most of them remembered. The fee would more than pay their overnight stay at their club. Charles was making his apologies and claiming a pressing engagement when the old boy laid a restraining and mottled hand on his arm.

'Just a point Bannister. I was talking to a mutual friend last night. In the club you know.'

The peer's watery gaze was intense, like a child trying to remember its poetry. Charles waited.

'And?'

The seventh viscount dropped his voice almost to a croaky whisper. The Central Lobby was a very public place.

'He tells me this Russian johnny is causing trouble. Know about it?'

'Go on.'

'Seems he wants to spill the beans. Bad business, Bannister. Bad business. Wouldn't do us any good at all.'

'You mean a certain book. I assume you've been talking to, eh . . .'

'Absolutely. You see, if he knows a thing or two, let's keep it to ourselves. Does no good telling the world what we know. Keep them guessing I say.'

Bannister bent his head as if considering the other's point. The old man hadn't moved. He expected some response. Bannister looked up and smiled, he hoped reassuringly.

'I'm perfectly sure the Prime Minister would never approve anything that would jeopardize our national security. Mm?'

The other man's stare became more watery. More intense, the old blue eyes almost opaque.

'Not talking about national security. Talking about damage to Party.'

Now Bannister was interested. 'Why should it do that?'

The peer shook his head in disbelief. 'Obvious. If we've been up to some jiggery-pokery, we don't want some Ruskie telling everyone. Now do we? Thought you'd have worked that one out for yourself.'

'It doesn't necessary follow that . . .'

The other man interrupted. 'Course it does. C has good reason. Sound man. Knew his father you know. Sound man. I tell you Bannister, we don't want this book. Understand?'

Bannister had the feeling he was being threatened. He scowled. 'We? No I don't understand. Who is we?'

The peer nodded in the direction of the Lords Lobby. 'In the other place. Listen, Ten's getting it all wrong nowadays. Any damn fool knows that except him. We don't need something like this. You can get away with almost anything when it comes to an election except a promise to put up taxes and incompetence.'

'What exactly did C tell you?'

'Quite a lot. If you don't know, then someone should tell you. If this little lot surfaces then you might as well promise to put up taxes.'

The old man gave a nod like an irritable squire bidding good-day to a liberal rector and with his stick trailing across the tiled lobby floor headed for the red benches and his attendance allowance.

'What's that old bugger doing in here?'

The mutter from his elbow surprised Bannister. Denis Wigton had the ability to appear and disappear like a ham in an opera chorus. One moment he was there and doing his best to steal a scene, the next he was retreating beneath the glare and voice of the principals.

'He's all right Denis. Harmless.'

'You've got to be ruddy joking. People like him should be put down.'

'A little drastic, but then, as you once told me, why smile when a snarl will do the job just as well and quicker.'

The two started for the Members' Lobby. They'd been on opposite sides, politically, for all their lives but liked each other enormously. Each recognized the integral honesty in the other. Wigton admitted that Bannister was in politics for what he could give rather than for what he could get. Bannister understood that Wigton was in politics to get for others what they had never had. In an obvious way, they had similar ambitions but came from different directions. Neither had succeeded, which was another point of understanding.

Wigton had something on his mind and paused just outside the double doors leading from the Central to the Members' Lobby. He put a hand on Bannister's sleeve. The look he gave the taller and younger man was almost earnest.

'I'm told you know Jules's dad.'

'George Cameron? Mm. He was my tutor at Cambridge. Why?'

Wigton scratched, then tugged his ear.

'Nothing much, 'cept she's bothered. She's not herself. I eh, I wouldn't like to see her hurt Charlie. Understand?'

'Not really. Why should she be hurt, after all everyone gets old, even old Cameron. She's not, well, she's not unbright.'

'I didn't mean that. You see Charlie, when people get caught up in grief, then they sometimes say things and do things they don't mean.'

'I'm afraid you've lost me Denis.'

'For the moment, maybe I have. But just think on't

when you're next speaking to her. She looks in charge, but she's not. That's all.'

By the time Bannister had retreated from the Lobby to his room in the House and then headed across to his much larger office in Party headquarters, or the Front Office as the more red-bracered young men on his staff called it, the matter of Grishin and his book and the blatant lobbying of Controller, Secret Intelligence Service, had been forced to the back of his mind.

He was wondering what Wigton had meant. More importantly, he wondered what it was that had prompted the northern MP to raise it. Bannister knew full well that Jules was under considerable stress, but she certainly had not said anything that would suggest to him that she could not cope. Bannister was thinking about her and wondering why he should be so concerned when he saw her coming down the steps of the corner building in front of him. It was the place where MPs and the media gathered. It was the home of the radio and television studios, the new and full time hustings which most Members, especially those in marginal seats, rushed to at the drop of a studio booking. It had to be the same for Juliet Cameron. Yet another television interview.

One of the daily gossip columnists had calculated that Juliet Cameron had appeared on more breakfast shows than any other Back-bencher that year. The gossip's suggestion was that since Juliet Cameron was far the prettiest Member of the Commons and even in the chill November mornings managed to wear skirts shorter than the latest couch bimbo hired by the ratings-seeking stations, she remained the only MP who could keep fathers from their commuter schedules and eldest sons wondering if there was something in politics after all. Now the legs were all but hidden as she huddled into a cashmere navy blue coat with the collar turned above her ears. He smiled.

'Don't tell me, yet another pundit's half hour?'

'You're only jealous.'

'Should I be?'

'Course you should Chang. They only ask you on when the children have been making fools of themselves. We don't have to worry about Party unity.'

'Really?'

'Really.'

'Because there is none. Mm?'

'A healthy exchange of views.'

'She told the *Daily Express*.'

'Right. Come on Chang. Don't look so serious. The Chamber's over there.'

His hands, deep in his overcoat pockets, clenched and unclenched, though far from angry. He enjoyed her banter, he knew they were both harmless enough. Bannister had been in the House for many a year. His family had always been in public service. Sometimes building empires, in recent years dismantling them. He had one view of the way in which the nation and its responsibilities should be governed. That view was not the same as Juliet Cameron's.

61

Now, and not for the first time, he wished that he knew more about this woman. He wasn't quite sure why he said what came next.

'I was serious about a drink sometime.'

'Christmas maybe.'

'It was not a seasonal offer.'

'And it wasn't a good idea Chang. I keep telling you, Front Bench mandarins don't dig dirt with opposition coolies. OK yah?'

'Now you're mocking.'

'Absolutely. Much safer that way. Bye.'

With that she was gone. He thought she laughed. He hoped it was not in mockery. He turned from watching her and continued down Great Peter Street. He nodded to a very athletic young man crossing the street. The wave of the other's hand had been very friendly although they hardly knew each other. At least Bannister did not think they knew each other that well. Nick, Nick, Nick something or other. Bannister could not remember.

He was one of Dougal's researchers. He really worked for Kay Bennet. Nice lad. Friend of Polly's, Bannister thought. Couldn't be sure. She had so many. But there was something about him. Probably been to the house.

Nick had been to the house. Quite a few times. But Bannister hadn't really noticed. As Mary once remarked, 'By the time Charles is old enough to be eccentric and absent-minded he'll have been that way for so long that the whole effect will be wasted. He'll be just another old fool.'

Charles Bannister was not really an eccentric before his time. He simply had so few interests outside politics that other matters either went unnoticed or were dismissed, although never with an unkind wave. Bannister would have been hurt if he knew that some, including his wife, thought him to be uncaring.

Charles Bannister, like his ancestors, believed in a caring society, although if pushed he would have had a tough time giving a clear explanation as to what he meant by one. It certainly did not occupy his mind as he crossed by the church and entered the discreet Party headquarters and gave himself to the immediate matter of his Party's and, in particular, the Government's popularity. Now, that was something Bannister really did care about, passionately.

The latest opinion polls had caused all sorts of difficulties for the Government and for Charles. As Chairman, it was his job to make sure the Party's machine ran smoothly. He had spent a great deal of time reorganizing it. Gone were the hangers-on, the so-called research officers who did nothing more than coat themselves with the icing of Party atmosphere and Yes Sir policies in the hope of being close enough to the centre to get on the precious list of potential parliamentary candidates. If a young hopeful were not on that list, then, given the way the Party structure worked, there was no chance of being considered for any constituency short list of PPCs – Prospective Parliamentary Candidates.

Just as Bannister had stripped the list of surplus

researchers, so had he sent packing many of the well-bred secretarial staff, up from the shires with a recommendation from a local treasurer that a job for old so-and-so's daughter would more or less guarantee that old so-and-so would keep clinking into the Party coffers. To Bannister it was a cynical way to run the office and he had systematically cleared out the passengers.

One senior official had been heard to remark that it was all very well getting rid of passengers but indirectly many of them were fare paying. He too had gone.

Bannister's reputation for fairness and sternness had survived and those left were no less hard working. His main problem was that although he was managing to get the machine geared up to fight an election, Cabinet policies seemed to be arranged to throw a spanner into his good works.

Rose tapped on the door and put a small wooden tray of tea on the edge of his desk with one hand and, with the other, a sheaf of computer print-outs on his blotter. She wheezed a smile of sympathy. When Rose wheezed and smiled at the same time, her nose pinched and her eyes screwed. The result was a sudden sliding of the heavy and enormously framed spectacles. Without them she was almost blind, with them she appeared as a caricature of some past agony aunt. With a thin but blunt-nailed finger, Rose pushed the frames firmly onto the bridge of her nose and squinted at Bannister as if anticipating his response to the uncreased documents.

'I'm not sure they'll do your temper any good, but they're accurate.'

She nodded to the pile of opinion poll analyses that he had asked for that morning. The new database system had produced them inside the hour. They did not make any better reading for all that.

Bannister nodded his thanks and while Rose poured tea scanned the conclusion which he now insisted should be at the top and not at the end of discussion documents in the office. Bannister worked on the principle that he was interested in an end product. He had told the office systems manager that his, Bannister's, task was to make sure that when the Prime Minister wanted to go to the country then the machinery was there to allow him to win the election. The policies and personalities might, as now, make victory less than likely, but the machinery to attempt it had to be ready at all times. The conclusion of any discussion had to be the base line from which came Party and administrative policy. Therefore Charles insisted that instead of a conclusion appearing at the end of a document, it should be at the top. In that way there was never any doubt as to the objective, and what followed was the justification for that objective. It was beginning to work.

Rose handed him a cup and went through his diary update. The weekend was supposed to have been clear. Down to the country on Friday morning. Surgery Saturday morning. A constituency dinner. That was it. Now it was not.

'There's a late invite.'

Bannister didn't look up from the analysis. He did

not accept late invitations unless they were from close friends or Number 10.

'Say no will you?'

'Thought you should know. You might like it.'

Bannister looked up. Rose was tapping a postcard-sized, gold-edged invitation. She smiled. The glasses slipped. It obviously wasn't a Party matter.

'Who's it from?'

She passed the card to his outstretched hand.

'Professor Cameron. There was a little note. Really nice. Said he was sorry for such late notice but it had slipped his mind, he was sure you would understand.'

'How curious.'

'Then he rang. This afternoon. Wanted to make sure you'd got it. Sounded a nice old boy.'

'He is. Or at least I think he is. I haven't really much seen him in recent years. But yes, nice old boy about fits him.'

Bannister ran his hand over the printed invitation. The Master and Fellows had great pleasure. This coming Friday. He wondered for a moment if he should accept. Jules would be pleased, he thought. It would be nice to see old Cameron again. What a coincidence. He imagined Mary would rather he went down to the country so they could dine together. It was something they rarely managed these days. Not in the country anyway. Not even during the recess.

Rose had calculated that during the last parliamentary year he had eaten one hundred and thirty Party dinners and two hundred assorted lunches. On five occasions he had attended two lunches on the same day. It was that sort of job. The Party Chairman soon became a dab hand at drawing raffles and developed an understandable loathing for chicken.

Bannister shook his head. A feast in his old college wasn't something from which he could slip away by ten o'clock. It would be midnight. It would be four hours before he reached the farm. Not on. But he sensed there was more than a social reason for the invitation. And once again he thought to himself, Jules would be pleased. He was not quite sure why that was important, not with everything else that was going on. He nodded.

'Very well. Would you telephone and say yes and then write?'

Rose's wheeze was a semitone lower than normal. It was her version of a contented sound. She smiled again.

'Do you good. Nice to get away to something harmless. You know what I mean? No handshaking. No division bells? I'll call now.'

She got up, shrugging the bobbled and woolly cardigan about her hunched shoulders. She paused at the door.

'Anything else?'

He shook his head. 'Don't think so. Oh, tell Professor Cameron that I won't be wanting a bed for the night. Tell him I'll have to leave shortly after dessert. Mm?'

'He's no chicken is he. 'Spect he'll be pleased. It'll be nice to see him after all this time, won't it now?'

'I imagine it will.'

Rose closed the door behind her and left him to a brief memory of sitting in an old leather corner sofa.

Even in those far off days, Cameron had seemed frail but with a mind which crackled with ideas and totally new ways of seeing old problems. Cameron had opened Bannister's mind but had never let him abandon his respect for the Establishment which for some reason, Bannister only realized years later, Cameron held dear. He still remembered the old boy's arm on his shoulder and his whisper of caution.

'It is the Establishment Charles, which allows the iconoclast freedom. The Establishment is the hall light left burning long after the rest of the house has retired. Go out on the town. Embrace the night and its pleasures. When you've done, well, you can come home. The light will be on. It will be a place you will trust. That Charles, is why you need the Establishment. Mock it for all you are worth. But take care not to destroy it. It is from whence you came. Leave it burning, even dimly, because you may never know when you might want to come home.'

Bannister smiled at a fond memory. Days long gone. A time when a serious Charles Bannister, more inclined to foils than sabres, knew little of the Establishment, for he knew almost nothing of anything else.

Now, he made a mental note to tell Mary of his change of plans and hoped she wouldn't mind, and also to tell Jules and hope that she would be pleased. He picked up the papers and turned to the desk light.

The opening paragraph was stark in its message to the Chairman. The Prime Minister's popularity was such that there was little or no chance of his leading the Party to victory. The Party could not expect to win. Instead it was hoped that the Opposition would lose.

Bannister removed his half-frames and rubbed the warm tortoiseshell frame along his nose. There was little comforting in the message and he knew that his task was to make sure that every department, and in particular Number 10, put on a credible performance of talking up policies in such a way that the Opposition appeared ineffectual and therefore was accused by the national media and, in the longer term, by the electorate of not looking like an alternative Cabinet even when existing Government policies were dull and capture prone.

Bannister was flipping to the summary sheets when he notice a sharp margin minute in Dougal Baxter's neat handwriting. The message was as simple as most of Dougal's: 'We need a feel-good factor and it has to be one which won't be forgotten and therefore one which cannot be subject to too much scrutiny and statistical reversal after a couple of weeks.'

He swivelled his high-backed chair towards the far wall and looked at, rather than saw, the small watercolour. D. C. S. Compton. That winning four. The Ashes won. An apolitical inspiration. A feel-good factor. Dougal was right. Bannister smiled. Oh for a World Cup success. Oh for victory with one glorious four to the square-leg boundary. Oh for Olympic golds and healthy urine tests. Ride the nation's cheers. We are the champions. Let the people sing. Let them go into the booths with smiles on their faces and carrying a cross. Let them lay that cross alongside the candidate's name. Another five years. Only there was no World Cup. No hopes at Lord's. No Wimbledon win. No hurdles to be crossed except for the long line of political unpopularity stretching along the electoral relay track.

Across the traffic, Big Ben chimed the hour, although Bannister, deep in his thoughts, never heard it. There had to be a solution. There always was. The document was correct. At worst there was the hope that the Opposition would once again lose an election, thus removing the need for the incumbent Government to win. But he knew that this time luck was not to be trusted. Not again.

In the back of Bannister's mind, there clicked a register of chance, possibility and probability. It was something that had been with him since the day he was first called to the Bar. It had been there as a junior Whip. It had survived during his time as Chief Whip. It was more than instinct. It was a deeper political nous which registered at the time seemingly irrelevant detail and then shuffled it when the moment was right. Shuffled carefully, professionally, the nous flipped out as an idea, even though the insider knew the deck was politically marked.

To Bannister, the view from Front Office was bleak. Yet there was something. Bannister experimented with a smile. What if there were to be a success of another kind? No grand sporting victory. No fairy-tale royal to cheer as had been the case in 1947. These were set piece occasions which risked back-firing if the result failed to please the crowds. What if there were to be an unexpected success? What if a famous spy were to show how brilliant had been the British counter-espionage effort? Would that be enough? Maybe not quite. But if it should show that inspired Government judgement had encouraged the SIS way of handling Grishin, then that would be a success with no come-back. A success with the Prime Minister's name written across each flattering paragraph. A quiet word of encouragement here. A nod of approval right on time there. Such lines and paragraphs could, presumably, be written into any manuscript sanctioned in London and carefully compiled in that tall, rather ugly stone house outside Bath. A quiet demonstration of the Bombardier's deeper leadership and one which neither sought nor expected plaudits. The right to govern because it was best that way. The way of showing that important departments and institutions trusted the Party's rights to form and administer the nation. Not perhaps the economic miracle that Bannister would have hoped for. Not even the way to get the nation singing from the terraces. But the tacit knowledge that there was only one Party to be trusted with the nation's security and wealth. It was thin. But it was worth a try. Grishin's book, correctly handled, could be the feel-good factor. Good old Dougal. Good old Grishin.

Bannister picked up the private telephone and called an unlisted number. Time, he thought, for a spot of Dundee cake and some strong tea in serious cups and a word in Henry's ear.

Twelve

Henry sipped his tea and watched his brother-in-law not eat his Dundee cake. From the walls, statesmen, generals and royal dukes captured in dull Victorian oils pondered the all but empty room. In one corner a long retired warrior sprawled and dozed, occasionally twitching as he refought a campaign of his youth. A grandfather clock kept the tempo of an archdeacon's nod as he listened intently to a right reverend's forecast of the likely make-up of the coming winter touring team for Australia. Simpson, who had served the club since the blitz, stood stooped and silent by the afternoon trolley, oblivious to the consideration of members who would never dream of letting him go to his retirement in Hornsey – wherever that was.

'Charles my dear, there is no twinkle in your eye. The cake is perhaps too dry?'

Bannister shifted. He was not certain how far he could manipulate the case of Grishin's memoir to the advantage of the Party. Should there be a slip, then the slide would not end until the last vote had been discounted.

'Tell me more about the book he wants to write.'

Colvil looked surprised. He certainly had not thought that Bannister would return so quickly to the matter. He flicked a crumb from his knee and removed the napkin from beneath his chins. Colvil enjoyed Dundee cake. But never more than one piece and never beyond four-thirty. It was five and twenty past the hour.

'It is not simply the book dear heart, it is the act of writing which is important.' He shook his head and his jowels mumbled through the next sentiment.

'You see, it allows us to give him a platform. He can then be free of our coffers and our exchequer of him.'

'So it's simply a matter of convenience. Then I really don't see the problem. Unless of course, there is something more?'

Henry Colvil dropped his voice and leaned slightly forward in his concession to the discreet nature of the subject.

'My Herod would say that the dangers of what he has to say should be observed. For our part, we, or rather some of my colleagues, would suggest that there is unfinished business which our visitor may be happy to close.'

There were times when Henry Colvil wondered how his brother-in-law had made such a name for himself at the Bar. On those occasions he reminded himself that the name had been in the chancery division where imagination was a distinct disadvantage. Colvil's blown sigh was that of a priest hampered by a weakling's heard confession. One's club was certainly not a place for explanations which required more than nods or silences of confirmation of secrets far too deep to exist beyond the twilight world of the Intelligence Services. His expression was patient, his explanation whispered.

'You see Charles, there are moments when some matters are best brought to the surface but not by our own fishermen. In the past, there have been moments of deep, um, treachery.'

Bannister shifted. He nodded. Headlines rather than heads flicked before him. Philby. Burgess. Maclean. Blunt. To Bannister they were traitors. He could understand some of the lesser names. They had been victims of greed and stupidity. The famous four had been members of his own sort. As old Cameron would have observed, indeed had done so, these folk had betrayed the Establishment under which the very fabric of British society and its finer values existed. Bannister sensed that Colvil's nudging towards publication had to do with that aspect of betrayal rather than the grubby secrets and wrongdoings of society's non-commissioned officers.

'You mean old man that there may still be names from the, ah, previous occasions? Names which have escaped public reprobation. Mm?'

'Indeed. Unfinished business. There are a few. Men who in times past have betrayed. Men who for reasons best known to those men in higher place, have been allowed to rest in peace.'

Bannister shook his head. Not in disbelief but in weary acceptance of so many wrongs that needed still to be righted.

'That's always been the case. Look at Blunt. Good God, we let the blighter carry on. He was even allowed to continued at the Palace. And a K – which we got back at the appropriate moment.'

Bannister sighed once more. 'We hardly give them on loan.' He shook his head. 'I don't see why your,' he looked around at the sleeping general and the concerned clerics, the shivering Simpson, 'I don't see why your Herod objects. Is it not in everyone's interests to bring these thundering people to book?'

Colvil raised his eyebrows. The world should agree. It rarely did.

'The problem Charles is one of degree. My Herod believes, um, sleeping curs are best left to lie. He sincerely believes that nothing is to be gained by sprinkling the, um, *meedia*, with insignificant names. His hypothesis concludes that questions will be asked as to why this business has been so long left unattended. Your very point about Blunt.'

Bannister sat back. There was something in this. They had gone through the whole analysis before. It was an extension of 'what did the President know?' and 'When did he know it?' On previous occasions when Parliament had been told, honourably enough, that betrayal had been belatedly discovered, MPs on all sides of the House had demanded satisfaction and noisily so. It was one of Dougal Baxter's more memorable comments that 'hell hath no fury like a Parliament scorned'.

Perhaps there was little to be gained by doctoring Grishin's memoirs to show the Government in a good light when the reason for the book was to make authority appear part of some unacceptable conspiracy of silence. Yet he was puzzled still.

'I see that Henry. There could clearly be more to lose that gain. But if this is so, why the split? Why do you and some of your friends believe C is wrong? It does seem to me that he could be immensely right. If he is, and you've more or less said that he could be, then why do you not go along with him? Mm?'

'Because dear heart, it is a question of unfinished business.'

'I know. You keep saying that. But I don't get the point.'

'It is one of honour. There are people who have never been brought to book.'

'Yes. Yes. Yes. A thousand times yes. I agree. But if we know who they are?'

'We most certainly do. Our visitor has told us, or rather he has told some of us.'

'And you believe they should be exposed publicly?'

'Most certainly. And so do you Charles. Why should they be allowed their secrets? After all, they did their very best to give away ours.'

Bannister's was an approving nod. 'I couldn't agree more. But in the present climate I simply cannot recommend to the Prime Minister that he overrules his head of Intelligence when there is no advantage to the Government.'

'And to the country?'

'The Government is the country. You cannot really

want to be governed by their lot. Certainly I can see why C is nervous of that. Presumably you have understated his objection.'

'I have put it as simply as I know how.'

Bannister smiled, he was not entirely taken in. 'Come on Henry, the Controller's argument is as plain as a pikestaff. If this had the political repercussions he imagines, then we would fall and your Service would be subjected to scrutiny and, worse still from your point of view, parliamentary accountability. Mm?'

Colvil clasped his podgy hands across his waistcoat, the fine gold watch-chain over his thumbs like some maharaja's head bangle.

'Of course there is always such danger. But my dear, we believe the importance of exposing these people is paramount.'

'Then why don't we do so? Why not bring them to justice in the normal way?'

Almost before the thought had left his mouth, Bannister knew the answer. Colvil had the grace to spell it out.

'Because Charles, any such exposure would have to be made by others. The, ah, clumsies.'

'You mean M.I.5.'

'Indeed I might mean those very souls.'

'And that would give M.I.5 a coup and you cannot tolerate the thought of them getting one up on you, especially now.'

Colvil looked away. Bannister, enjoying himself, went on.

'Because they are making a good case for taking over the whole intelligence operation in the UK and this would give them the chance of embellishing their case for doing so. And what's more,' Bannister paused like some great conductor triumphantly poised with the symphonic chords under his baton, and then swooped, 'because M.I.5's already onto this aren't they? They've found out what's going on haven't they? You want to get in before they do.'

He leaned back in his chair. The sudden movement caught Simpson's eye and Colvil waved the old servant away before more tea might be brought.

'Which Charles, would make so many look a little foolish.'

'But if it's published in his book, that's going to happen anyway isn't it?'

'Certainly not. He is our visitor. As matters stand, everyone must and will undoubtedly accept that we could have told his tale many moons ago. Should we have so wished. We thus protect ourselves from the silly accusation that we didn't know. You must Charles, convince your Herod to overrule mine.'

'And in exchange?'

'As you have observed my dear, it would be most helpful for all concerned if a few paragraphs showed Government to have been on top of the matter for the past ten years.'

Bannister was wary but happy to explore the idea.

'And presumably a statement from the PM that your people have long had the situation under control and had very good reason to let the scallywags remain at large would go unchallenged and would serve your cause well. Mm?'

'Most certainly. Five could hardly make any capital out of it.'

Bannister was warming to the idea at last. It seemed that both M.I.6 and Downing Street had much to gain although he still did not quite understand the Controller's caution. He had forgotten one thing. The list.

'One small matter old man. If this were to go ahead, and I'm not saying it will mind you, but if it were to, then of course I'd need the names well in advance.'

Colvil's slow blink of disapproval was obvious.

'Very difficult Charles. For the moment at least. I feel that gallery of rogues should remain uncovered until we know if your Herod approves.'

'It could help make up his mind.'

'But Charles, he employs you to do that. A loyal, a good and a faithful servant. Not the thought and reputation of traitors.'

'Nevertheless, one or two names would be helpful.'

'I'll see what may be arranged.'

Bannister was not done.

'After all, if they're minnows, it can't be that important. Is there anyone interesting on the list?'

'Not to most people.'

'Then to whom?'

The grandfather clock struck the half hour. Colvil's sense of theatre was satisfied.

'I'll not tell you yet Charles, but let us say there is one name which will most certainly amuse you.'

'I'm not at all certain I would be amused by the name of a traitor. But from what you're saying, it must be someone I know.'

'So it must Charles, so it must. And in good time you shall decide for yourself how amused you might be.'

He signalled to Simpson. Perhaps there was time for one more pot from Assam.

Thirteen

Bannister walked into Dougal Baxter's office to find it empty except for Kay Bennet standing on tiptoe on her boss's desk. She was stretching to the ceiling and holding a glass in one hand and a postcard in the other. The stretching had shortened even further her very short black jersey skirt. Bannister was embarrassed. She looked down as he came in, smiled, said she wouldn't be a moment and then with a mutter of triumph cupped the tumbler to the ceiling and slid the postcard between the plaster and the glass. A large black spider plopped into the trap and she took Bannister's offered hand and stepped elegantly down. She held up the specimen.

'Dougal can't stand them. He hates anything creepy-crawly.'

'I must say I've never been keen myself. But it's

something one learns to live with. I was brought up in a rather large house. Full of them. Then of course school.'

She smiled again, opened the window and dropped the spider to the ledge. She closed the window but continued to watch the spider.

'Full of creepy-crawlies I expect.'

Bannister started to answer and stopped. He was being teased. Kay wasn't watching. Her spider-trapping had laddered one leg of her tights. She was running a long-fingered hand along and up her leg. It was a slow motion. For his benefit. The way she was balanced, her legs were slightly apart, the skirt tighter than ever. Most of the men in the outer office might have dreamed of watching her. Bannister looked away. Unmoved. Laddered tights reminded him of scruffy courts and tarts.

'Where is he?' His voice was business-like.

Kay looked up. She sensed the mood change. She liked Charles Bannister and wanted to be accepted by him. No one knew she was Baxter's mistress. One day, maybe, there would be a time when she and Baxter would be together. He would never divorce his wife. His Church would never allow that. His wife, Ros, would be amused to keep him on a string until it suited her to let go. But one day. Kay pulled at her hem. The action only tightened the soft material over the tops of her thighs. Bannister did not want to, but he looked away. She coughed as if to help change the pace.

'In the Department. He said he'd be over, but he's got a delegation of American lawyers to see.'

Her voice was almost accentless yet somewhere there was a trace of Georgetown, where she had finished her Master's degree in international relations, and the beach talk of Tel Aviv where, as the daughter of a widowed archaeologist, she had been brought up. It came together as a natural, not contrived, huskiness. It was a warm voice. It was the voice of her mother whose maiden name Kay had taken when she returned to England in the belief that Arrens had been an unnecessary complication in an already complicated life.

Bannister's embarrassment had turned to tetchiness.

'I can't quite see why the Home Secretary has to see lawyers. Surely that's for the Attorney or someone else in the Department.'

'Northern Ireland? Extradition?'

Bannister nodded. He should have thought of it. The Home Secretary's brief was wider than many thought. Also Dougal Baxter was fascinated by all things American. He claimed to dislike them as a race but was almost childlike in his attitude to them individually. Mary Bannister had said it was because Dougal only met rich Americans and it was wealth that fascinated him.

The door banged open against the hat stand. Nick Potts, Dougal's chief researcher.

'Seen the chief then, Bisto?' He stopped. 'Oh sorry. Didn't realize.'

Nick was for ever on the move. He talked in his own language, often made up on the spot. A conversation would be peppered with advertising slogans. To Kay Bennet it was infuriating. To Polly Bannister it was hilarious. To Dougal Baxter it was immaterial because Nick's reports were quite different from anyone else's. Concise and pertinent.

Dougal Baxter's best speeches did not come from the Department team but from Nick's enthusiasm and Kay's ability to organize and direct the young man's energies. Theirs was a sometimes difficult relationship. Nick was probably the only male member of the staff who didn't drool at the sight of Kay's every movement. He felt sorry for her. They were two of a kind. In some sense both outsiders. Political offices like Dougal's could normally handle one outsider, rarely two.

Bannister nodded to them both.

'I must go. Please ask him to call me as soon as possible.'

As he started for the door which Kay now held open, he caught her scent and the movement beneath her silk blouse. He said nothing more. Bannister felt more at ease with women who rarely strayed for their wardrobes beyond sensible shops that sold costumes and frocks.

'What's the matter with him?'

Kay shrugged.

'Nothing. He's always like that. It's that stiff collar and waistcoat. Same as the military? Give them a uniform and officers act like officers.'

Nick flopped into his swivel chair and started tapping at the computer terminal. 'He wasn't in the army.'

She looked across from the filing cabinet. 'I didn't mean that. He's a type that's all. Anyway, how do you know?'

'Know what Jaffa?'

'That he wasn't in the military.'

'Just do that's all.'

She closed the door and sat down at her desk opposite his.

'Come on Nick. You don't just do anything. How d'you know?'

'Well. It's hardly a secret is it? No big deal. *Who's Who* would know and it doesn't so he wasn't. Bisto?'

'But why bother to find out in the first place? He's nothing to do with us.'

Nick continued tapping. He was working on his own disk and on his private Apple Mac instead of the office IBM system. He double-clicked a file. Within seconds Bannister's biography and closest friends appeared on the screen, only the file was not marked Bannister and the Party Chairman's name did not appear in the file. He looked up. Kay was waiting for an answer.

'Everyone's to do with us luv. Right? You never know when the Chief's going to need info.'

'And you've got it? Even on his closest friends.'

Nick added two lines to the file. Locked it. Cleared the screen and shut down.

'No one has close friends, not in this business Bisto. Not in this business.'

Fourteen

Juliet Cameron put down the telephone, frowned in worry rather than annoyance, picked up her handbag and an armful of files, hurried into the Commons corridor deep in thought without acknowledging the greetings of two of her colleagues, turned the corner and crashed into Bannister. The files went one way and her clutch-bag the other.

'We're going to have to think of something else you know.' His tone was affectionate. They were both crouched picking up scattered papers. Sharpe, the badge messenger, came up, helped, then discreetly went on his way. Messengers develop sixth senses. Sharpe's were finely tuned.

'What is it?'

Juliet Cameron looked wary. She did not want to let this man into her thoughts. She told him anyway.

'It's Pa. I've just been talking to him.'

She paused. Bannister did not want her to.

'And?'

'And, well, I don't know. That's the problem. What he says is fine. It's his voice. He's miles away.'

Bannister handed back the files. 'He sent me an invitation. Did you know?'

She shook her head. Bannister told her about the dinner.

'I'll try to talk to him. But I'm afraid a feast's hardly

85

the place for a heart to heart. The last person one talks to is one's host. Perhaps if I get there early.'

'Couldn't you stay over? They'll put you up in college won't they? Or you could always stay at the house.'

Bannister wanted to say yes he would. He wanted to say all sorts of comforting things. Bannister wasn't very good at comforting, so much so that he avoided asking after anyone's health in case they told him.

'We'll see.'

'Difficult?'

'I must be back first thing. I've got a surgery at midday.'

Juliet Cameron nodded. She understood. She should have been going up to her own constituency. She could drive from her father's home to Norwich in an hour, especially on her motorbike. The agent disapproved. Said it was the sort of gimmick they could do without. Juliet had been driving bikes since she was seventeen so she didn't take too much notice. This weekend, she would put in an appearance, but only if her father were well.

'Try will you? He's just told me he doesn't want me to come this weekend. Most of the time he's complaining that I never come to see him. Now . . . well, I just don't know what to think.'

'Will you be there?'

Her gaze was steady. The eyes non-committal.

'Yes.'

'I see.'

From the tall desk George Sharpe watched the Party Chairman and Opposition Back-bencher deep in conversation. From where he stood, Sharpe couldn't hear what they said. Apart from the distance, MPs soon learned to talk in confidential voices without any conspiratorial air. But the badge messenger had been around for a few years. He knew a thing or two, he did. He knew how to pick up signs and he said as much when he saw Bannister's assistant, Rose. He was delivering uncollected messages.

'Didn't realize they knew each other.'

Rose had been around for just as long and she knew a gossip when she heard one. Even though she disapproved, the Commons existed on gossip and everyone listened. But Rose knew how to play the game and knew its rules. She wheezed before sipping at her twentieth cup of tea that day. She didn't offer George Sharpe a cup.

Rose worked on the principle that where the carpet started badge messengers stopped. Now she sipped once more and carefully put down her cup into its saucer and then put both on the desk before replying – carefully. Sharpe had something on his mind and she wanted it.

'Most Members do, don't they? Once they've been here a bit.'

''Spose you're right, Rose. 'Spose you're right.'

He made for the door. She knew he wouldn't go. He didn't. He turned. Rather handsome, she thought, in his white tie, tails and stiff front with his gold chain and badge hanging over his midriff. He had something else to say. He'd hoped she would have given him a prompt. She didn't. He spoke anyway.

'It's just that they're not on any committees together, opposite sides so to speak.'

'Mm?'

'Well, it's just that most Members stick to their own.'

'Is that it?'

Sharpe tried another card, saving his trump.

'Course the papers say that she's a bit wild you know.'

'Do they now.'

'Oh yes. Of course with her looks . . .' He tailed off. Rose did not.

'She would be?'

'Naturally. And according to a couple of blokes down in Annies, well they say she's got something going with another Member. Only they're discreet you know.'

'In other words they don't know.'

'They say whoever it is is pretty high up. You know, in the Government.'

Rose thought it time to pounce. 'Well just between you and me, George Sharpe, Mr Bannister has known Miss Cameron for a long time.'

Sharpe looked over his shoulder. The door was closed, but you could never be sure.

'Oh yes?'

'Oh yes. You see, Mr Bannister's known her since she was a babe. Her dad was his teacher or whatever they call it at Cambridge. Now will that do you? You'll do me a favour if you'll stop dropping hints about schemes and romances. Okay?'

Sharpe bobbed his head. He'd been clobbered. He didn't want to get on Rose's bad side.

'Is that so? Oh isn't that nice now. Very nice.' He was opening the door and with what he hoped was at least an equalizer looked back with what passed for a smile. 'Funny what she calls him though, isn't it?'

Rose raised an eyebrow. It was enough of a question for Sharpe.

'Funny she should call him Chang. Never heard that one before have you now? Friendly though. Don't you think? Perhaps it's something from way back, you know, when they were in Cambridge. Well, as they used to say on *The Glums*, "Hello, Hello, Hello". Or in my case goodbye, goodbye, goodbye.'

And with yet another half-remembered saying from his beloved Light Programme, George Sharpe, who often loitered in the darkest parts of the Commons and overheard all manner of conversation which he stored for future use, was gone. He was careful not to bang the door. Another habit of his.

Rose picked up her cup and saucer. No she hadn't heard that one. Chang? She wondered where it came from and looked through to Bannister's open door to the empty inner office where the photograph of the Bannister family stood loyally on his desk.

Downstairs, in the bowels of the Commons, Nick Potts, on his second pint, was deep in conversation with Eamon the barman. The subject was horses. Eamon knew more about horses than anyone Nick had met.

Eamon had the inside on every stable, every jockey and every trainer's thoughts, ambitions and manipulations. The only problem was, Eamon was rarely on a winner. He often knew who was going to win and then he would back an outsider. Eamon, in short, avoided favourites because they would never return what he said was 'an interesting profit'. He turned the *Racing Chronicle* and pointed to a horse with two thirds and a second that season.

'Wouldn't you be excited skinny if that came in at 33–1 young Nick? Now wouldn't you?'

'I'd be excited if it came in before dark. The last horse you gave me bit the lad and was withdrawn.'

'That he did. But did you see the ugly fucker? I'd a bit him meself given a chance and an eighth.'

When George Sharpe came in, Nick was onto his third pint and twentieth poorly place bet of the evening. Sharpe on the other hand knew which gee-gee to back. Only he was not a betting man, but he knew Nick was.

Keeping in with people like Nick could show a profit. They often heard things in the private offices. Give them a couple of pints and they might even tell you. So a good two-way was always handy. There was a grey jumping at a northern track the next day that would see Nick a favour for a ten pound note. It was a mare by the name of Chairman Mao.

'Funny about Chinese names. They come up everywhere.'

Nick nodded. He supposed they did. And so George Sharpe told him about Chang.

Fifteen

Dougal Baxter was in his finest form. He had what he called a scheme running. Baxter's schemes were never to do with anything else but the future prospects of Dougal Baxter. In spite of limited intellectual ability, a sometimes abrasive nature and perhaps because of a total disregard for almost anyone, Dougal Baxter had succeeded thus far. He had become Home Secretary at a time when the obvious candidate for the job would have possibly used it as a springboard to Number 10. The Prime Minister had been tempted and would have made the appointment had it not been for eleventh-hour advice from one of his most loyal colleagues. That loyalist, with great deference to the PM's judgement, had suggested that the ruthlessly ambitious candidate for the Home Office would possibly form a schism within Cabinet and therefore pose a threat to the leadership. The Prime Minister, fiercely loyal to those he implicitly trusted, had thanked Dougal Baxter for his wise counsel and had given him the Home Office.

Baxter saw now that stage two of his scheme was nearing port. Baxter, who had never been nearer to the oceans than a ferry ride and one short visit to the royal yacht, was nevertheless fond of sailing metaphors. They gave him, or so he felt, that hint of machismo to round off his public image. They did not. But Baxter's arrogance was sufficient to believe that if he believed something then others would be equally easily convinced. He now sat back in the largest armchair in his Commons room and eyed Bannister with jovial suspicion.

'Come on Charles, you know the time's not far away. There are twenty-eight Back-benchers, our own Back-benchers mind you, who are willing to stand up and be counted. You must know that. My God I hope you do. You are Party Chairman. Or had you forgotten?'

Bannister sighed, as he so often had since the day they had first met at school. Even then Dougal's ambition had been beyond disguise. He had done well by scheming, often because others were not interested enough to stop him. But he had never reached the top. Never would as far as Charles Bannister was concerned, especially in the House, where, although luck played its part, without the Party machine deciding what was proper, no number of high straights and full houses would allow even the most ambitious gambler into Number 10.

'Dougal, I tell you, there is no chance of this working. Nor should it be encouraged.'

'Charles, you have three or four pet phrases, most of which I have heard once a month since we were thirteen and all of which are supposed to maintain the *status quo*, even when it is clear to everyone else that the *status quo* is untenable.'

Bannister stood and, his arms folded like some

Victorian academic demonstrator, started to pace the room.

'I have already told you that there is every sign that the economy is coming together. You saw what happened at the conference. There was no serious opposition.'

'Only because it was beautifully stage-managed by you.'

'My God Father James. Those days are gone. One can manage so much but with all the media attention of the past couple of years, that is no longer possible.'

He paused. Baxter was spinning a paper-knife as if it were some marker on a ouija-board. His face was the picture of ambition. Bannister knew also that to some extent that his old friend was right. But he was not right enough.

'Dougal, you must accept that you are in the same position as the too ambitious candidate for ordination. You are in danger of having a huge "Not Yet" marked on your card. That will do no one any good at all. This is not the time to put up against the Bombardier.'

'The annual election? Oh I wasn't thinking of standing. Oh no. Not me.'

Bannister sat down. 'You can hardly expect me, or anyone else for that matter, to take seriously the claims of your famous twenty-eight. There isn't a name between them.'

Baxter laughed. Or he made the sort of noise he kept for occasions when he was trying to laugh. Baxter only laughed at either his own jokes or the misfortune of others.

'No. No. No. Charles. Not them. Not me. You.'

Bannister headed for the door.

'Now I know you're off your chump.'

He paused, his hand on the knob.

'I'm seeing the PM about this Grishin affair after dinner tonight. You can come with me. We're dining at eight. All right?'

Baxter wasn't so easily dismissed. His voice was theatrically quiet. 'They're asking for you Charles. So am I.'

Bannister left the door unopened.

'To stand against the PM at Leader Election. Nonsense. And you know it. I would never contemplate such disloyalty, certainly not at the behest of a bunch of, of, well I can't bring myself to describe them. Dougal, I am very angry at all this.'

Baxter indicated the chair beside his. 'Sit down for a moment Charles.'

'There is nothing more to hear. I've heard enough and it is nonsensical.'

'Charles, please.'

Bannister sat down. Baxter was speaking even before the cushion had given way to Bannister's angular frame.

'Tomorrow morning *The Times* will be carrying an article saying that the time has come for change.'

'When doesn't it? Every serious newspaper seems to have a dozen sad fellows in the Lords willing to write some such nonsense for a fee.'

Baxter waved his hand.

'Hear me out Charles. Hear me out. This is not one of those pieces. This is the leader column. It will be saying that there is a great deal of support for change, that the country needs it. Europe needs it, the banks need it, the pound needs it and therefore the economy needs it if confidence is to be restored. As you said yourself, if the economy doesn't come right then we don't.'

Bannister was long on frustration and short on energy. He had enough on his mind.

'This has nothing to do with me and if what you say is true, well, thank-you for the warning. I shall prepare myself to trot off to Broadcasting House and tell Peter Hobday and the rest of the country that it's all nonsense. But really Dougal, I've enough on my plate without these silly games.'

'Don't be so pompous.'

'I'd hardly call my attitude pompous.'

'Of course you wouldn't Charles. But it is.'

'If by that you mean a sense of how we should behave, how we should at least go through the motions of decent behaviour, how we should rehearse our ideas of loyalty, if you call that pompous, then I accept that you have a point. But I do not regard fundamental loyalty to leadership until such times that that leadership is unworkable as an example of pomposity. And I must say old man, this scheme of yours, and I assume it is yours, I must say I regard it as a very silly exercise indeed.'

'Not silly Charles. Reality. Elsewhere in the paper will be a news story which says that there is an increasingly influential body of Party opinion which is demanding that we get back to old values . . .'

'Including loyalty?'

'Including loyalty.'

'It most certainly doesn't sound like it.'

'We are talking about loyalty to the Party. That's more important than loyalty to the individual, especially when the individual in question is damaging the Party's chances of remaining in government. Which is exactly what you were talking about just now but you can't see we've already arrived at that point.'

'And what has any of this to do with me, excepting of course that I'm the one who has to go out into the market-place and calm nerves?'

'Everything Charles. Everything. That other article, which is bound to be followed up by all the other papers, and the television will be saying that you are the unanimous choice as an alternative leader.'

Bannister drummed his fingers along the arms of the chair. He was fighting for self-control. He was very angry.

'How in blazes do you know all this?'

'Because I have, let us say, arranged it. I've had a word with the right people and the right people have responded. There is a Lobby system Charles, or had you forgotten?'

'I'll not have this. I'll simply not have this. You have

no right to interfere in the way we control our relations with the Press.'

'Our problem stems from the fact that we don't. We don't control our relations with the Press. We have failed to be anything but objects of criticism. We both know why. Our policies have been botched. We have had little in the way of leadership. But most of all it's been the failure to sell ourselves to people who are supposed to be on our side.'

'And you believe that I should stand against the Bombardier. How crass. You have not even had the courtesy to consult me.'

'You'd have said no.'

'Of course I would.'

'Then there's your answer.'

'I will not allow my name to be put forward for the ballot.'

'Naturally.'

Bannister stared at Baxter's smug expression and for the thousandth time wondered why it was they had remained Baxter's version of friends.

'If you knew that, then why are we going through this charade? With modesty, I'm a little too senior and too long in the tooth to allow myself to put up as a stalking horse. I could name you a score of Members with safe seats and reputations for acceptable eccentricity who would do that.'

'You? A stalking horse? Whatever next?'

'I'm beginning to wonder.'

'You will not have to be Charles. Listen to this.'

Dougal Baxter snuggled into his chair as a story-teller might when his children are about his knees by the firelight.

'My plan is for you to be seen as the alternative. Good old-fashioned values. Scion of the Party. Would never do anything to rock the boat unless you thought it absolutely necessary. No record of ambition. Wonderful sense of public duty. A wonderful sense Charles, you really have. I much admire it you know.'

'Get on with it.'

'The momentum from that will take over. One of those dreadful lawyers from Washington today had the right expression. He called it the "Big Mo".'

'Dougal. Please.'

'You, of course Charles, deny that you're interested. The more you do, the more people will believe you are because elsewhere we shall be keeping the "Mo" rolling. And then Charles, at the last moment, guess what happens.'

The Party Chairman was in no mood for guessing. He did not. Baxter didn't mind continuing.

'Very simply, when the momentum is overwhelming in your favour, it will mean in truth that it is in absolute favour of the Prime Minister going. The PM will see sense, or be encouraged to, and that Charles, is the point when I, reluctantly mind, step forward and agree to take over.'

Bannister shook his head slowly. It was a quietly expressed sense of exasperation.

'And why Dougal, why should he not see this coming a mile off?'

Baxter's expression was one of genuine pain.

'Why, Charles, because he trusts me.'

Sixteen

They dined at eight. The Bannisters, when they were together during the week, always dined at eight. Being together was not something Charles, Mary and Polly managed very often. Charles was usually at some official function and then rushing back to the House for a division at ten o'clock.

Although she had to play the Party Chairman's wife at black tie dinners and after-six cocktails, Mary found herself more and more spending long evenings, as she put it, 'curled up with hot chocolate, a good book and my neuroses'. Polly had her own life. She had dropped out of her final year at the Guildhall. She didn't want to be a cellist nor did she want to spend the rest of her life teaching children not to be cellists. Now she was doing occasional work in Dougal's private research department, something which he had, against all advice, kept going when he became Home Secretary.

Dougal was not dining with them. He was supposed to have done but had cried off at the last moment. He'd been quite sorry but something had come up in the Department. Mary had sighed like goodly Mistress Bannister, mentally adjusted her mob-cap and then, in one of her 'sod it' moods, had left Dougal's place set. It was that sort of meal.

Every so often the other guests would glance at the empty place, the laid cutlery and folded napkin, with all the secret thinking of a Hitchcock thriller. Bannister himself took no notice. But then he rarely took notice of anything at home unless it was an account to be settled or a bathroom not spotlessly cleansed. Bannister's personal neurosis was dirty bathrooms, in fact household grubbiness of any sort.

By the time the guests had gone, it was almost time for Bannister's midnight meeting with the Prime Minister. Late sessions were not encouraged by Number 10. The PM liked to get to bed as early as possible and then rise by five to work on his boxes. Also he feared that late-night visits would be seen as crisis meetings.

This evening, Bannister was in no great hurry. He walked across the park, nodding good-night to a bovine Back-bencher heading determinedly in a northerly direction and to a small flat off Hill Street where he would enjoy himself until the early hours. Bannister's lip turned in distaste and he made a mental note to have a private word with the Chief Whip. Thanks to Henry, Bannister knew what went on in the flat and other erotic predilections of the Back-bencher. The Chief Whip could either warn off the man or save it for a time when he appeared to be wavering over a vote and use the information to force him into the right lobby at ten o'clock.

Bannister had telephoned ahead and without fuss he

was let into the garden entrance of Number 10 and within two minutes his coat had been taken and he was upstairs in the private apartments of the Prime Minister. Dougal Baxter was already there, comfortable on the sofa with a glass of fizzy water in his hand. The sitting-room was surprisingly small. The Bombardier's wife, known to other Cabinet wives as Missie Mouse, described the flat as cosy. She spent as little time as possible in Downing Street, preferring the comfort of their family home with its executive downstairs cloak-room, its net curtains and smell of lavender spray furniture polish. An enterprising publisher was helping her put some early poems in order and really wanted her to do an illustrated Number 10 cook book. She smiled at Charles, asked him if he would like some tea, put a hand on her husband's shoulder, told him not to stay up too late and said good-night. The Bombardier watched her go admiringly and felt annoyed with himself that he had not kissed her good-night. They kept separate rooms.

He pointed Bannister to the firm armchair and set down a scarlet-covered file and folded his hands, neatly, in his lap.

'Well Charles. You now think we should go ahead with this Grishin fellow. I thought we'd agreed the best thing was to do nothing.'

Bannister nodded. He was wondering if Grishin was at all relevant to the real question on his mind. Baxter was beaming. For the moment Bannister ignored him.

'I have arranged that the Grishin memoir will

contain very flattering paragraphs about the way in which the Government has handled the whole Intelligence gathering operation during the past ten years and in particular about the way you have personally overseen the most delicate matters. I believe that we, as a Government, and more importantly, you as a Prime Minister, come out of this rather well.'

'How nice.'

The Bombardier was smiling. Bannister did not understand.

'How nice?'

'Yes. How nice. Don't you think so Dougal?'

'Absolutely. I particularly like the part which shows you in a good light. How clever Charles. How very clever.'

Bannister wished he were standing. He always handled these situations much better on his feet. In court he had been much more impressive than in chambers. When Charles stood up in the House, there was the same feeling. Now he felt unsure, especially about Dougal.

'The idea is that this will provoke a round of good news for us. It'll show we're sure-footed.'

'Which we are of course.'

The PM turned to Dougal, still smiling. He liked Dougal. He trusted him. Unfortunately he did not like his Party Chairman. He never doubted his loyalty or his competence. But Charles Bannister was, well, very superior. The PM always felt inadequate in Bannister's company, and confused too because after all he was

Prime Minister and Charles was not. What he could not quite work out was why Charles did not want to be. The PM could not understand how anyone in politics could be without ambition for Number 10. But Bannister was not ambitious. He did not need to be. The family had money, innate social position in almost any society they chose to enter and a long history. The PM had none of these things. He could never warm to Bannister but neither did he see him as a threat. Until this evening.

'You think it'll show me in a good light do you?'

'Most certainly.'

'Give us a boost. Get the ratings up do you?'

'Not dramatically, but it will help consolidate our position.'

'And mine?'

Baxter was still beaming. Charles nodded again.

'Undoubtedly.'

There was a pause. The PM's smile was still there, but it had not quite reached his eyes.

'Then how do you explain *The Times* leader column and the Lobby piece?'

Baxter looked suitably serious and rocked his head in his best courtier's fashion. Baxter would never be sage-like but on these difficult occasions he tried very hard. The PM's smile had gone. He was waiting for an answer from his Party Chairman. Bannister thought slowly and sensibly before he spoke.

'I'm afraid I'm not sure to what it is you're referring.'

The PM reached for the scarlet folder and two

photocopied cuttings from the edition of *The Times* just starting to circulate for the morning and which the late evening television shows had picked up in their reports of the early editions. Charles had not seen the papers, had not heard the news, had not been telephoned from Front Office by those who had heard, seen and read. He had not forgotten about the planted story and briefing that had produced the leader column, but with other matters on his mind he had made a small yet significant slip. He had thought more about the ambitions of Dougal Baxter than about the consequences for himself. He now realized why Dougal had not been at dinner.

Bannister glanced at the cuttings the PM handed him. They were more or less as Dougal had told him they would be, including the article which suggested that a growing Back-bench and grassroots opinion showed that he, Charles Bannister, was the leading candidate to restore the Government's fortunes with his senses of decency, moral courage, old-fashioned values and quiet and godly governance. It was all there. Cranmer himself could have written it.

The PM was still waiting. Baxter was perfectly Baxter.

'I'm sure Charles has had no part in this if that's what you mean. Let's not, if I may say, lose sight of our main objective. We need to restore the atmosphere we once enjoyed when the electorate and the newspapers were sure we were heading for the right port even if they disagreed with the course we were setting.'

The Prime Minister was not going to be distracted from his need to get a response from Bannister. He understood Dougal's attempt to smooth things. The PM had never gone along with a widely held view at Westminster that Dougal Baxter was ruthlessly ambitious and hoped that one day he would be PM. The Bombardier accepted that Dougal wanted to be PM one day, but that he could understand and accept. But he knew by instinct that his Home Secretary's first loyalty was to the Party and to the present PM.

Now he wanted Bannister to deny that he was attempting to undermine Number 10's authority. He hoped he would deny it. He wanted to be sure. He knew full well there was nothing that he could do to sidetrack Bannister. Sacking him as Party Chairman was out of the question. That would be seen as a panic measure and therefore a sign of the PM's weakness. He was sure he had many enemies. In fact he believed that most of his so-called colleagues were really enemies. Thank goodness for Baxter. He might be ambitious but he wouldn't usurp their friendship and trust to achieve that ambition. When he spoke the PM's tone was uncompromising.

'Well Charles. What do you think?'

'Frankly, I think there is mischief afoot. I believe, in fact we both know, there is a Back-bench cabal, and that's all it is, a cabal, which is intent on causing damage. Yes, perhaps they want to get rid of you. There hasn't been a Prime Minister in this country who has felt safe when the economy was on the run. And the three of us know why Members become disloyal when they think their seats might be in danger at the next election. Mm?'

The PM still wanted to hear him say it. 'What about your own position? What do you think?'

Bannister knew how to handle the PM. He had been his Chief Whip. He knew exactly what to say and he had recovered his ground. He pretended he had not understood the sense of the question and answered as any loyal colleague would.

'Frankly, I don't think they'll get very far. I imagine everyone with an ounce of sense knows I'm the last person to float in this nonsense. I suggest we ignore it. We certainly don't allow anyone to respond in any way If, and it will, if it comes up in PMQs then I suggest you simply dismiss it. I'll certainly be at your side when you do.'

The Bombardier relaxed. He had heard what he wanted to hear, but you could never be sure. For the moment the response was adequate. Dougal Baxter's slight throat clearing was that practised by close advisers since Walsingham.

'Dougal?'

'Nothing really. I was simply thinking that Charles might find himself in a difficult position. He is bound to be asked questions on one of the silly radio programmes.'

'I think old man, you may leave that safely to me. I will be the first to make it clear that the whole thing is utter nonsense and that there is no question of any change.'

106

Suddenly the Prime Minister was standing. His cardigan was lambs' wool and neatly buttoned. He was a very neat person.

'I must get to bed. Lots to do you know. Lots to do.'

The other two rose to their feet. Bannister wasn't quite finished.

'Just one small matter now this *Times* nonsense is out of the way . . .'

The Bombardier interrupted him. 'Is it?'

'Why certainly.'

Dougal was not going to be left out. 'But Charles, these matters are never out of the way until something else has been put in their place. You know that.'

The PM was smiling again. Good old Dougal.

Seventeen

Baxter's bodyguard had been waiting in the chequered hall of Number 10 and had followed them through to the back, into the garden and out towards a deserted Horse Guards. It was difficult for Bannister to say what he had to with a keen-sensed detective inspector within earshot. At the corner they stopped. Bannister kept his voice low.

'Dougal this has got to stop. I will not have it. I will not be party to your miserable little game.'

'Charles, you're so sensitive. It'll be quite painless. Trust me.'

And with that he waved a goodbye and was gone.

By the time Bannister arrived back at the flat it was almost one-thirty. The light was on in their bedroom and Mary was just finishing a telephone call. Bannister entered the room just as she was replacing the receiver.

'Who was that?'

'Hello darling. How are you? You're looking ravishing tonight. Thanks for a lovely dinner. The fish was splendid. Sorry I'm late. Any messages?'

'I'm sorry. Thanks very much. Yes it was. Splendid. The fish I mean.'

'Of course you do Charles. My pleasure.'

'Who was on the phone?'

Mary snuggled beneath the blankets. Her voice was muffled.

'A friend.'

'I'd have thought it a trifle late for a friend.'

'It's never too late for a friend darling. That's what they're for.'

'I see.'

Bannister went through to his dressing-room. Mary sensed his mood. She pulled the blanket down from her chin.

'Trouble at mill?'

'Mm. Mm.'

'Dougal?'

'How d'you know?'

'It usually is, when it isn't Polly.'

Bannister reappeared in a bathrobe. 'He's up to his old tricks.' He opened their bathroom door.

'And is the Bombardier?'

'What?'

'Up to Dougal's old tricks?'

'He doesn't know what to think. As usual, it's all in the paper. You'll see in the morning.'

She could hear the water running. She raised her voice. 'I know. It was on the midnight news. The papers have been on and the *Today* programme want you to call them.'

There was a pause. Bannister came back to the door. He looked strained. Stripped of his white stiff collar and tightly tailored blue pinstripes, Bannister also looked older than his fifty or so years.

'When was this?'

'Three or four times.'

He looked at the bedside telephone, walked over to it and switched off the bell.

'Blast! Blast! Blast!' Each word came out evenly spaced and with enormous feeling. 'They can go to hell.'

'Oh they've been there darling. That's why they're calling.'

Eighteen

As Party Chairman, Bannister was in something of a dilemma. Part of his job was to put the media straight on rumours. The PM's Press Secretary was the Downing Street spokesman. Charles spoke for the Party. He was the troop rouser. He was the organization man. He was the man to trot out the denials, the pained expressions and the Clap-Hands-Here-Comes-Victory speeches. He was the warm-up man for the main act – the Prime Minister. For most of the next day Bannister was being forced to speak at a personal level. The problem was obvious. The parliamentary journalistic mafia, known as 'The Lobby', knew there was something behind the story. They knew there had been a briefing although only one of the pack knew from whom. Bannister did not wish to ridicule the whole matter but recognized that he must distance himself and the Prime Minister from the mess. By the evening he believed he had.

As he headed his Alvis towards Cambridge, the six o'clock Radio Four news was playing down his part but emphasizing that there were those at Westminster who believed that Government Back-benches had made their first move in unseating the Bombardier. The leadership elections were in three weeks and for the first time there was a suggestion they would hold more interest than usual.

By the time Bannister swung into the Master's car-park he had discarded for the moment his political worries. It was good to be back. It always was.

The college porter who showed him to a guest room was well aware of the political gossip and was itching to give the celebrated old member his opinion. Fortunately for both of them, the porter confined himself to passing on the message that Professor Cameron would call on him at seven-thirty.

Bannister lay in the long deep bath and thought back to the days when he had, as a young undergraduate, wondered about the future and being away from this place. He'd always known he would go into public service. First had come law. He had never enjoyed it. He'd done well, taken silk quite early and had married sensibly.

He looked up to the badly painted ceiling with the damp patch in the high corner and the brilliant white pipes, thick and liable to violent juddering when stressed by the simple act of someone drawing a bath. He loved the solid feel of the place and wondered how long it would all last. The college had been there more than four hundred years. It was far from one of the older houses, but old enough not to feel the need to rush matters. Yet there was, he knew, a new breed. On Bannister's last visit the Master had offered the thought that the running of the college by the Fellows was done through the governing body and 'not through the governing mind'. He probably told it to all visitors, but there was an element of truth. Times brought about the changes to things Bannister wished left unchanged. But as he towelled himself in front of the long mirror, Bannister knew that was a great deal to do with his own ageing and his fears of what getting old might mean.

Bannister was not a vain man yet he worried about his thinning hair. His hands had started to look older than his face. Even bruises took longer to heal. He did not want to be an elder statesman. He did not wish to be a grand old man of politics. When the time came to go from the House, he hoped that he would be fit enough to go without fuss and then disappear from public view. Just another old man with problems in the waterworks.

The knock at the outer door, the oak, brought him back to the evening and he opened it to find an uncertain Cameron tugging his chin as if he were not sure of the address.

Cameron pumped his hand and shuffled by him with a rustle of his scarlet gown. Bannister felt underdressed in his dinner jacket. Cameron eyed him.

'I can find you a gown if you wish.'

'Is it necessary?'

'No. Nothing's necessary.' With that he flopped into an armchair, the flop of an old man, thought Bannister. The flop of a man with few strong muscles to control his motions.

'You're looking well sir. Very well indeed.'

He was not. Cameron knew he was not but he did not mind Bannister telling him he did. He grunted something Bannister did not catch and smiled, the dull light of the standard lamp not quite catching the watery eyes. When he spoke, he did so with the preciseness Bannister had never forgotten.

'I'm well you say?'

'Yes sir. You are.'

'Do you mean I do not normally look well.'

'No. I meant that you looked well and how pleased I am that you're not looking, eh, otherwise.'

Bannister had almost forgotten the ritual of exact

112

meaning on these occasions. He remembered coming to Cameron's rooms one afternoon at the start of his second year and being genuinely happy to be back and with his tutor. He remembered saying that it was nice to see him and Cameron stopping in his tracks, looking quite bewildered and asking, 'Do you mean it is sometimes not nice to see me?' It was a game. Cameron was speaking once more, gazing through the window as if expecting an unconventional visitor though the tall Georgian frames.

'And you Charles. What of you? I expect you are kept busy by the events of this day. The Master tells me there was something in the paper concerning you. Do you enjoy being in the public prints?'

Bannister had never considered whether or not he actually enjoyed appearing in the papers. He suspected that he did not, but it was something which came with the rations of the job.

'Not enjoy, but it no longer concerns me.'

'When did it concern you?'

'Well I suppose it always has. It depends what they are saying.'

'So you are a thespian. You look each day to see if you've received good notices. You must have many critics.'

'Thousands.'

Cameron squinted. Then it dawned. He chuckled and his head dropped at an angle as if remembering times past.

'Mm. The electorate. Very good. Very good. Being

accountable to anyone other than oneself is disagreeable. Don't you think?'

'I'm afraid there is always someone who knows something.'

'And sometimes too much?'

Bannister smiled. 'If you mean too clever, perhaps. If you mean that there's always someone who knows the truth, then yes. "He is the freeman whom the truth makes free"?'

Cameron's look was sharp, the suspicious glance of the old and wary. Then he relaxed.

'Oh yes, your dear poet. But be careful how you use him. He also observed that "wisdom is humble that he knows no more". But yes, yes I suppose truth does free us from . . .'

The pause was long. Bannister sensed conflict. Uncertainty. He waited for Cameron to continue but the old man seemed to have forgotten what it was he wished to say. Bannister felt slightly uncomfortable.

'But then I suppose we should be asked to define freedom and ask what is truth.'

The lamp's light was in Cameron's eyes. Bannister could not imagine what was on the old man's mind but he looked worried. He was about to ask what time they were expected across in hall when Cameron wagged his finger at him.

'You, Charles, need not define nor ask. You know when you are free and you know what is, at the time, truth. Both are luxuries, neither are guaranteed. There is no certainty left.'

114

Bannister was puzzled. There was an energy in Cameron's tone that was not simply in the younger man's imagination. He probed, but gently.

'Are you disturbed by what you imagine to be truth? Perhaps we reach an age when we feel a more urgent need to define truth. That means we recognize how quickly time runs out. I was thinking only this evening . . .'

Cameron interrupted with a wave of a finger. 'I have, most of my life Charles, been quite certain that I did not understand truth. I have always known that truth is but a convenient label which allows us to point to something unacceptable and accuse it of being untrue. I am not a scientist and therefore I have none of the scientist's convenient definition and laws which make truth irrelevant and only complex or simple equations important as long as they may be balanced on a blackboard or, I suppose now, on an electronic apparatus.'

'You're saying that those, or some of those things you thought to be true, or labelled as truths, are, are, are what?'

'They are unfaithful Charles. I am a foolish man and an old and foolish man is quite vulnerable to unfaithfulness and far beyond the thought "that truth lies somewhere, if we knew but where".'

'Cowper.'

'Yes Charles, your friend once more. He was writing of hope, if we knew but where.'

Bannister crossed an elegant leg, first setting aside the immaculate crease in his trousers. He was out of

115

his depth. He had not come to talk of truth and freedom yet he knew from memory that the old man rarely floated a thought unless he wished to develop it. Bannister shifted in his chair.

'Ahm, Jules, Juliet suggested you wished to talk about something. Mm?'

He might have shouted 'Fire!' In a moment Cameron was struggling from the armchair and making for the door and the scrubbed wooden staircase.

'Come on. Drink.'

The moment gone. Cameron was stumbling down the wide stairway, the door slamming behind him. Bannister, surprised and wondering, caught up beyond the chapel where a top-hatted head porter ushered the straggling Fellows and the guests into the ante-room of raised and quickly drained glasses.

Very few dons would drink in their own rooms that night. Being a feast, the dinner wines were all paid for from an old endowment. This was a college night, it tickled the meanness in them all.

Dinner was noisy. The Elizabethan hall was a great shoe-box and its acoustics would have delighted a concert master. Rows of conversation made it impossible to hear very much. The evening would have been an adventure playground for a speech therapist. Bannister was on the top table and sat between a philosopher and Cameron. The philosopher had the peculiar skill of talking about his own work whether or not there was any indication that his neighbour listened. He was working on metaphysical expression when Bannister switched off and resorted to constituency trained how-wonderfuls and indifferent food.

On Bannister's left, Cameron said very little. During each course he would eat at a furious rate and with his head bent to the table. Cameron's soup had gone almost before Bannister had picked up his spoon. The first sorbet disappeared in three mouthfuls. The plaice fillets were bunched, swept about the cream sauce and stuffed in his mouth with a great deal of spillage and choking sounds. The venison was attacked before Bannister had been completely served. By this dish, the philosopher had tired of Bannister and had turned to his own guest, a Dr Morrison, a stunning black woman from Harvard.

When Bannister had been introduced to her in the ante-room she had said nothing but 'Yes' and 'No' in answer to what he had hoped were polite questions. When Bannister had asked what she did, Dr Morrison had said moral philosophy in such a tone that it was assumed by her that he would not understand and by Bannister that she was right. Now the philosopher and the good doctor were engaged in furious debate. Yes, she had been right.

Cameron was talking, but Bannister missed most of what he had to say. The wine had been good and the professor emeritus had quaffed rather than sipped, so much so that Bannister could only admire the servants who kept the various glasses topped. He noticed that Cameron's was refilled more than those about him. Cameron had come up in 1938. The servants knew his ways. But tonight he seemed a little the worse for the college's drink.

Twice Bannister bent to the old man's side, but over the din found it hard to understand him. In fact he said little. His precise remarks had become codes. Bannister picked out phrases but none made sense. Later the Master told Bannister that he was concerned for Cameron's health but did not say why; the philosopher said 'Good night Mr Bannerman' and the lady from Cambridge, Mass. gave him a number three smile and said 'Goodbye', but so distantly and when she was looking elsewhere, that even Bannister felt insignificant.

Bannister had, in spite of half-promises, intended to pick up his bag and press on to his home in Hampshire and his hoped-for weekend. But the cold night air had done little for Cameron's resistance to San Patricio, fresh Chablis, dry claret, sweet Sauterne, the college port and the third passing of the single malt. Bannister had abstained. He helped Cameron into the front passenger seat and with directions from the night porter set off along the Hills Road searching by moonlight for the promised "igh 'edges and three funny chimneys'.

He had almost forgotten she would be there. Juliet opened the door and took her father's arm and helped him in his slow progress up the wide Edwardian staircase. Twice he stopped and turned. Twice he slowly blinked at Bannister waiting at the foot of the stairs.

'We must talk some time.'

The words came out slowly and with pain. They

118

came with a sweep of an arm which would have done for his balance if it had not been for his daughter's own arm about his sagged shoulders. The scarlet professional gown had long been discarded. The dinner jacket was double-breasted, stained and the tie askew though not undone. This was no academic drunk with wine but an old man frightened by time and memory. Bannister felt sad as he watched them onto the landing. He felt he should go. He felt an intruder.

He did not go. Instead he went into the drawing-room where the last of a fire smouldered in the black grate. The room was as he remembered it. Dark with books and long, wintry, rust-coloured velvet curtains. The sofa in front of the November fire was piled with cushions; on the hearthrug, hot chocolate and a face down open paperback of *To The Lighthouse*. He could just make out symphonic tones from the speakers either side of the fireplace. From somewhere in the house he heard bathroom noises, followed a short time later by a closing door and a cheerful but softly called goodnight.

Jules came in. She was smiling. Her red hair was loose and fell on the shoulders of her woollen dressing-gown. She waved at the sofa and he sat and said no to whisky and to coffee and to tea.

'I'm afraid he enjoyed himself. I couldn't really leave him there. I hope you don't mind.'

'Don't be silly. It was very sweet of you.'

She caught his expression.

'Oh dear. Sorry. Changs don't do sweet things do they? It was really thoughtful. Really.'

She touched his knee with her hand. It might have been a friend at a coffee morning. Or even family. More likely family. It was not a provocative gesture. She didn't leave her hand on his leg, nor was it withdrawn quickly. Bannister coughed. His cough was an alternative to 'I see'. It covered a multitude of confusion.

'I, eh he, that is, didn't say whatever it was he wanted to say. Mm.'

'Nothing at all?'

'No. Have you any idea what it was?'

Jules shook her head. She had not. Somehow they managed to talk about her father's old age and the possibility that he was tired. He told her about the discussion about truth and she laughed and said it was always a discussion in this house. At one point he must have said yes to a whisky.

The music, the third tape, stopped. He said that it was time that he was going. He said that two or three times. Twice she made coffee. And they talked of her early days and disappointments and he remembered his days as an undergraduate and she said how she had wanted to go to Ruskin and how she had taught at Birkbeck which he hadn't known and he told her about a great cricket match in 1947 at Hastings when a record was broken that would never be beaten and who D.C.S. Compton was and they laughed a great deal and soon it was three-thirty in the morning and it was cold and he did not put his arm around her as he wanted to.

She stood at the door while he drove the throaty Alvis from the gravelled drive and he hoped he hadn't woken the neighbours and she put the tips of her fingers to her cheek. It would have been silly to have simply shaken hands.

Across and down from the house, the driver of a dark parked Ford yawned and rubbed his bitterly cold hands and made a note on his clip-pad.

Nineteen

The Cabinet Secretary cared to be at his desk by seven o'clock. He was not an early riser by nature, he would have left his podgy frame undisturbed until a reasonable hour. But like the nineteenth-century warriors he studied, he preferred to choose and walk the battlefield while his opponents remained encamped. The Cabinet Secretary had chosen Whitehall while still at Oxford. To him the Civil Service was not the dull bureaucracy perceived by the public. To the Cabinet Secretary Whitehall was a treasure of Chinese boxes each to be carefully manipulated with the finest of instruments until they were set in place – changeable but not flexible, movable but without a rattle.

This true mandarin believed politicians to be the means of gaining the public's unwitting consent for the bureaucracy to run the State, not on behalf of the electorate or the elected representatives but according to the interpretation of the most senior bureaucrats.

Fortunately, the Cabinet Secretary was blessed with having no detectable sense of humour and if asked to be generous with the truth, he would have listed his single pastime as intrigue. He had never bothered to play with Whitehall metaphors and indeed he regarded chess as a far too public game inasmuch as that after every move all the remaining pieces were on display. In the Cabinet Secretary's pastime, nothing should be obvious, positions were never open to examination, opponents' moves were ever made without exact knowledge of his own position – unless of course he decided that would be to his advantage.

Every morning, the Cabinet Secretary went through his Private Folder with a relaxed yet uncompromising view of life. The Folder contained those notes, memoranda and indications which were only one below the secrecy normally reserved for quiet and uninterrupted walks in St James's Park or discreet remarks in the Athenaeum.

On this Monday morning he laid two slips of paper to one side. He would shred them before leaving the room. The third, date-timed forty-eight hours earlier, he read through twice. For a minute he stared at the face of the rosewood-cased clock. Its single hand suggested five past seven. At five and twenty past, a reasonable hour but still early enough to indicate to others the sense of urgency, the Cabinet Secretary picked up his private telephone and without reference to his desk book, dialled Henry Colvil's home number.

Twenty

The weekend had been a little tense. Mary had been short with him for reasons neither of them understood. Polly had picked up the atmosphere and had been unwise enough to ask what was wrong. As neither of them knew, the answer had been along the lines of 'nothing darling'. That had made Polly mad because she felt she was being treated like a child by two adults who were being childish. She had spent most of Saturday evening on the telephone which made matters worse, and instead of joining Charles and Mary at Matins on Sunday morning, an obligation she usually honoured for her father's sake, Polly had been picked up by Nick. Mary was surprised and sufficiently on edge to show it.

'I didn't know you were with him now. What happened to the drummer?'

'Oh Mummy. Do you have to? Nothing happened to the drummer as you call him.'

Mary had shrugged and looked hard done by. 'Sorry I asked. I didn't know you and Nick were, well . . .'

'For Christ's sake! We are not anything. He's in Southampton and he's simply giving me a lift back to London. No big deal. Satisfied?'

Mary had gone into the garden to find Charles who

was having a bonfire. The gardener who kept the place tidy during the week always made sure there was something for 'the boss', as he called him, to do. He knew that, as much as a time waster as it was, the boss loved nothing better in the garden than bonfires. Bannister liked the smell and the satisfaction of the fire. The gardener understood also that prodding, feeding and staring into a garden fire was the boss's way of relaxing. When Mary found Charles, he was staring into the fire. She mentioned Nick and asked was it not sad that Polly was going back so soon. Charles had said that he supposed so. He was not really interested.

'Penny for them.'

Bannister looked up from his bonfire as if seeing her for the first time that morning. His look was distant and had nothing to do with the crispness of the late autumn.

'What?'

'I said penny for them. What is it?'

Bannister said nothing for a moment. He could still smell the scent of her bath oil. He wondered what had happened. He had wondered all weekend.

'Oh nothing. Few problems that's all.'

He tried a smile of reassurance but it did not quite work. Mary, he thought, looked very county in her tweed skirt and Barbour. Very reliable. He supposed they were. He said something about its being time for church, tossed another load of leaves on the fire and trod in the fork. She followed him in and they hardly spoke for the rest of the day. They were not angry with each other. It was simply another of those weekends which had started full of promise. There was nothing to say. There hadn't been for some time.

The telephone calls started on Sunday evening and although the PM said there was no need to come back, Bannister knew it was going to be one of those weeks.

Instead of driving up to London on the Monday, Bannister went by train and left the Alvis with Mary. She had decided to stay down for the week. He did not ask why. On the train, he read the papers and knew that he should have gone back the previous evening. Another bad opinion poll. A story of an impending scandal and, on top of it all, a leaked memo from the Home Secretary which, if it were true, should never have been written, never mind leaked.

At Number 10, the Prime Minister was surprisingly relaxed. Bannister could not think why. Baxter had already told the Bombardier that the memo was genuine, but that he should not worry about it because he, Baxter, would turn it to their advantage. The Prime Minister trusted Dougal to do so. But that morning's opinion poll had been scathing and Bannister could not quite understand Number 10's apparent lack of concern.

The poll showed, as they well knew, that the Party was trailing the Opposition by twenty points and the Bombardier's personal rating was on a par with the hapless England football manager. Even the loyal end of what used to be Fleet Street was questioning the wisdom of either of them staying on. Bannister knew nothing of soccer although he did subscribe to the Wilson hypothesis that when the English team did badly, voters subconsciously took it out on the Government. And then there was the scandal.

The *Guardian* was claiming that a massive security scandal was about to break. 'Another example of Government incompetence,' had been the shadow Home Secretary's predictable but nevertheless damaging comment on Radio Four.

Both the PM and Bannister had asked the Cabinet Secretary if he believed the *Guardian* was referring to Grishin. Both had been reassured that considering the Grishin episode was supposed to be in the good news bracket it could not be that. Moreover, there was, according to the Director General, Security Service, and the Controller, Secret Intelligence Service, nothing in the Intelligence tea-leaves which would embarrass anyone. But the story was running and because every editor loved a good spy scandal and every reader, listener and viewer wanted to believe them, there would be follow-up stories for days to come. Charles advised against sitting it out and suggested a statement dismissing the matter as pure imagination. The PM wasn't so sure especially as the Cabinet Secretary observed that there was no need to make a public pronouncement until all avenues had been inspected.

On his way out, the Cabinet Secretary mentioned to Bannister that he would care for a private word. A somewhat delicate matter, he had said. Could they perhaps slip into his room? They might have done had not someone from the Private Office caught up with them. The PM wanted to see the Cabinet Secretary again. Immediately. Bannister had not waited. He took his umbrella and left.

He was walking through the Members' Entrance as Juliet Cameron was coming out.

'Hi.' Her smile was warm. Her eyes were uncertain. He was pleased to see her and said so.

'How's your father? Hangover?'

'He's beside himself with worry. All last night he was wandering about downstairs.'

'Doing what?'

'He's got some paper and notes. I went down and he got quite ratty. It's terrible. He accused me of spying on him.'

'Older people are sometimes very suspicious of their children's motives, especially when they're concerned. I shouldn't worry too much if I were you.'

Juliet heaved her shoulders in a sigh. 'Yes you would. Of course you would. But he didn't say anything to you did he?'

'No. But when you think about it that's hardly surprising. We hardly saw each other before dinner and high table is not the place for a heart to heart. By the time we were in the parlour well . . .'

'He was drunk.'

'I would not have put it that way.'

'Course you wouldn't Chang. You're not his only child. You don't feel frustration the way I do.'

'And anger?'

'Right. He's asked me to ask if you'll go up and see him again.'

Bannister did not understand what was going on.

'Do you want me to?'

She looked at her feet. Her voice was uncertain. 'Please.'

'Will you be there?'

She looked up. Nodded slowly, not taking her eyes from his. 'Yes.'

Above them Big Ben started its chimes for the hour. He looked about him.

'Look, how about a drink or something? Later I mean.'

Juliet started to shake her head. But she didn't. 'We'll see. You've got a lot on your plate just now.'

'What?'

'Come on Chang. Some of us on our side can read you know. I'm one of them. Perhaps later. Bye.'

He walked on and into the House. He wanted to look back and watch her go. That would have been quite unbright.

By the time Bannister looked into the Chamber the third element of the Prime Minister's bad day was being given full throat by Opposition MPs and not a few of the Government's own supporters. The baying and calling from the green benches described and dissected the leaked memo from the Home Secretary to the Employment Secretary.

Dougal Baxter had, it seemed, suggested that some drastic action should be taken to help young people find 'interesting work and not dole office aspirins'. Unless action were taken, Dougal had written, crime among the young would increase. The memo had concluded that the Home Secretary felt a 'deep and moral obligation not only to the community but to the young people of our nation to whom we shall look for our common prosperity in years to come'.

The leaked memo could not have appeared on a more awkward day as the Home Office was top for questions – that daily routine in the Commons starting after prayers at two-thirty when a Department answered MPs, as laid down in the Order Paper. Dougal Baxter, as Home Secretary, was on the Front Bench doing his best to answer the set questions but found it difficult to avoid the one everyone was asking: was the memo genuine and, if so, why was he so concerned as to interfere with the affairs of another Cabinet Minister.

Dougal Baxter handled the whole matter with style and his version of concern. He refused to discuss a document which was a private affair and was nothing more than a discussion point between two Ministers. It had nothing to do with Government policy, there was no attempt to mislead the House, certainly not to usurp the authority of Parliament. Therefore, there was nothing to say but he hoped that members opposite and indeed on his own side would support the sentiment of the memo and in the meanwhile he could deplore the actions of those who had chosen to leak the contents of this document. The leak amounted to a betrayal of trust, and trust and partnership were the key elements in resolving so many of the nation's problems.

By three-thirty an almost jubilant Baxter was in Bannister's room in the Commons. Rose offered tea. Baxter, almost in a single breath, made quite something of saying no thank you and how he was still restricting his caffeine intake and that she would be advised to do the same and while about it give up the disgusting smoking habit.

Rose, who had been rolling her own cigarettes for thirty years, gave an extra wheeze and slipped a message in front of Bannister with his tea cup and two gingernut biscuits. Henry had been trying to get him. It was most urgent. Bannister folded the note, which Baxter was trying to read, and sipped his tea. Over the rim he eyed Baxter's lounging and smile.

'Well old man? What the hell is going on?'

Baxter was enjoying himself. 'Why Charles, everything. Everything. It's working. Don't you think it was marvellous in there? They have fallen for it hook, line and sinker.'

Charles replaced his cup and tugged at his waistcoat. 'The PM tells me the memorandum's genuine. Is it?'

'Of course.'

'Blast! Blast! Blast!'

'Of course it is, Charles. It's part of the plan. If I'm to be seen as the obvious candidate when you step aside, then I must be seen as innovative, caring. Which of course I am.'

'But this is nonsensical.'

'Certainly not. My Department has figures to show that juvenile crime can be directly linked to unemployment.'

'We know that.'

'But we never admit it.'

Bannister looked amazed. 'Of course we don't you dunderhead.'

'Charles, please listen a moment will you?'

Bannister was steaming. 'No Dougal, you listen to me. That memo suggests that unemployment and crime are related. We never admit it. Why? Because we would be open to the charge that a failure to reduce substantially the unemployment figures means that we are responsible for the most dastardly of crimes. You should not have put that in a memorandum. Definitely not. Mm?'

Baxter was well back in the chair, arms folded across his chest in a comfortable pose rather than defensive.

'Of course I should Charles. As I keep telling you, it showed how much I care. Once people found out what I was really thinking then they would see how wise it will be to follow me. This little scheme will get us more support than anything you've managed to dream up this year.'

'And you imagine they'll line routes and cheer?'

'All the way to Number 10.'

'Or the scaffold.'

'Not when the headlines come in tomorrow's papers. The timing is perfect.'

'You make it sound as if the whole thing was planned.'

Dougal Baxter held out his arms. He could have been at La Scala. It took a couple of seconds, but then it dawned on Bannister. But he had to hear it from Baxter.

'Who leaked this memorandum Dougal? Tell me, who?'

The pleased-with-himself smile on Baxter's face was enormous.

'Why Charles, I did of course. Don't you think it's brilliant?'

Twenty-One

All his life Charles Bannister had been in charge of events about him. He was not a schemer by nature, nor would he have been the dashing captain of a wartime submarine chaser. But he would have made a good admiral.

Bannister stepped from problems he found distasteful but not before he made sure someone else was dealing with them. This was partly compassion, where necessary, and partly his omnipresent sense of duty, but mainly because he did not wish to see the problem before him again. Consequently Bannister kept control and would always have people about him to flog miscreants and pay off beggars before they touched at his coat. Mary Bannister took care of his private life, Rose his public life.

That day Bannister felt weary. Too many things were going wrong. Too many things were getting through. At about six o'clock Rose had come in with the usual pile of late letters for his signature just as he was pouring a sherry. She had wheezed through a joke about it being a bit early for that. He had snapped at her.

'What's that mean?'

Rose had looked surprised. Mr Bannister was never sharp with her. He sometimes was sharp to her about others but he never had a go at her.

'Sorry. Just joking.' Bannister had recovered and had attempted to make out he had been playful. He had not been and they both knew so and his excuses only made her embarrassed and Bannister more annoyed with himself.

'Things are a bit whatsit aren't they?' She squinted through the heavy spectacles and tugged her cardigan about her. She only needed curlers, slippers and a garden fence and Rose would have been set for a gossip.

Bannister dropped into his desk chair and waved Rose to the captain's. He raised his sherry glass and at first she was going to say no because she didn't want one but said yes because that would have reinforced her accusation that it really was a little early. Bannister poured.

'Cheers.'

He sipped and settled back. 'I'm afraid they are. And I'm not sure what's going on.'

'That stuff in the papers about the Prime Minister. Nothing new in that is there? I mean, we all know we're in shtuck don't we?'

Bannister nodded. They all knew. But no one was doing anything about it. A large part of his job was to suggest what should be done especially in questions of presentation. But after the midnight meeting with the Prime Minster and Dougal, Bannister felt that any advice he offered would be seen as a ploy to advance his case. And yet there was Dougal blatantly scheming to launch, or better still to get someone else to launch, a palace coup.

'And we both know that these sort of headlines hunt in packs. I'm sure there's more to come. But, well, as you've seen, I spend the whole day in meetings and nothing comes of them.'

'How did lunch go?'

Bannister had met the editor of the newspaper which had questioned the PM's position and had carried the story about Bannister's suitability as an alternative leader. The meeting had been a sensible discussion, but had not got Bannister or the Party very far.

'An opinion poll is an opinion poll. As he said, the evidence is there. It's not their evidence.'

'They don't have to publish it.'

Bannister's was a wry laugh. 'I'm afraid Rose, we count on their support but we do not edit their paper. Anyway, all he was really interested in was whether I was going to run against the PM.'

'Are you?'

Bannister looked and sounded genuinely surprised at the question. 'My God Father James, of course not. You of all people should know that.'

Rose sipped for time. She didn't really like sherry. It was a drink for funerals and bored ladies. 'There's a lot round this place who say it'd be a good idea.'

'Who's saying that? Nonsense.'

She shook her head. She could have done with a roll-up. 'Plenty of them. George Sharpe was in earlier . . .'

'The badge messenger? My God what does he know? He's hardly chairman of the Back-bench Committee. Come on Rose, the future of the Party is not going to be decided on the say so of, well, of a doorman.'

Rose took a final sip and put the empty glass on the desk in front of her. 'I tell you one thing Mr Bannister, George Sharpe may not be chairman of this or that committee, but he's got the biggest set of ears in this place. There isn't a corridor he doesn't walk. He's down in Annies bar most nights. And there isn't a cupboard he hasn't opened at some time or another. And I'll just say one thing: George Sharpe says that there's talk of someone else standing by. He reckons if it comes to a proper race then that someone else will be in the frame, not you.'

Bannister closed his eyes. He really had had enough of the whole affair.

'And does he say who this mystery horse might be?'

'No he doesn't. But I reckon he knows, or thinks he does.'

On the way out Bannister saw George Sharpe in the Lobby. He put on his affable voice.

'Evening Mr Sharpe. How's the Navy then?'

Sharpe had been a Chief Petty Officer, a communicator. To be a Chief Radio Supervisor you had to be an intelligent man and a bright one. The instincts of a communicator were to find out what was going on. The instincts of a Chief Petty Officer were to make damn sure you knew. Information on a mess deck meant power. Sharpe had been a powerful man, which in the Royal Navy had meant he had had enemies because others knew how powerful he was. He was still powerful. The difference was that few knew that and so George Sharpe had no enemies and, as he pointed out to Rose one evening, 'friends always want to tell you something – even when they've got nothing to tell'. Now he smiled, albeit formally, at Charles Bannister. Bannister was an officer. Chief R.S. Sharpe, as he had been, knew how to treat officers.

'Fair to middling sir. Fair to middling. And yourself?'

'We live in interesting times, as I imagine you've noticed.'

'Blimey yes sir. Still not to worry, worse things happen at sea.'

'And tell me Mr Sharpe, apart from taking to the boats, what would the Navy do in these circumstances?'

Sharpe screwed up his face in a Chief's serious look.

'Well sir, you could always pipe hands to dinner. Most of the lads couldn't eat and think at the same time. Bit of a breather so to speak.'

They both laughed and a passing Back-bencher looked at Bannister and wondered about the future.

'How wonderful Mr Sharpe. How wonderful. And what happens when they've finished eating?'

'Well sir, then I reckons a good skipper might run an exercise. A good one.'

'I see. Take their minds off things.'

Sharpe shook his head. 'Oh no sir. Just the opposite. It's all about concentrating their minds and what they're supposed to be really doing. You run yourself a good, say, Sweepex, you know, looking for mines, and the ship's company really has to turn to and get itself sorted. Yes sir, that's what a good captain does, a good work up so every man jack of them has to give it everything. That way you clear their minds, them what has them of course, and you remind them what they signed on for.'

'What did you call it? A Sweepex?'

'Well that's only one of them. But yes, looking for mines so the bigger ships can get through. If you don't mind me saying so sir, I served with a smashing Jimmy once . . .'

'A Jimmy?'

'Sorry sir, that's the first lieutenant, sort of general manager in the ship. Anyway he had a good saying. "Nothing like making a man sweat his bollocks off to stop him playing with himself". Begging your pardon sir. But I tell you, he was right.'

Outside the House it was dark although many people had yet to leave their offices. Bannister turned from

Pall Mall into St James's Square and mounted the short flight of steps to the Army & Navy Club. He pressed the door-buzzer, waited, there was a click and he pulled the glass door and entered the surprisingly modern lobby. The uniformed porter said good evening and expected no reply although Bannister nodded. He turned to the right and into the cloakroom. Coat pegged and tie checked in the wall of wash-room mirrors, Bannister mounted the stairway beneath Captain Carew's curiously horned greater kudu, turned right once more and went into the library. He paused. The room came from some grand house. Leather reading chairs scattered for a family. Small round tables lit by lamps and left for coffee and wine. The white net curtains at the long windows formed an eerie backdrop and before it Colvil sat waiting at a broad writing desk. There were no others in the room.

'Ah Charles, come sit.'

Colvil indicated a leather chair close by. He took a white handkerchief from his cuff and dabbed at his nose.

'A cold don't you know.'

'I didn't. I'm sorry to hear that.'

Bannister sat. He crossed and re-crossed his long legs. he felt uncomfortable. Colvil was moving his mouth and completing a minor impression of a goldfish. It was, to Charles at least, a sign that his brother-in-law was about to say something which he felt to be important. Bannister got in first.

'Tell me Henry, you know about these things. What's a Sweepex?'

Colvil looked surprised, even in the half-light.

'Well my dear, it is something small ships have to do. Mine-hunters. They all get together and have a jolly sweeping exercise. Pinging and towing and cutting things. They're actually doing what it says, they're sweeping for mines. May this one ask only your interest?'

'Nothing in particular. Someone mentioned the phrase. I suppose minefields are emotive subjects.'

'Especially the acoustic devices dear heart. I'm afraid those for whom pinging is a somewhat discreet pastime bring disturbing echoes.'

'Phone tapping? Don't want to know old man. Nothing to do with me. Try Dougal, he's in charge of clumsies.'

'That is quite another matter. No Charles, this is far more serious and it does concern you. I'm afraid it does.'

Bannister's chuckle was entirely without humour. 'Isn't everything? I've got Dougal scheming behind my back, the Prime Minister virtually accusing me of sticking a knife into his, a very polite editor asking very politely if I'm about to run for power or cover and now you banging on about your precious Grishin. Come on old man, what now?'

The library door opened and one of the last members of the Rajputs stomped in, sat at a table at the far end of the room and, with his failing and only eye close to the flimsy pages, began to scan *Who's Who* for a colleague just passed on. Colvil viewed the crouched figure and lowered his voice to almost a murmur.

'Charles, I have a little difficulty with which you could help me enormously.'

Bannister held up his hand. 'I have done everything I can on that matter. I have recommended publication, but I'm afraid it's not entirely in the PM's hands. Sorry.'

Colvil's head went to one side as if Bannister were a portrait contemplated on varnishing day. 'Yes, yes, Charles, that I understand. This is a smidgen more sensitive. You ah, you dined in your college on Friday, yes?'

Bannister looked on mildly surprised. It had been no secret.

'So what?'

'And then you took, or rather helped, your old tutor back to his lodgings.'

'I took him home. Yes. They're hardly lodgings, he's lived there for years.'

'Without owning them. But that's by the by. You took him, ah, home. Yes?'

'Go on.'

'And then you left in what I believe are sometimes called the small hours.'

Bannister was sitting very upright.

'How the blazes do you know this?'

Colvil was playing with his watch-chain, flipping it against his very round tummy. He was not enjoying this moment.

'Charles, this is very painful for me. You left the, eh, house, at, eh five and twenty to four o'clock. Um, in the morning.'

Bannister said nothing. Waited. Colvil looked over his brother-in-law's shoulder. The Indian Army colonel, uncertain on his cane, was wobbling from the library.

'I only wish I had known that you were meeting Cameron. It would have been helpful.'

'I'm not sure I understand what you're saying Henry. Damn it old man, are you telling me I've been followed?'

Colvil blinked furiously. 'My dear heart. Perish that thought, oh please do so. No, no, no a thousand times. No Charles, not you, Cameron.'

Bannister was now totally confused. 'Whatever for?'

'The list Charles, the list. Don't you understand? Your old tutor is the leading light on friend Grishin's list. He was recruiting for the KGB right up until the late 1950s.'

'I don't believe it.'

'Of course you don't Charles and if I may say so, that is a very commendable response. Sadly though, I'm afraid it is true. Cameron is nothing less that a traitor.'

'Is? You said was.'

'So I did. But then I think you would but agree that time does not heal treachery. So dear heart, you may imagine also my concern when your name appeared on our surveillance report this morning.'

'Surveillance report? What report?'

'He is ah, the subject, ah, of some considerable interest. You must not Charles, under any circumstances see Cameron again.'

Twenty-Two

The Division that evening was unimportant. Bannister was paired, but he could have easily voted. Rose brought through another coffee and told him he was drinking too much of the stuff and poured him Malvern water. He looked preoccupied and she told him so. At first he did not hear, which proved her point.

'What? Oh yes. Things on the mind that's all. Just things.'

Rose was unimpressed. 'Well at this time of night why don't you make one of those things a cab and get home for an early night? Mrs Bannister called ten minutes ago. I said you were about.'

'I'll call.'

'Cab?'

Bannister did not like to be pushed. Rose was indispensable, but even she was going too far. She knew that, but she was worried about him. She was fond of the Bannisters. She had baby-sat when Polly was a tot and Mary had insisted that they would not have a nanny. She had been there on the day he entered the House. Yet Rose would never presume to think of herself as a close friend even though her sense of loyalty extended to concern, which is what she now felt.

'Something up, isn't there.'

It was a typical Rose statement. Not a question. And she expected an answer.

'So you keep asking. I'm sorry. But when isn't there? You know Rose, there are times when I honestly wonder why I've stayed in this place. It used to be fun. But now?'

He raised his hand as a victim might at the sight of a ransacked home. Bannister's memories, the trophies of the young days seemed worthless, even gone. On the desk, photographs of Mary and Polly. On the small table the Great and sometimes the Good smiled as they shook his hand. The old newspaper headline of his first election victory, now framed and hanging from the wall lest he should forget the people who put him there. Now he wasn't certain that he wanted to be there at all. There was more to being Party Chairman than pretending that you liked nothing better than eating two chicken lunches a week. And now there was Dougal on the power rampage. Ten, even five years ago, Bannister would have taken it in his stride. He would have slapped Dougal down just as he had at school. He would probably have anticipated it. But now? Now he had that feeling of being out of control. On top of all this, Cameron.

But what gnawed at his subconscious was not Cameron but those peaceful hours after midnight in a hardly light Edwardian living-room. The freedom. The freedom to talk about things that really had nothing to do with either of their lives but which, for that moment, mattered to them.

In the background of his thoughts, Rose was pushing him. She was still worried. He could hear her voice but could not make out what she was saying. He wasn't listening. Only hearing. He swung back and came in halfway through a statement.

'. . . gets to a point when nothing seems worth it. Don't you think?'

'Sorry. What does?'

'What you're talking about I suppose. Course it was fun. You didn't have to mind your P's and Q's. Now everything you do is watched.'

'What do you mean by that?'

His tone was sharp. She carried on as if she hadn't picked up the sentiment of his question.

'You get on the radio, the telly. People see you and know who you are. You go to a restaurant and even if they don't know exactly who you are they think they do. You've got to be careful. If you want to have secrets you've got to be double careful.'

'What sort of secrets?'

'Same sort of secrets that other people don't have to keep secret. Bit Irish that, but you know.'

He supposed that he did. Henry Colvil, his own brother-in-law, had proved that not six hours ago. And now Rose. What did she know? You never knew in this place. Bannister looked at this curious woman. He felt in a weft of slow motion sounds and almost blurred visions. Her lipstick was thick as it always was and now looked grotesque. Her eyes squinted from behind the thick lenses. They were menacing. Her bobbled cardigan, gathered about her bony frame, could have emerged from a grey ghetto. Or, more dramatically, she could have been an interrogator carefully posed beneath a bare bulb in some dank Madgeburg cell, relentlessly questioning him while the 16th Shock Army rumbled over the concrete streets above.

Bannister's mind was whirling tricks of light, sound and imagination. He felt overwhelmed. He needed air. He needed to get away from the House. He stood, ignoring the coffee she had left on his blotter, and moved to the door. He wanted to chide her. But his self-control had not deserted him. He was angry with himself. His spent a great deal of his life being suspicious of others. He did not like the thought that for a moment he had included Rose, dear Rose, in the same basket of suspicion. He tried to smile

'I'll see you in the morning.'

As he left, Sharpe appeared at the outer office door. He flattened himself against the wall making way for an officer such as Bannister, who, with a nod, swept into the thickly carpeted corridor. Rose looked tired.

'Fancy a swift one then Rose my love. Just time before they close.'

She came into the outer office closing Bannister's room to Sharpe's prying eyes. She was packing odds and ends into her handbag and didn't look up.

'Very kind, but no thanks. I've got my bus to catch.'

'Oh.'

The voice was disappointed even though Sharpe knew that Rose was not one for the Westminster bars. He tried again.

'Just thought you'd like a bit of a black so to speak.'

'Black what?'

'You know, black cat, chat.'

'Oh rhyming slang.'

He grinned. It was a nice grin she thought. Still cheeky, even at his age.

'No. Just made it up.'

He was, even at his age. She smiled for a moment and took out her small, silver tobacco tin. She fancied a roll-up. Not here though. Anyway, she was fed up of being taken for granted.

'Tell you what Mr Sharpe, I wouldn't mind a small ginger wine somewhere. Not in this place. Okay?'

She might have told him he was the first lottery millionaire. The grin became a broad smile.

Twenty-Three

Bannister crossed Millbank and ignored the tempting flag of an empty taxi. He would walk. He had things on his mind which were best sorted on foot. He was starting to believe Baxter. He was losing his grip. When that happened it was time to get out. Stay in the House, but get out of the front line before he made the sort of mistake that would condemn him to the Lords. Another cab slowed, its orange light welcoming him aboard. Bannister ignored it. The cab moved on towards the brighter lights of Victoria. Then it started to rain. It came from nowhere. One moment a cold damp London night. The next, sheets of bitterly cold driving rain.

Bannister cursed his own stupidity. No hat. No umbrella. No taxi. It was a sharp, spiteful rain, a month early. He hunched deeper into his large overcoat and ducked into a doorway. Three cabs went by. One with its 'For Hire' sign lit, but the driver did not see the tall, cold man with the dripping hair and the grumpy expression. Twice he went to the kerb in search of a taxi. Twice he retreated to the doorway, the second time after being soaked from shoe to knee by a kerb-hugging BMW. Bannister had just decided to ignore the weather and head back towards the Embankment when a hurrying figure beneath a huge umbrella dashed into the doorway, turned to close her umbrella and then jumped back with fright. It was Kay Bennet. He apologized for frightening her. She said it didn't matter but what the hell was he doing lurking in the doorway?

'It's raining.'

'Really? So that's what it is.'

'I mean. Well, I suppose that's it. I'm sorry, I didn't mean to startle you.'

'No problem. Look you'd better come in.'

She was tapping out a key number on the brass-plated entry pad.

'In where?'

She was holding open the door. 'In here. I live here. Come on.'

Bannister was flustered. 'That's very kind of you Miss Bennet. But really.'

'Come on. Don't worry. I'm not Mae West. I'll call you a cab.'

'No really.'

'Suit yourself.'

She did not wait for an answer. He followed her in.

The lift was out of order. She said something about an electrical fault and by the time they reached the fourth floor and Kay Bennet was opening the light, oak veneered door, he was quite out of breath.

Her flat was 1930s large. There was even a bar complete with quilted fascia in one corner of the square living-room. Bannister winced, but took comfort in the fact that he was not surprised. The furniture was Italian with lots of stripes and coloured whirls set against the startlingly white carpet, all looking like a banana republic's presidential uniform. At one end, chrome chairs at a smoked glass dining-table and a Persian grey cat, comfortable, where there might have normally been a bowl of synthetic fruit.

Kay slipped off her shoes and left him standing at the edge of the hall and living-room and staring at an enormous unframed nude on the far wall. The fall of the dark hair, the full-breasted voluptuousness was mesmeric. It was hardly a scruffy and hazy modern painting but something out of the air-brushed New York fifties. The model was far from American. He was

148

still staring when Kay reappeared with a large green fluffy towel. She handed it to Bannister, caught his gaze and his embarrassment. She half smiled. He wasn't the first man to blush. He felt foolish. She did not let him off the hook.

'Hang your coat over there and you can leave your shoes in there.'

She pointed to a half-open door. It appeared to be a darkened kitchen. Bannister protested that he only wanted a cab. She shrugged.

'Okay. There's the phone. I'm getting out of this lot.'

Kay Bennet disappeared again. He went to the telephone. There was no directory. He thought about calling Mary. He thought it a bad idea. It dawned on him that he didn't even know where he was. From another room, Bannister could hear a powerful shower. He took off his coat, a soggy heavy woollen mass, and dropped it and his shoes on the kitchen floor. He had dried his hair as best he could and was attempting to rake it into something like its well-ordered way when Kay returned. She was running a comb through her long straight black hair. He handed her the towel, it matched her overlarge bathrobe.

'I'm afraid I'm very wet.'

'I'm afraid you are Mr Bannister. Without wishing to sound forward, would you like to take off your trousers.'

There was a long silence. Then they both started to laugh. There is a certain foolishness in arrogance and Bannister had just seen his joke. He said no thank you, he would, if she did not mind, keep his trousers to himself and she understood. But he did say yes to a whisky.

Bannister sat in an armchair and felt uncomfortable with wet legs, but did not change his mind about his trousers. Kay stretched out on the ivory leather sofa and wriggled into the warmth of the zigzag coloured cushions. Each time she crossed and recrossed her ankles to get comfortable and balance a tall glass of white wine, her robe slipped and she took her time covering her very long legs. Bannister found it disturbing.

But they talked and he stayed and he accepted her offer of a second whisky. She half rolled, half rose out of the deep cushions and the robe parted even further. Bannister looked away only to be confronted yet again with the unframed nude.

In the mirror behind the padded bar, Kay saw his second glance at the painting and smiled to herself. She thought him quite good-looking in a stuffy sort of way. He would, she thought, have made a good Army officer. Tall, upright, no fat on him, good with men, always looked after the horses, probably somewhere deep down a sense of humour. She liked Army officers. They tended to be uncomplicated. She wondered what he was like in bed. She had seen Mary Bannister but had never been introduced to her. She seemed an obvious wife for Bannister. Good type. Pretty. Clean hair. Hilditch blouses under cashmere in the winter, Harvey Nichols shirtwaisters in the summer and just old enough to have frocks rather than dresses. No nonsense. Sensible shoes but with buckles. Sensible tights but aubergine.

Kay added a splash more whisky over the ice cubes and deliberately let her fingers catch his when she handed him the tumbler. She wondered if he were possible. When she sat back in the cushions she took her time with her robe and decided that Charles Bannister was entirely possible. Having decided that, she rather lost interest.

Bannister spent the next couple of minutes metaphorically clearing his throat and they talked about her job and how she had come back from Brussels where she had been translating to find that Dougal needed someone to set up his private research office.

'Did you know him before you came back?'

She shifted and rested an arm on the back of the sofa. The right fold of the robe drooped and he could see the swell of her breast.

'Vaguely. We met in Brussels when he was at Environment. EC stuff.'

'And he offered you a job?'

She shifted again. So did the robe.

'Sort of.'

Bannister waited. It was a technique he had learned successfully in court. There are those people who feel they have to say something more. Kay Bennet was not quite that sort of person. But she did say more and he wondered why.

'It's being on the circuit you know. You hear about jobs and well, knowing him . . .' She paused. There was obviously something else. Bannister wondered, but not too deeply.

They talked about the Department and about young Nick and about how good he was and that Bannister should not be fooled by the green braces and odd-ball lingo. But every time the conversation might have got to her, Kay Bennet moved it along. She was an expert at being non-committal and sufficiently anonymous to make herself uncomplicated for her employer. The House was full of such people, like coats in transition from one hanger to another, many of them using the House for what it might lead to. Some, however, were more like Kay. To them, mostly attractive young women, the House was the alternative to the European Community of super-qualified mostly single secretaries and most of them dreading the loneliness of the middle years.

Bannister was on his third whisky. He was surprised how much he liked her. He was, in his very Charles Bannister way, surprised at her intelligence. He had always seen her as an obviously attractive woman who wore rather obvious clothes. Bannister supposed that some would regard her as, well, desirable. He probably meant sexy, but was not sure and would never readily have used the word. Sexy was not in his vocabulary and he would never have wanted anyone to believe it might be. But the more they talked, the more Bannister knew what he thought of Kay Bennet.

Bannister, as Mary knew full well, liked his women uncomplicated, from his own circle and sexually conventional. Kay Bennet was desirable even to Bannister and even Bannister was beginning to think so. She seemed almost asleep and her voice was far-away. The Persian grey had curled into a soft muff on her out-stretched lap and as she lay there, gently stroking the purring animal, the warmth of the flat and the whisky and the murmuring of this almost complete stranger, nestled in the deep cushions and soft leather sofa, left the hideous rain far away.

She had put on music, quiet music from a corner and they were content to sit back and listen. The moment was disturbed by the sound of a key turning in the front door. He heard the door open and Kay, quite startled, tried to move the cat and struggle out of the cushions at the same time. As she swung her long legs from the sofa and started to her feet the robe fell away almost to her waist. The front door closed and Dougal Baxter walked in.

Twenty-Four

The porter had been across with the morning mail. Another envelope. It was a white envelope and square. The handwriting was the same. Cameron recognized it at once. He left it on the dark mahogany table along with the *Reporter* and notice of the death of a former Fellow. He looked at the obituary card and wondered if they would say prayers and to whom. Christians had so many others to blame for their sins, he thought. He walked across to the long bookcase, slipped on his wire-framed spectacles and uncertainly mounted the library steps, gripping tightly the steadying pole but wobbling still as he opened the glass-panelled door. He took down a volume he had no wish, no need to read. He closed the door and stepped down almost slipping on the bottom and most worn step. For an hour Cameron sat in the high-backed chair and dipped into Gilbert White. He turned the leaves and thought of the past and its wretched happiness. He wondered so deeply about mistakes and not having the courage to see them and stand aside. And then he came to the page where the other envelopes were marking chapters and he put down the book.

It was odd. He knew the envelopes were there all the time. Of course he did. He had put them there. He could feel them. But his mind had tried to fool him. His mind had pretended they were not there, like knowing the result of a contest but watching the replay and hoping that matters will turn out differently.

Cameron picked up the white envelope and tapped it on the palm of his hand as if weighing its contents. He picked up his paper-knife and then changed his mind and put both back on the table and went into his gyp-room. He ran the cold tap until it splashed noisily in the deep Belfast sink and he scrubbed at his hands with the hard green soap. There wasn't much lather and he did not feel cleaner as he dried on the roller-towel behind the door. He filled the kettle and lit the gas ring and went back to the letter.

The document was simple in its tone, cruel in its message. It was from the same person. He did not understand why. It had been a long time ago. He had believed, he still believed the system could be changed but only by a true understanding of the social revolution. Now they were coming. He had always known, somewhere deep inside, that one day they would want him. What would they do? That he did not know. And why was someone telling him? Why these letters? Who was coming? Who wanted him to know? And why after all this time? Why not before? These were too many questions for an old man. Too many about himself. Too many without answers or the defiance of belief, for now he believed in nothing.

He needed to talk to Bannister once more. Bannister, of all his undergraduates, had done well for himself in that sort of circle. Bannister knew the Prime Minister for goodness' sake. Bannister knew everyone and one of them would know why. He had tried at the feast. But there was nothing he could say. It was the wrong time. It was the wrong moment. He was, anyway, a coward. He knew that. That was why all those years, so many years before, that was why he had helped. No money. They could never accuse him of that. No real ideology. Simply the need to change. Change what? The system? Not even that. Had it not all been about disillusionment? He no longer knew that either. It was too long ago and his mind was too good; how could he know what he had really thought. He came back to the letter.

He muttered to himself as a priest at his devotions. His unbelief was helped but his mind echoed to the chant of confusion. The same questions as before. Why did someone want him to know? Why did someone say these things? Why did they not simply come and do what they were going to do anyway? Or was it a cruel hoax? But if it were, then whoever played this joke knew, presumably, everything.

The sudden scream of the kettle frightened him and he dropped the letter. He stood looking down and wondered, why now? After all these years? Why now? And who?

Twenty-Five

Bannister was not sure when he had been so embarrassed, if indeed he had ever been so embarrassed. His explanation of being caught in the rain and the coincidence of the doorway and Kay's return was as lame as Dougal's claim that he was dropping in to talk to her about tomorrow's debate and that it was quite natural for him to have the key to his office manager's apartment. Bannister had bid both a strained goodnight and Dougal had petulantly questioned Kay for an hour after he had gone. By the time the two men met over coffee the next morning, it was time to reach an understanding.

Bannister would normally have not wished to raise the matter. Baxter most certainly did wish to clear the air. He waited until Rose had closed the door before he spoke and then it was about Rose herself rather than the night before.

'Is she all right?'

'Who? Rose? Yes, why?'

'Well you haven't mentioned last night to her have you?'

Bannister nearly spilled his coffee in his anger. 'I beg your pardon. Most certainly not.'

'Sorry. It's just that she's very cool this morning. Very cool. I didn't even get a good-morning from her.'

'That, Dougal, is largely because Rose does not like you.'

'Really? Oh good. I thought it was because, well, I thought it might be that she knew something. Oh that's all right then.'

Baxter took another sip, then changed his mind and drained his cup and set it on Charles's polished desk next to the tray Rose had left. He was ready for business.

'Now Charles. About this business. We need to understand something.'

Bannister was looking out of the window. He could see the sky and buildings across Parliament Square. He longed for a sturdy walk across the hill by their Hampshire farm, or even a week right away on the narrow boat he had bought for them the previous year but had never used. Baxter was speaking, Bannister was half listening.

'Charles, it's very simple. As you know Ros and I

have an understanding. We both have our careers and well, Ros understands that mine is the more important and that an official parting would not be, eh, convenient.'

Bannister put down his cup and saucer on the tray. 'Really old man, this is not at all necessary.'

'Oh but it is Charles. As you are aware, the arrangement I have with Kay Bennet is, well, a temporary arrangement. Obviously I wouldn't normally wish to get mixed up with someone like her.'

'And abnormally?'

'Very funny Charles. But you do know what I mean.'

'Probably, but I'm not sure I wish to know any more. What you do with your private life Dougal holds no interest for me. No interest whatsoever. I'm sorry I've disturbed your nest, but you may rest assured that your arrangements are quite private until they concern the Party. You have my word.'

'Why Charles, that's very understanding. And of course I shall not mention the other matter.'

Bannister's look was sharp. 'What other matter?'

'Come now. Neither of us is that naïve.'

'I simply do not know what you're talking about.'

'Miss Tartan Drawers.'

'What the blazes are you talking about? Miss who?'

'Miss Tartan Drawers. The delightful Miss Cameron.'

Bannister gave Baxter a hard look. He was determined not to react.

'If I knew to what you referred, this conversation would be simpler. As it is, it is infuriating. I do not care to be infuriated. There is already too much on my mind, so if you do not mind, Dougal, you must allow me to get on.'

'Have it your own way Charles, or should I say, Chang?'

Baxter was smiling broadly as if they were a couple of sailors ashore with two good telephone numbers.

'Dougal, I'm not certain what you're suggesting, but if I were you I would be careful. You are treading very heavily on our friendship.'

The other man shrugged. He had made his point. He did not wish to pursue it and he had already made a mental note to congratulate himself for listening late one night to young Nick's account of a minor coup on a race at Redcar. Dougal had no interest in horses but he did like gossip. He was now glad that he had not hurried on when Nick started to tell him that it was funny about horses that have Chinese names. It had turned out a good two-way bet.

Bannister realized that the Cabinet Secretary knew about Cameron. When they met in the hall at Number 10 neither man mentioned the subject. The Cabinet Secretary never raised a matter unless totally necessary and Bannister had nothing more to say, certainly not to the Cabinet Secretary, although he would have wished to know if the Prime Minister knew. If he did, then the Bombardier gave no sign when they met in the Cabinet Room. It was not a Cabinet meeting, just the two of them. The PM called Bannister to sit beside him and began by apologizing.

'I've been thinking about the other day Charles. I don't want you to get the idea that I thought you were against me. If I gave that impression, well, you know me, sometimes I'm not always that clear. Anyway, hope you didn't get the wrong end of the stick. Okay?'

Bannister murmured something about the PM being able to count on his loyalty at all times just as he always had. He continued when he noticed the Bombardier enjoying this declaration of political brotherhood and added that his luncheon with the newspaper editor had drawn no evidence that would lead to the identity of the person who had suggested Charles Bannister as the man most likely to take over at Number 10.

'And you Charles. What do you think? You know what's going on. Any private thoughts?'

Bannister nodded. They both had private thoughts, but in the circumstances, his silence suggested, it might be best to keep them that way while the political knives were stropped and the sharpening reverberated throughout Westminster. It was another horrid Chinese game. Bannister's explanation reassured the PM because they both understood that the Bombardier hated decisions which would lead to unpleasantness.

'I think that at this stage you might allow me to sort the matter. If I may say so, a suitably warned off malcontent may become a loyalist at the mere drop of a threat of, say, deselection at the next election?'

The Bombardier smiled his quiet way. He really quite admired the way Charles Bannister was such a Party mandarin about the Palace of Westminster. Even when he had been Chief Whip, Bannister had managed to control the unruly Back-benches through persuasion and inside knowledge of their less noted lives, rather than some of the bullying tactics used by his successor. The PM knew that, although effective on the night, the stronger approach tended to produce Lobby fodder which later turned to resentment, whereas Charles Bannister's style was to convince a rebelling MP that he was indeed one of the inside team and that the PM of all people would not forget. It had often worked, even with a relatively small majority.

Bannister, watching the bobbing, smiling head, wondered if the PM knew of Dougal's involvement. When the Bombardier spoke, Bannister decided that he could not possibly know.

'Dougal tells me that you are really quite popular.'

Bannister must have looked surprised, even pained. The PM laughed and slapped Bannister's arm.

'I'm sorry Charles, I didn't mean it like that. I mean that you've got a big following. We're going to have to use that following aren't we? Make sure your friends are our friends.'

Polly was right. People often said the PM was lightweight, but you did not get to be leader of the Party if you were lightweight – somewhere there was steel and presumably ruthlessness. Bannister hoped so. The Party was going to need it. His mind went back to his conversation with George Sharpe. It was time for hands to dinner perhaps, most certainly it was time for a Sweepex.

'Might you consider a new campaign? Might you consider the idea of something more than a rallying speech? Something which would get every Member and every senior member of the Party working on a grand project. Something which would catch the public's imagination?'

'You mean something like "Buy British".'

Bannister's sense of humour was almost exhausted. So was the Bombardier's. When it came, it came with the steadiness of the realist who had won the Party the last election against the odds but had disappeared beneath the avalanche of bad decisions and inept presentation.

'I'm sorry Charles, but really! We have an economy that's in the next worse thing to a mess; a foreign policy which no one understands and is three parts humiliation and one part waiting for a new president; unemployment which has been at this level for so long that everyone forgets to feel bad about it unless its them; a national health service that exists on a care and maintenance basis only and the dilemma of what to do with a society which'll have more than one million people over the age of eighty within five years. Charles, the days when you could think up a slogan and jingle and then tell them they've never had it so good are long gone. Half of them have never had it at all and the other half are scared witless they'll never get it back. Any other ideas on that theme?'

The Prime Minister sat back, still with the benign smile. Bannister was surprised.

'I see.'

'Of course you do Charles. Now, if you really think you can find me something which will mobilize the troops, fine. You get on and do it and so will I. But when it comes to voting, slogans will sound hopeless.'

The Bombardier stood. Bannister smiled and started for the door. He felt as if he had been dismissed. For the first time, he felt the junior partner. He looked back. The PM was sitting again and going through notes, ticking and scribbling in his precise handwriting using the slim French fountain pen the Bannisters had given him as an election present. He looked up, still smiling.

'Why don't you have a word with Dougal. He seems to have a good idea somewhere. See if you can work it up into something will you?'

Bannister nodded. Dougal!

'Oh and Charles?'

'Mm?'

'The Cabinet Secretary mentioned something to me. Something about an old friend of yours.'

Bannister waited. The Bombardier was head bent, back at his notes. But the message was far from muffled.

'Steady as she goes Charles. That's what the Navy says isn't it? Steady as she goes. Don't want a man overboard do we?'

Another smile and then nobody's fool bent over his papers and another agenda.

Twenty-Six

Baxter was slumped on the Front Bench half listening to a Point of Order and waiting to take questions when Bannister slid in beside him.

'What's the bright idea of yours Dougal?'

Baxter gave his sickliest of grins.

'Which one did you have in mind?'

'I didn't. The Bombardier seems to think that you have something worth working on.'

The Chairman of Ways and Means was giving good reason why he would not allow another intervention and would rule on the Point of Order at a later time. The interruption had made its own point and Dougal and his team stirred themselves. Dougal was about to star. This wasn't the time to talk.

'Law and order starts in the home. All good stuff. I'll tell you about it later.'

He sprang to his feet and with a bright smile of confidence pronounced a well-rehearsed answer and then threw in a successful jibe at the Opposition which the shadow spokesman only made more successful by looking hurt. It was going to be a typical Dougal question session – full of take and very little give. Each of his answers would have been crafted for a headline followed by a nine-second television sound-bite while

164

each of his juniors was lumbered with serious answers and even one or two which, by their dullness, were designed to slip by unremarked.

Bannister left the Chamber through the swing-doors behind the Speaker's chair. He was heading for the Whips' Office when, unexpectedly, because it was not her territory, he met Jules. He smiled and meant it. She really did make him relax. He wasn't quite sure what it was, but it happened. Thirty years earlier he would have put it down to romance. Charles Bannister had never quite come to terms with the concept of love which he regarded as best left to literature and an emotion reserved for one's daughter and, years earlier, for his nanny. To Bannister, romance was not the same as love, in fact it had little to do with it and therefore he had felt quite strongly that romance was a reasonable and even pleasant state. It was uncomplicated. It allowed a structured and slightly irresponsible relationship to blossom into close friendship which he believed more likely to survive than anything as fleeting as the deepest of emotions. He was not sure how he felt about Jules, but it was certainly more tantalizing than simple friendship. He felt a little younger when talking to her and very pleased to see her.

'Hello you. How about that drink this evening?'

Juliet looked about her. Just then they were alone. 'We'll see.'

'You said that last time.'

'And we did and you didn't.'

Bannister felt guilty. 'I'm sorry. It was raining.'

'What had you in mind Chang? Pimms on the terrace?'

He wanted to tell her about Dougal knowing his nickname. He did not.

'Look. After the Division.'

'I said we'll see. I'm not sure this is a good idea.'

Bannister heard the swing-door.

'I do. I want to talk to you about your father.'

'I'm going straight back to the flat.'

'I'll call you.'

Bannister was still feeling at rights with the world when he entered his inner office. Rose was piling letters onto his desk. There were also three 'While U Were Outs' from Henry. It was urgent. Mary had telephoned twice. She was back at the flat. He wondered why it needed two calls to tell him that. Rose shrugged.

'Oh and the Cabinet Secretary called. A private word, he said.'

'He never has anything else. The only time he's ever said anything on the record was to wish the Prime Minister a happy birthday. Then he spoiled it by saying "I'm sure you will have". That man has developed superciliousness to an art form. It's a wonder he hasn't been onto Heritage for a grant for his smile.'

Rose wheezed her amusement. It was good to hear her boss in song once more.

'What started that. I thought you two got on.'

'Not when he wants something.'

'Does he?'

'If he calls here? Of course he does. He never makes telephone calls in case he's listening in.'

Two minutes later there was a laugh in her voice as Rose put through the Cabinet Secretary. Even that required one-upmanship. The Cabinet Secretary was a grandee of the highest order. Charles Bannister was a member of the Cabinet. The simplest form would have been for Charles to call him on his private line. Rose, however, enjoyed the games of Westminster and Whitehall. She telephoned the Secretary's private office who at first tried the 'Could he call him back?' routine. That did not work, so the Cabinet Secretary found himself saying 'yes' on a dead line, followed by 'Just putting you through sir', followed by Charles, sounding slightly surprised that he was there and almost giving the impression that he had forgotten he had called him. For Rose, a perfect piece of Whitehall theatre – but not farce.

'That matter I mentioned. I understand that the Prime Minister may have made reference to it himself.'

Bannister liked less and less the way the Cameron affair was developing.

'He may have done.'

'In that case may I add my voice to the warning, in the most respectful way of course.'

'Of course. Go on.'

There was a pause. Bannister was right. The Cabinet Secretary rarely spoke on the telephone unless he were forced to. When he spoke again, the voice was terse.

'That is all. I simply wish to add my voice. I imagine

we understand, it is more serious than we imagined. If you wish to call by, then I will explain further, but for the moment . . .'

Bannister said thank you. He said it politely. But he was furious. And he said as much again when he met Henry Colvil in the Reform.

'My dear heart, we must not become overly excited. Really we must not.'

'But I've had enough of this Henry. Absolutely enough. I'm told I am entered in some disgusting log-book by one of your thugs as if I were a common villain. I'm told whom I may and may not visit. I have the Prime Minister treating me like a misbehaving fourth-former and now I get him, him of all people, being damned pompous. My God Father James, what exactly is going on?'

Colvil looked about him rather nervously as one or two members looked across. They had probably not heard what Bannister had said but they had picked up his tone and they certainly knew who he was, which made it even more interesting.

'My dear Charles. There is quite a lot, as you put it, going on, otherwise why would I presume to speak so cautiously about your old friendship? Your Cambridge friend is under enormous suspicion and will be dealt with.'

Bannister moved his head from side to side in frustration and undisguised annoyance.

'But he is an old man. He's a frail and rather sad old don who is coming to the end of his days and now he's being hounded to, well, he's been treated rather badly.'

Henry blinked slowly at his brother-in-law and took a small sip of his afternoon Madeira.

'He is, Charles, a traitor. He betrayed his monarch, his country and the trust others placed in him. He tried, probably successfully, to recruit young men and in one case, a young woman, to the cause of an alien, an offensive and an overtly hostile state. Treachery has no more uncompromising witness than this man.'

'All the same . . .'

'There is no same Charles. None whatsoever. Furthermore, it is but a few days since you would have told me the same thing. Why you find yourself able to utter this bewildering liberalism is beyond me. You should know that I find it remarkable and, may I say, deeply disturbing.'

Colvil took another sip at the thin wine. This time it was with a jerky movement, the whole action was medicinal rather than pleasurable. Bannister sighed and removed a speck of cotton from his chalk-striped trouser leg.

'Henry I am not for one moment condoning what Cameron may have once been. But the truth is, he is exactly how I describe him. He's old and uncertain. I shouldn't wonder if he's not long for this world. Why hunt him down?'

Colvil carefully placed his small and now empty glass on the wine table at his elbow and entwined his plump fingers across his belly. His eyeglass dropped and rested above his hands. It was the action of a country solicitor about to do his duty by a widow with an empty will. He coughed.

'Dear, dear heart. It is not I, it is not we, who hunt him down. It is his treachery.'

Colvil looked once more to left and right in the most casual of manners and then leaned forward and tapped Bannister on the knee.

'And I'm afraid, Charles, there is more to come.'

Bannister nodded for his brother-in-law to continue.

'Go on. What?'

Colgil was as far forward as his dignity would allow and when he spoke it was in a whisper.

'For some time we have known about Cameron. In fact there are those who have known for some years.'

'Then why has he been allowed to continue teaching. Why wasn't he sorted along with the others?'

'And Blunt?' Colvil's small mouth twisted in a sneer. Colvil, as Bannister knew, was one of the SIS people who had never agreed to Blunt's amnesty. They wanted him exposed and sent to prison. But they were overruled. So Cameron too had been allowed this curious freedom. But why? Colvil continued.

'As I say, Cameron has not been a secret for some time. But what we have never know is the identity of some one or even some persons Cameron recruited. Most attention is placed on the recruiter, but little on the recruited.'

Bannister shook his head in disbelief.

170

'Come on old man, that Hollis and Co stuff is old hat. It wasn't true anyway, we both know that.'

Colvil gave a short wave of his hand. Bannister's voice was once more showing his frustration.

'Charles. Please. Yes, we know that. Poor Roger had no black marks other than those splashed on him in spite. What we long suspected is that Cameron may well have recruited the odd one or two who disappeared through the net, probably in the late 1950s.'

'After Stalin?'

Colvil's chins shimmered when he nodded assent. He was feeling happier with the conversation and made a discreet signal for another Madeira. Colvil was perhaps the only member to be waited on in such a manner. No one knew why. Colvil did not wonder at it. Now he was in full flow.

'Absolutely, my dear. Absolutely. The coronation, Everest and the death of Stalin all in a few months. What a wondrous year. A wondrous year. If only there had been a decent claret. But certainly Charles, Cameron was busy recruiting into the brave world of Khrushchev and his successors. Do not forget the disillusioned after Suez and so much more. Thank God, and one does, for the Cuban missile affair. It finally brought a lot of somewhat silly people to their senses.'

The Madeira had appeared and Colvil took his first sip. It was unusual for him to take a second glass in the afternoon, although he always did on October 21 when he quietly toasted the Immortal Memory. Bannister had lost much of his anger but not his sorrow and confusion.

'You're clearly suggesting that Cameron managed to recruit people who have since gone into high office and may still be there.'

Colvil replaced his glass. 'Indeed I am Charles. Indeed I am. Although I would add that you are correct up to a point Lord Copper. Up to a point. We, I, suspect that there is thus far undetected but one survivor of the Cameron school of charm. But one.'

'Who is?'

Colvil shrugged with his jowls.

'Truly I do not know. Which is why we have such differences of opinion. C believes that by leaving Cameron be, the political stability which he craves for the nation, or perhaps for his higher knighthood, remains.'

Bannister picked up the thread. 'But if Cameron is blown, then he may take everyone with him, hence instability.'

They both paused like monks considering a gospel for the day. It was Colvil who broke the contemplative silence.

'Indeed, Charles, indeed. What is more, I happen to understand that in spite of your best endeavours, your Herod has changed his mind, if that what it is, and has once again told C that Grishin must take up knitting comforts for the troops or some such similar and harmless pastime.'

'No book?'

'No book.'

'No book. No exposure. Henry, doesn't that strike you as curious?'

'Most certainly my dear. Most certainly. Which is why we have not given up and which is why you must stay from Cameron's staircase and instead pursue our cause with your Herod.'

'And you? What will you be doing?'

'Ah yes, what indeed. We shall be going about our business.'

Bannister sighed. It was the deep sigh of one very sad.

'About your business. I bet you will.'

'But our business is not treachery. Please console yourself with that point and Charles, do try to remember your rightful indignation when I first mentioned that unfinished business needed tending. I must say I prefer your first reaction to your present one. Indeed, I find that a smidgen worrisome.'

Twenty-Seven

Mary Bannister had bathed. She preferred bathing in the London flat. She liked the warm bathroom with its heated towel rails and bowls of soaps and smellies. She disliked the healthy, draughty and spartan barn of a bathroom at the farm that had been created from a middle bedroom with sloping ceilings and low windows.

Visitors thought it quaint in the summer but never in the winter when the night frosts formed icicles on the insides of the windows. The farm had two bathrooms. The other was a recent addition to the main guest room and was almost modern, give or take the odd damp patch from the eaves and an end chimney which should have been capped but never had been. When there were no guests, Mary used it instead of the family one, but it too had the feel of what she imagined she might find in a holiday cottage. So one of Mary Bannister's first actions every time she returned to London was to soak for as long as she could in the luxury of her clean, fully tiled and warm-towelled bathroom. For Mary was a London person.

Everyone, or almost everyone, insisted that Mary Bannister was brilliant in the constituency. She dined the Party groupies, fed the vicar on Sundays, put the Tio Pepe away when the hunting set came to swig at lunchtimes and bought at almost every stall when it was time for fairs and fêtes. She could be seen, heavy-booted and rosy-cheeked, yomping through woods. She could be seen and heard singing in a pleasing mezzo on Sunday mornings. She could be seen pricking out when it was time to prick out, pruning when it was time to prune and even bottling (or so it was said) when it was no longer fashionable to bottle. And she hated it.

Mary Bannister regarded the country as a place to catch one's death and the nosiest and most boring neighbours imaginable. But everyone was right on one count. She remained a good constituency wife. She had been brought up in the world of politicians. Her father had sat on the Back-benches until the day before his death. Her maternal grandfather had been active in the Lords and a second cousin and his brother-in-law had both been Ministers, one remained so and yet another member of the family sat in the Lords on the Bench of bishops. So she did the okay things with grace and much of the time without thinking.

But ten years earlier Mary had tried her hand at writing. Charles had never been a great public figure. He was, according to Mary, something of an acquired taste. He had neither the personality nor the desire to become a media politician. George Sharpe said he was part of the old school. In some ways that was good for the Party and good for Charles, but not much help to an aspiring authoress and her publisher.

There had been a brief period of notoriety when her second book appeared with a raunchy cover and three or four pages to back it up. But the publicity season on Mary was short lived. Most books of her type had three or four pages on which there wasn't explicit sex. At the same time, Mary regularly made a decent profit in soft-back. But more and more she was finding that the freedom she enjoyed from writing and being her own person had great moments of emptiness. She really would have preferred to spend more time with Charles and, at one time, with Polly. Her friends told her that now Polly was in her early twenties they would become friends. Perhaps they would one day. For the moment

Mary's mumsy tag was written in frustration rather than affection.

Now, as she sat feet curled beneath her in a sensible night-dress and dressing-gown with the *National Geographic* magazine on her knee, Mary Bannister wondered if it were not time that she went in search of the African red-bummed something or at least the Seychellois coco de mer. The telephone interrupted her dreams and saved her from a decision. It was ten forty-five. Charles? It was not. It was the Cabinet Secretary.

Charles Bannister sat in his Commons room and wondered about Cameron. Henry was probably right. But only about Cameron. The yellow stickers on his pad reminded him that he had not called Mary. She was engaged. Ten forty-five. Blast. He turned over the private directory in front of him and dialled a Dolphin Square number. It rang three or four times.

'Are you in?'

There was a long sigh at the other end.

'Yes.'

Her voice was soft.

'See you shortly.'

He replaced the handset, looked at the yellow sticker, got up, switched off the main light and went in search of a cab.

Henry Colvil was sitting up in bed and reading Proust. His Man had replaced the blue coverlet with the green. Colvil believed the green to be a more sympathetic match for his aubergine pyjamas. His Man understood this and had changed the linen accordingly. Colvil was holding a dark almond-shaped chocolate ginger in his fingers and was about to slide it between his lips when the telephone burbled. Colvil looked at the gilt mantel clock. Five minutes to midnight. It would be improper to let it ring and cause RLS to answer. RLS stood for Rotten Little Sod.

On the one occasion when Henry Colvil had allowed himself to swear, or even thought to do so with any feeling, it had been some fifteen years earlier and at His Man. He remembered the incident rather well, although he chose never to tell others. His Man, instead of being offended, had beamed at Colvil's splutter and cry of 'You rotten little sod'. For some reason Colvil had from that point called His Man RLS. No one but Colvil, and of course RLS, knew what the initials stood for. One lady friend had assumed it must be a continuous sound, not a set of initials and therefore a common Nepalese name. Colvil had never said otherwise. RLS most certainly had not. He now lay in his cot, eyes open, until the ringing stopped and he knew from the click on his extension that his master had picked up the bedside receiver. RLS closed his eyes and was instantly asleep.

Colvil was far from asleep. A call so late in the evening from the Cabinet Secretary was a disagreeable event. Colvil would normally expect telephone calls at that time in the evening from unthinking family or the Department. He found the Cabinet Secretary an obnoxious fellow but a necessary ally and so tried to put a modicum of pleasantness into his voice. It did not come willingly.

'No, not at all. I was reading. What a delightful surprise.'

He listened a while and felt the surprise was just that, but hardly delightful.

'I see. But he is in a difficult position. You and I understand the need for discretion, but although he is, as you rightly point out, the only connection we have, we are sailing somewhat dangerous waters if we ask for such cooperation. May I ask what prompts the urgency?'

He listened. He understood. He was sympathetic and was glad the Cabinet Secretary had telephoned. He suggested they met shortly before nine o'clock and strolled in St James's. Yes, where they would normally meet.

Colvil replaced the receiver and stared ahead at the long gold-lacquered dressing-mirror on the opposite wall. He wondered why the Cabinet Secretary should take the side of his Department and not the Security Service. He wondered also why the Cabinet Secretary should involve him and not talk directly to Controller. Having wondered for some moments, Colvil reached for the dark chocolate which he had abandoned by his velvet sleeping mask. He popped the confection into his mouth and returned to his book, wondering only if he too should take a muffler the next morning in case Zephyrus and Boreas vied with each other. He supposed he saw the connection.

Twenty-Eight

Kay Bennet was naked beneath the duvet. Through half-closed eyes she watched Dougal Baxter dressing. She had never understood him. She had never really tried. For most of their relationship, she had avoided any serious examination of their future other than the obvious fact that, as a Catholic, Dougal never considered they had what he called 'a permanent arrangement'. She knew also that Dougal would never leave his wife.

Ros was rich, her family even richer. Dougal enjoyed his wife's wealth in many ways. The money meant that although he was comfortable in his own right, his future was reasonably assured. Also, he liked the idea of the small Iberian villa kept, maybe surprisingly, since found by one of Ros's ancestors during the Peninsular Wars. Dougal enjoyed the long Christmas holidays at her family home in Scotland even though he detested the weather and the heartiness of her friends. He refused to shoot or stalk, not because he felt sorry for the grouse or for the deer. Dougal was simply the most unsporting of people. That his wife should own two thousand acres and a turreted granite pile big enough to give most of Inverness bed and breakfast – and rheumatism – in one clear weekend was a pure irony of Dougal's life. His own family had money through publishing. His half-brother was for the moment chairman of the company. They both knew that if Dougal lost office then the half-brother would move over. Until that moment, Dougal planned and plotted the downfall of anyone who might challenge his political and private future.

Dougal Baxter had no sense of loyalty other than to himself. He had no qualms about hurting others as long as they could not retaliate. When he pulled back from hurting or unseating it was either because he recognized he would not succeed or because of his innate cowardice. Now, as he finished dressing, he sat on the edge of the bed and stroked Kay's bare shoulder. Very gently he massaged the soft flesh knowing well how it aroused her. He talked quietly and with his most sincere smile.

'You have to understand, my dear, that if our little ploy's going to work, then you and I, especially you, must be very careful. Last night was very silly you know.'

She moved under his hand. He knew what happened when he stroked her like that. Dougal, she accepted, was a bastard. Dougal knew so and was sufficiently a bastard to believe that was part of his attraction.

'But there was nothing in it. I promise.'

'Of course you do. But you know it's very disturbing to walk in here and find you naked with my closest friend.'

'I was not naked.'

'You were better than that. Don't you know that men of his age need the stimulation of scanties. Most fetching.'

180

She stirred beneath the duvet.

'You have nothing to worry about. He's too nice anyway.'

'For what?'

She snuggled further in. Actually she thought she fancied Bannister. Or she had.

'Well you know.'

'I most certainly do. Let me tell you young lady, Charles Bannister may appear all strait-laced and wouldn't say boo to a goose, but don't be fooled. Charles is something of a swordsman.'

Kay looked at him. She was interested for more reasons than she would wish to show Dougal Baxter. And she knew exactly how to get out of him what she wanted to know.

'Oh ho. Here we go again. Dougal Baxter's fantasies. Charles Bannister's an old fuddy who'd blush if he saw a pair of knickers on the line. Don't talk nonsense.'

Baxter fell for it.

'You'd better not tell Miss Tartan Drawers that.'

'Who?'

Kay had rolled over on her back. Baxter's hand was beneath the duvet and she moved against him.

'Miss Tartan Drawers Cameron that's who.'

'You trying to tell me they've got something going? I don't believe it.'

'Frankly my dear, as the man didn't say, I don't give a damn what you believe.'

She wanted to know more, but she knew he wasn't ready to tell otherwise he would have. But she knew also that he would, perhaps even that evening. Baxter liked to play games. He liked power at any level of friendship. He needed to be seen to be powerful, especially by his few friends. Too often he went unchallenged. She often tried it and failed. Like the night they had been dining in a restaurant and he suddenly called for the bill and insisted they went immediately even though she was only halfway through her main course. She had refused to go. So he had walked out. The staff had looked embarrassed at first and then had smirked. At her. He had gone. She had followed. It was his simple way of saying that it was he who dictated their relationship when it was obvious that he did anyway. Perhaps he played these games because he knew she suspected or knew his weaknesses. She did but she rarely exploited them, although she knew he could be relied on to tell her most things on their pillow. Or at least that's what she thought.

Slowly he moved his fingers beyond her hip. She closed her eyes. From her muffled lips came a gentle moan of pleasure. And then, just as she knew he would, as he always did, he was gone. He spoke from the bedroom door.

'I'll see you in the morning. Don't be late. I need you and Nick to put a speech together by the evening.'

She eyed him from the warm bed.

'On what?'

'Family values. The PM thinks its a good idea. Bye.'

She heard the front door close and knew that he would walk down the four flights of stairs though the lift was now repaired. Even, or perhaps especially, at two in the morning, Dougal Baxter believed caution to be the better part of indiscretion.

Kay reached into the bedside drawer and beneath a soft layer of handkerchiefs. She found what she was looking for and snuggled down. She lay, moving slowly and whispering to herself in a dreamy voice, and then dozed. Her dream woke her. She was sorry. She got up, went into the bathroom and switched on the shower. As she slowly soaped herself with the giant primrose bar Kay thought of Charles Bannister. Juliet Cameron? She could not believe it. Yet there had been something there. A spark, a moment when he had relaxed. Not just the whisky. She turned the shower full on and laid her head back into its stream.

Twenty-Nine

The three men walked slowly through St James's Park. Every few moments they would pause in the unexpected early morning sunshine as one of them made a point that needed emphasis, that needed explanation. The tallest of the three, his hands deep in his overcoat pockets and in the centre, said very little. The shortest, nearest the lake's edge, carried his silver-topped cane at the trail like a very round Victorian dragoon and looked across the water as he listened. The third man was speaking, his hands gripping his unfurled umbrella behind his back, his eyes almost closed and his head half in the air.

'It is quite impossible for this matter to be, ah, restrained. I believe the PM will agree when it is explained once more. The necessary, ah, measures are in place. Once the writing is done, then there is what I am told is called an editing period.'

'By whom?'

'I really do not know Charles, I really do not. But I am informed that the procedure is to make the whole thing sensible and entirely commercial.'

The Cabinet Secretary when in flow had an ecclesiastical pronunciation and commercial emerged as commerc-ee-al. He continued to annoy Bannister.

'By this I mean that an agent has been chosen, one in whom we have confidence, and a publisher has accepted the task. The editor will, I imagine of course, be trustworthy.'

Colvil glanced from the view across the lake and nodded once. He approved thus far. Nevertheless, he decided it time to bring the conversation to the reason for their meeting. He stopped and the other two turned towards him, Bannister, more hunched than usual, the Cabinet Secretary, his hands still behind him and almost seated on his umbrella. Henry blew his cheeks into a puffball.

'I am afraid dear heart that the three of us need to speak of more delicate matters, although inextricably related to friend Grishin.'

The Cabinet Secretary took a half-step backward and

assumed his normal pose of letting others bleed their thoughts and concerns. He quietly nodded as Bannister looked at him to see if he too were in the same frame of mind as his brother-in-law. Clearly the Cabinet Secretary was part of the ambush. Bannister said nothing while Colvil made short humphing noises before continuing.

'We would care to know exactly what communication you have had with Cameron, in any form whatsoever.'

Bannister looked surprised. Colvil knew everything about the meeting in Cambridge.

'But you know, Henry. Hardly any communication at all. The poor old boy was clearly agitated, but frankly by the time we'd got to pudding, well, he could scarce remember the Master's name. *In vino* blindness rather than *veritas* I'm afraid.'

'But we imagine it would be possible that he could say things in some other manner.'

Bannister shook his head. 'I don't see how. Jules, eh, Juliet his daughter, seems to think that he would like to see me again, but that's all.'

'Exactly my dear, that is exactly what we had in mind. The delightful Miss Cameron may be a conduit for her dear father's thoughts.'

Bannister started to walk on and the three fell in step. It was a slow march, without the faltering pauses. The three men stared ahead and spoke quietly, Bannister with a growing sense of frustration.

'I'm afraid one of you must stop playing games and

tell me what it is that's bothering you. It would be very helpful if you took me into your confidence rather than your very curious interrogation technique. I must say Henry, I would have expected you and I to have this sort of conversation in private.'

The Cabinet Secretary made a rare intervention. He swung his gamp behind him and cleared his throat.

'But Charles, this is in the greatest confidence. The greatest privacy. After all it is one of those conversations which is not taking place.'

Bannister dug deeper into his huge pockets and his patience.

'I feel there is something quite important that you're not telling me. Why do we have to have this, this, frankly this melodrama? I accept what you say about Cameron. He is, or rather he has been, a traitor.'

'Is.'

'Very well, have it your own way...'

'It is not my way, my dear. He is a traitor. I'm afraid treachery is most certainly akin to being black or white. One is or one is not.'

The Cabinet Secretary hummed his liturgical assent to the heavens.

'You see Charles, ah, we imagine that some of what friend Grishin has to say may not be published. There are other, ah, other, ah consider-ae-si-ons.'

Bannister sighed, stopped with a grate of his steel-edged heels.

'Am I to be let into this secret? In fact is it really a secret or are we going through yet another piece of

186

nonsense which comes to nothing when the truth's known?'

The Cabinet Secretary cleared his throat once more. It was shortly after nine, and therefore late in the morning for the bureaucrat.

'I must leave you both. But let me assure you that there is no nonsense in what we have been discussing. Grishin knows much that he has not told us. Of course he does. You understand as well as I the system of insurance. He keeps an, ah, an important piece of information from us. What it is I do not know. He has not said. Therefore it is vital that anything Cameron should tell you, directly or indirectly, should come to us as soon as is poss-i-bul.'

The last syllable allowed him to be return-ed to his speech affectation. But having given what was, for him, almost an address, the Cabinet Secretary touched his finger to his black Homburg and, humming, set off along the path towards Horse Guards.

Bannister watched him go and then turned to his brother-in-law.

'Come on old man, what in blazes is going on? What's this directly or indirectly nonsense. What's he talking about?'

They continued their walk towards the gates opposite St James's, turned as if meeting some invisible barrier and strolled towards the bridge once more. As they crossed, Henry Colvil raised his hat to a matron he thought he might know and ignored a slim young man he most certainly knew.

'Charles, we must not excite ourselves.'

'I am not excited, I am concerned that something important is happening, that I am somehow involved and that I am not told the full story.'

In his anger, Bannister's stride had increased. Colvil's foxtrot had trouble keeping pace. He touched a grey-gloved hand to Bannister's arm.

'Wait Charles, wait. Hear me quietly.'

Bannister glared at the cloud that had hidden the winter warmth and pulled his scarf higher about his throat.

'Go on.'

'It is very possible that Cameron retains the name of someone, someone in a very high place.'

'Yes. Yes. Someone he recruited years ago. I know all this Henry. My God Father James, you've already tried that. I'm also far from stupid. You must have a reasonable idea who it is.'

'Perhaps.'

'What does that mean?'

'It means we have spent a little time going through not just the college but the whole University members' book for some five years. We have made a reasonable assessment of all those undergraduate and graduate students whom he might have met.'

'And presumably you have gone through his supervision list. If it exists, which I doubt. And I suppose you've been through personnel and registry here so you know which of the more senior men appear on your Cambridge list.'

'There are three and one-half dozen names.'

Bannister started along the path stepping aside for a brace of prams that must have strayed from Kensington Gardens. Colvil caught up.

'You see Charles, we believe that the name Cameron has, well, its bearer is still active.'

'Oh yes. Well that should make life easier. All you have to do is go to the reason for thinking that and you've got your man.'

'Or woman.'

Bannister halted.

'Why woman?'

'Why not?'

Bannister stared hard at Colvil and gave him an elementary lesson in Cambridge social history in general and Cameron in particular.

'Because old man, in the time you're talking about, Cameron would not have had any women undergraduates. The college did not have them. He never saw any, on principle, from elsewhere.'

'Maybe the one we had in mind had, let us say, slowly maturing sympathies for Cameron's ideals.'

'I can't imagine how. He was notoriously rude to women. He barely tolerated them in the university. Hardly does now, and he certainly did not in those days.'

Colvil shrugged his shoulders. The hand was back on Bannister's arm.

'With one exception dear heart. One, ah, exception.'

'I don't believe it. Who?'

'His daughter.'

Thirty

By the time Bannister had reached the Commons he was confused. He was certainly angry. Denis Wigton was coming through the Members' Entrance at the same time.

'Got a moment Charlie?'

The voice was sternly Bradford from the Navy Cut blackened throat and the severe stare beneath the shaggy eyebrows. Bannister was brusque.

'Sorry. Can it wait?'

'Not really.'

Bannister stopped and glared.

'If it's any more of your folksy advice Denis, then keep it to yourself.'

'Happen the only thing I keep to meself is me temper. But no, I was wondering if you fancied a swift one later. Maybe in the Kremlin.'

Bannister found Wigton's suggestion that they met for a drink in perhaps the seediest of the Commons' bars quite ludicrous and he said so.

'Whatever for? I must say I'm not in the habit of having a swift one as you call it and certainly not in that place.'

Wigton looked a little put out. But not much.

'Quiet chat over a cup of tea then?'

'Denis, one of your more endearing, if at times frustrating, talents is the way you say what you have to say. Would please mind telling me why we should be arranging to have tea of all things?'

Wigton smiled. He liked seeing Bannister agitated, not for any political reason but simply because the Party Chairman made him laugh when he was hot under his stiff collar.

'Okay Charlie. You see, I've been asked to write a book about this place.'

'Congratulations.'

'No need to be sarcastic.'

'I wasn't. I meant it. I look forward to reading it. I imagine your own brand of parliamentary understanding will give fresh light to the place. Now, if you don't mind, I must press on.'

He started to go. Wigton tugged at his sleeve.

'Just a minute. You see, I was wondering if you would make a contribution to it.'

'Me? My God Father James. Whatever for?'

'Well, it's like this. It's difficult to explain in a couple of minutes, but I'm not writing it all, I'm sort of editing it I suppose and then writing a commentary which leads into each chapter.'

'This is all too complicated for this time of the morning Denis.'

'That's what I meant. Well, the book's not a tourist thing and it's not a tract. It's a book about integrity and how certain values have survived in spite of everything that goes on. You see Charlie, I reckon some people are in this place for the right reason, what I suppose some folk would say are old-fashioned reasons. You know, integrity, public duty and that.'

'I hope you're right, but I sometimes think it's a dwindling band, if it exists at all.'

'That's the point and that's what the publisher likes. Any road, I'm asking a few people to write their own thoughts, people I eh, well, frankly Charlie, people I respect. And well, I know we're on opposite sides, but I do. I respect what you have to say.'

Bannister looked for a sign that Wigton was setting him up for a big put-down. The other's embarrassment made it obvious that he was not. Bannister too was embarrassed.

'Denis that's very sweet of you. I'm flattered and I promise you, I'll give it some thought. Now I must go.'

'Fine and thanks.'

Bannister started for the Lobby and then paused.

'Oh just one thing Denis. Your concern about Jules. I know I was annoyed but I want you to know my concern for her is my concern for her father. I've known her since she was a slip of a girl although I did not realize it until she came into the House. Don't worry about her. My intentions, as the Victorians would have said, are entirely honourable.'

He did not wait for a reply and turned towards the door at a faster pace than he would have normally taken. He wondered why on earth he had made the point to Wigton. He certainly knew that it was not true. Could no longer be so.

Rose was waiting with the usual long list of telephone calls and the reminder that he was supposed to be making his second visit to Cambridge. The Party had lost the seat at the last election. It had gone to a good Opposition candidate who had since been making a name for herself both in the House and in the constituency as a hard worker, a campaigner and above all a listener on local issues. Her Saturday morning surgery was so popular that after a great deal of negotiating with its conscience and with its controller of policy, the local radio station had started broadcasting the hour-long session. The other local Parties had objected on the grounds of political bias. The radio station had said that it was quite willing to broadcast any surgery they put together. As none of the other Parties had yet chosen a potential candidate this was impossible. The protest had only given the sitting Member more publicity especially as she very wisely made a point of saying and advertising that she represented all the voters and that everyone would be welcome. The result was a jammed surgery which had to move from the local Party offices to a school sports hall every Saturday, an enormous amount of free publicity and an almost unprecedented increase in the MP's popularity rating.

Charles was well aware that these sort of bold ideas were not coming from any of the local Party managers. They were stuffy and in his view arrogant. So he had decided to see them, give them a talking to and hopefully take away the lessons for use in seats they did hold. Rose was in charge of Bannister's diary and she had made a series of appointments for him in the region.

Charles Bannister in many ways was a bad choice as Party Chairman. He hated small talk and a large part of the job was exactly that. In truth, Bannister was like most senior politicians. He regarded the work of the constituency as important but depressingly boring and in many cases, the local Party officials as petty and arrogant. So when he went anywhere, he insisted that he kept on the move, covered as much political and social ground as possible and could justify not returning for some time, if ever again. Rose had fixed such an itinerary for Bannister.

She apologized that this was to be yet another occasion when he would have two lunches. He would start at a manageable buffet just outside Cambridge at twelve-fifteen and as it was a stand-up-and-how-are-you affair he could be ten miles away in time for the one o'clock sit down chicken and salad and get his breath and digestion back to make the well-done-keep-it-up-we-could-not-do-it-if-it-weren't-for-the-grassroots-support speech. Then there was a visit to a regional political agents' briefing seminar at Madingley at three. He needed to be away by four-forty and a car would take him to a meeting of his college's fund-raising committee by five.

Charles regarded this as the most important event of the afternoon, not because he had an overwhelming loyalty for his college but because he intended to convince one the college's richest and most generous old members that now he had bought his honorary Fellowship a similar amount might go down well with the Party under the heading 'contributions to politics'. No promises mind you, no actual mention of the honours system, but after all it was a system. With an election on the horizon and a wretched bank balance, the Party's need was greater than the college's, which in any case was as rich as it was considerably mean. Bannister had no qualms about hijacking a source of funds.

From the committee meeting Bannister would enjoy the stroll to another college where at six-forty-five he would give a speech to the Party's student body, from which, he supposed might come a future Party Chairman and possibly a Prime Minister or two. Then at seven-thirty, with apologies to everyone, he would leave and probably head for an evening meeting or home.

'What d'you want me to do about travel? Going up by car?'

'Mm?'

Bannister was thinking about Wigton, about the walk in the royal park.

'You going to stay or come back?'

'I'll come back. There's Cabinet first thing.'

Rose nagged at an irritating suspender.

'You go up by train I could always put you into the University Arms or somewhere. Get a room in your college couldn't you? You could come down on the morning train. Good night's sleep.'

At this time of the year, finding a room was not difficult. He was sure that should he mention the matter, he could always stay with the Master, an old family friend. He shook his head.

'Don't worry. I'll drive and if I change my mind I'll put up somewhere.'

She pushed some papers his way and waited as he unscrewed the top from his fountain pen.

'You could always stay with your friend, old Professor Cameron.'

There was something in her tone which suggested that Rose was probing, maybe making a point. Bannister ignored her suggestion and scratched his signature on fifteen letters and nine memoranda.

In the Central Lobby George Sharpe was having a word with one of the junior doormen. Interesting job being on the door he had told Rose. She had sipped her green ginger wine and listened at first with polite interest and then with unease. Lots of people do things without taking notice of the furniture, which was why the policemen in the Commons and the doormen often knew more than many imagined, as Sharpe had mentioned, very casually of course.

'Party comes out and takes the next cab up. Says to the cabbie, Fred's caf if you will my man. Bit later, out comes a Member, takes the next cab up, says to the cabbie, Fred's caf and make it rapido. One and one makes two. Yes? One and one makes a very interesting two. Know what I mean?'

Now Sharpe was hearing some of the night's goings and goings. It was interesting who went where from the covered porch where the taxis drew up in the cobbled yard beneath Big Ben's gaze, especially late at night, when you might have thought most places were closed.

When Juliet Cameron came through the lobby with a casual smile for Bannister who was coming the other way, Sharpe and his friend looked on without expression.

Thirty-One

They had arranged to meet in the Embankment gardens. The promised clear skies had come and the leaves, yet to be swept by the zealous keepers, made pleasant scrunching sounds beneath their feet. It was a silly meeting. They risked being seen by so many people who knew them, but for the moment both still believed anyone would accept a logical explanation of even the most obvious contradiction.

Bannister was nervous, not because they had met, nor for the growing relationship which had now wandered that extra mile beyond friendship. Bannister had been unnerved by Henry Colvil's suggestion that Juliet Cameron may have been so influenced by her father that she too would have adopted his belief that the system under which they lived was so corrupt that it was only right that it should be betrayed. Charles Bannister had called this nonsensical reasoning. Colvil had insisted that the sins of fathers could be visited on daughters as well as sons. He mentioned Juliet's record as a student socialist, as a volunteer flying picket, as a banner carrier on miners' demonstrations and, something Charles had never known about, the long summers spent with her father visiting the shrines of Moscow, Leningrad, as it then was, and the lecture tours in Bucharest. With such a background, or so Colvil wondered aloud, was there any reason to believe that Juliet Cameron might be anything but contemptuous of the society which had given her such opportunity.

Now, as they walked, too close together, Bannister knew that he would have to distance himself from this quiet, reassuring woman almost half his age and for whom he had developed a disturbing fondness. But he could not possibly tell her why.

'Your father, is he any better?'

'No. Why should he be?'

'I don't follow.'

'Well, you asked me last night.'

'I suppose I did.'

She stopped. He walked an extra pace and turned to face her. She saw in his eyes an agony that had not been there before. An anguish that would have been impossible the night before.

'What is it Chang?'

'What is what?'

'Tell me.'

'Nothing.'

'I'm a big girl you know. You don't have to believe

the end of the world is nigh. I'm not a kiss-and-tell if that's what's worrying you.'

Bannister shook his head. It was a mournful day. How he wished it would end. How he wished it would go away and he could wake up again and find himself years before, still in chambers with the warmth of the fresh white gloss paint, the terracotta walls, the deeply shone oak desk and its lamp with its soft glow beneath the dark green shade and the reassuring hiss of the gas fire. How he wished for the days when complicated ambitions had yet to intrude into his life. His voice was truly mournful.

'I simply do not understand what is happening.'

'Do you have to?'

Bannister looked genuinely puzzled.

'Naturally. Don't you?'

'No. That's something we find out for ourselves. It takes time Chang. If you ask too many questions now, then you ask the wrong questions, you risk smothering something that may be there and you risk forcing something which really isn't. Let's stay friends. There's no need for great self-examination.'

'It isn't that simple.'

She walked on, wanting to take his arm but knowing she could not. A tug-boat set a busy bow wave of brown and grey, hooted as it approached the bridge and they paused again, watching as a black-hulled police launch rocked side to side in the sudden wake.

'You know Chang, nothing to you is simple. You're so ordered that if anything in your life steps out of line, especially your emotions, then you're about to call up the United Nations or at the very least the Samaritans.'

He did not laugh. He wanted to. He wanted to tell her that her father was under suspicion. He wanted to tell that his own brother-in-law had suggested that she too might have worked for the enemies of the State. He wanted to tell the most awful thing of all was that Henry had asked him to report anything she might say about her father. He wanted to tell her that he had been asked to spy on her. He wanted to tell her that he had been angered by Colvil and had torn up his nonsensical suggestions and flung them in his face and that he would defend her and her father from anything that was said against them. But he did not because he had not flung those accusations in Henry's round, supercilious features. He had instead agreed to help Henry because if he had refused to do so then he would have drawn attention to the depth of their friendship.

As they leaned on the wall overlooking the Thames, he imagined the warmth of her arm. He felt also the terror of what could so easily follow.

Bannister straightened. It was a sudden movement. It clicked from his character like so many decisions he made. He had second thoughts but the decision became easier once made. But when he thought of the options, the consequences – it was intolerable. Bannister did what he always did when the most horrid decisions had to be made, he retreated into his instincts.

All his life Bannister had taken refuge in his severe and lonely background. He had once confided in Mary that he had hated his prep school and had hated Eton. (His comfort was that he soon believed that his hatred was ill-founded and a sign of weakness. He disliked weakness, particularly his own.) Mary had said nonsense and so he had shown her it was not. Had tried to shock her. He had when he told her how he had vomited the first time he had witnessed buggery. But not the second time. In his second year he had chosen not to know that it happened.

That year he had remarked to a friend that the secret of the school was that it was a product of the boys and their parents, not of the system. And so Bannister, so mature, had learned to feel comfortable in an ordered system where those matters outside were best left there and a sense of duty covered cracks in a too often uncaring and uncared for society. The recipient of Bannister's remark was a new boy, Baxter.

Years on, when they remembered that conversation and so knew why they had fallen in so easily with each other, it was Baxter, by then a man, who in his straightforward manner remarked that society needs abattoirs but most of all it needs butchers. There was, Baxter had offered, little worse than a badly butchered joint. So Bannister came to feel that society needed both a political system which felled democracy at the point before it got out of hand and it needed therefore politicians of their persuasion who would butcher the

201

acts of the Party's apostles into appetizing and palatable joints.

It was with this simple understanding of how and why his own emotions were completely and rightly controllable in all things and his belief that his personal position mattered above all things, even above his own ambition, that Bannister now looked sympathetically but uncompromisingly at Juliet Cameron.

Juliet's father was in trouble, she was deeply disturbed, she needed his sympathy and understanding. She had both, but she could not have his support. His personal position did, after all, matter more than anything.

'I must get back. There are things to be done. I'm sorry.'

She nodded, saying nothing. She understood that whatever doubts he had had were now daubed with an emulsion of guilt and nervousness. She had asked for nothing. She had nothing.

Bannister wanted to leave but he could not bring himself to until she said something. She knew that. She did not make him wait.

'You don't have to make excuses Chang.'

'What does that mean?'

'Nothing more than that.'

'I'm sure it does.'

'I know you are, but it does not. As I said, I'm a big girl now. Friends?'

'Of course we are.'

'No, not of course. There's no such thing as of course.'

He looked at his well-buffed toe-cap. Sensible shoes. Strongly laced in lines, not criss-crossed. Polished insteps. As life should be. Chang. He should have said something earlier.

'Look Jules, you probably think this is irrelevant, especially at the moment, but you remember I said that you shouldn't call me Chang? Well, I meant it. Dougal, well, Dougal mentioned it the other day.'

Juliet Cameron looked surprised, then sad.

'I'm sorry.'

Her voice was as soft as it had been that evening when he had said goodbye.

He tried a smile, did not quite succeed, and turned and headed along the Embankment towards the safety of the one place he perfectly understood. The House. As he walked, he once again wanted to look back, even turn back. He did not. Bannister had a different courage.

From the other side of the wide road and from where he had stopped, just as they had, a sturdy figure in a British warm looked for a moment puzzled and then checked his watch and filled a line in his mental notebook.

Thirty-Two

Two streets away from where Bannister had left Juliet Cameron standing in the new drizzle, Dougal Baxter was holding forth in the warmth and safety of his research office.

At the word processor, Nick Potts, his green braces hanging in loops about his buttocks like a young hussar at his ablutions, tapped into quickly blinking and changing data sheets.

Kay Bennet, enormous tortoiseshell-framed spectacles on the end of her nose, ran through a list of printed quotes from eighteen philosophers. Dougal paused as Kay shifted in the high-backed leather chair and crossed her seemingly longer than ever legs. He stared at the tops of her thighs as he spoke.

'Now this point about family values will tie in nicely with the law and order speech. I shall make it the same one. What d'you think?'

Kay looked over her glasses and nodded.

'You could. You've got to come up with something to please them. You completely failed last time.'

Baxter never responded well to the truth, especially when he knew it to be exactly that and particularly when it concerned one of his public performances and therefore a reflection on his political nous. Nick kept gazing at the screen waiting to interrupt if the bitterness which he noticed more and more in the Chief's voice showed itself in response to Kay Bennet's simple observation. He need not have worried. Baxter was in charge, for the moment.

'What you fail to remember is that all Home Secretaries become Daniels when they speak to the Police Federation. Okay?'

No it was not. Kay said so.

'But Daniel could handle the lions. You didn't. Well, not last time you didn't.'

Nick was not sure what was going on, but it was time to move in. He tapped two more lines on the screen and swivelled on the backless stool. The backflip of his slicked hair completed his notion of the spot-on research assistant. Nick Potts would truly have been happier working for an American senator.

'Tell you what Chief, you out this law and order in the home thing then you'll get a standing happy hour from the plods. No probs. It's a natural.'

Dougal, for reasons no one else understood, was perfectly at home with Nick-speak. He gave the impression he was.

'Of course.'

Kay had not expected Nick's support, but neither had she expected such a quick put-down.

'I can't see why. You'd be telling them that they can't handle crime prevention and detection. That's pretty insulting isn't it?'

Nick did not wait for Dougal to defend himself.

'No way Bisto. No way. You'd be telling the plods it isn't their fault. That gets the heat off them. Then you wang in with mucho police reform without them being screwed up before you begin. I'd say you'd ring the clanger and get the coconut on this one Chief.'

'Or the bird.'

Dougal had a proper regard for Kay's intuition. He saw Kay Bennet as a survivor. They both knew that she amused him and when they were alone she did things to him that made him wish for a lasting self-control quite beyond his shallow capacity. But he understood well this sense of survival she showed in the most difficult of circumstances. He could and had, humiliated her on more than one occasion. There had been the time when they had been sleeping together for more than a year but well before she had come to London and he had been introduced to her at a British delegation cocktail party in Brussels. He had pretended not to know her. Furthermore he had deliberately turned his back on her so she was left standing by herself in a diplomatic group of mainly men and mainly those fawning over the Minister. On another occasion, he had told her to get out of the taxi half a mile from the Commons so that no one would see them arriving together after a long lunch in her then flat. Now he showed his annoyance even though he understood that she was right. She knew and he knew that unless he got the speech right on the nose, he risked getting the annual raspberry reserved for the Home Secretary by the Federation.

'My dear Kay, what you fail to remember is that you

two are supposed to produce the words which will make me a hero, not a cretin.'

She smiled sweetly and recrossed her legs watching, with satisfaction, his greedy eyes.

'Oh we'll produce the words, we more or less have, but it's not the words, it's the way you tell them.'

Dougal felt, with considerable justification, that his knockabout style and glimpses of foresight were highlights of Commons interventions and conference speeches. Dougal Baxter never left out facts, but he made them sound like decrees and his joking and leg-pulling together with his pig-sticking of an increasingly tired sounding and looking Opposition made him a headline performer in a Parliament sadly lacking the orators of the very recent past. Kay's point had not been at all well received, but before he could put her down, she continued.

'We're talking about a hostile audience. Blame it on the parents if you wish, but that doesn't take it off the streets. I've been looking through the reasons for this speech. You've got to please the police, please the public, please the Party and presumably please your chances of Number 10.'

Baxter looked to the ceiling. He liked bluntness in himself, not in others.

'That is quite unsubtle my dear.'

'I'm not your dear.'

The sharpness in her tone made Nick glance up from his screen. Obviously the Chief had been giving her a hard time. Nick wondered when that had been. The Chief was cooling it.

'A slip of the tongue which I'm sure you'll forgive.'

The in-joke was lost on Nick but not on Kay. She gave him a bitter look, but it did not last and they both looked forward to the late evening. She continued before he could.

'You've got to promise them something.'

Nick tapped the screen with the long slim German ball-point in his mouth. He removed the pen and wagged it at them both.

'Exactly Bistos. Exactly. And you know all it would take? A promise that you'll come up with more plods.'

Dougal looked from one to the other and then shook his head.

'And who is going to pay for them?'

Kay stood and stretched with her hands clasped behind her head. Her silk blouse could have popped a button at any time. Dougal looked down at his papers.

'Well? Is no one going to tell me?'

Kay came down from tiptoe and walked across the room to the water cooler and stooped to fill a plastic cup. She looked at neither of them when she spoke.

'They do. The police. You tell them and the world that the parents are to blame, which most of them know anyway. You say that to help the police you're preparing to authorize more numbers. Then you say that you're inviting the police themselves to come up with savings to pay for them because you know full well that they see it makes sense.'

The telephone rang. Nick handed it to Dougal.

'Number 10, Chief.'

Dougal listened for a moment, said yes a few times and then without blushing told the Prime Minister of his plan.

'Actually, I was thinking about it all night and I'm going to speak on law and order, home and parent values and the need for more police on the beat.'

There was an obviously agitated interruption, which was how Dougal Bannister had hoped the conversation would run. He slipped in as smoothly as he needed to and gave the PM his reassurances.

'Of course, I shall make it clear that they have to make room for the new people and that the public will expect them to do so.'

There was another pause and Dougal beamed.

'Why thank you. That's very generous.'

He replaced the handset and sat on the edge of the desk.

'As I expected, the Prime Minister likes my idea.'

He smiled once more and headed for the coat stand and the door. He turned.

'And I expect it'll pick up a national mood, don't you think?'

The other two nodded. Kay was speechless. As usual, Nick was indifferent. Dougal was moving into great form. He closed the door quietly. Perhaps he did not wish to break their line of thought. After all, Dougal Baxter wanted the speech ready by five. Had he not said so?

•

Thirty-Three

His Man had prepared Henry Colvil and Bannister a light luncheon. The quails' eggs were just warm and wrapped in a nest of light blue linen. The oysters were already in centre table, tangy with lemons on slivers of ice and the Chablis not over-chilled, not iced. As he munched, Colvil wondered if his brother-in-law was quite himself.

'Of course I am old man. What a funny question.'

Colvil had seen no humour in his thought nor his enquiry and said so.

'Is it? I surely think not dear heart. You seem under considerable strain.'

Bannister brushed the last of the mottled shells to the side of his plate and dipped his egg in the salted mango sauce. He looked up. Colvil was contemplating him in a most un-family manner.

'Henry you really are a prize chump some times. Of course I'm under considerable strain. One minute I'm trying to tell the Prime Minister how to stay out of trouble the next I'm . . .'

Bannister tailed off his explanation. Colvil had heard it all before and if he had not then Bannister had most certainly heard every sodden syllabary. As he listened, Bannister felt weak and miserable. He was about to go on the attack when a hardly seen hand removed the shell-cluttered plate and slid his oysters in its place, together with a fresh napkin.

Both men waited until they were alone. Colvil lifted a shell and swallowed with a practised throat the delicious mollusc, swilled his mouth with the white wine and gasped his satisfaction at the pleasure to be repeated eleven times. Bannister spoiled the moment and the occasion. He pushed away his plate, the oysters untouched. Colvil raised an eyebrow and dabbed at his sticky lips.

'Something amiss? I do hope not.'

Bannister heaved his discontent.

'You know full well there is. I have melodrama for breakfast and now farce for lunch. God knows what we'll be getting for dinner.'

Colvil was not easily disturbed from his luncheon. He took another oyster and another sip of wine and then quietly and not without a certain moment of theatre that did justice to the faded puce and turquoise of his Garrick tie, he rested his napkin as some phallus by his plate and tapered his podgy fingers in an imaginary pyramid.

'Dinner? Well I hope by then we will have sense, though I fear it uncommonly unlikely. You see Charles, I feel it is time that you and I have a little family conversation. I feel too that for the moment, and one hopes for all time, it is best kept between the two of us.'

Bannister gazed once more at the ceiling. For the first time he noticed its fine Wedgwood blue and the chalk white cherubs smiling from their corner hide-aways among grapes and elaborate laurels. He wondered which one of them they mocked and which one they urged on to merriment and even beyond. His eyes rested on Colvil's quite uncherubic features. Not for the first time he noticed how the other man's eyes could close into slits of sinister watchfulness. Not at all the chubby, good-natured, if slightly ridiculous, club bore whom Bannister valued as close companion at lunch in the Reform or tea across and down the Pall Mall way in the Rag.

'Henry. Please?'

'Very well Charles. Very well. It is simply this. We have, as you might imagine, a sensible and unobtrusive surveillance system within the Department. Yes?'

Bannister nodded. He supposed M.I.6 did indeed have such a system even though London tended to be regarded as the bailiwick of the Security Service, or the clumsies as Henry and his Friends chose to call M.I.5.

'Go on.'

'So I shall my dear. So I shall, but I must say regretfully.'

'Is there a point to all this Henry?'

'Sadly, I'm afraid there is. You see the surveillance process produces a log of events as, of course, you might hope it would.'

Bannister was beginning to feel uneasy, less confident, less belligerent.

'Mm. Mm.'

'Well, imagine my surprise when to my hand this morning fell the recent pages of that document. Imagine further, and I say this with enormous sincerity, my distress when my eye fell upon your name.'

At this point, Colvil's Oxford popped from his eye and dangled from its green silk tape. The silence lasted thirty seconds. Maybe more. Thirty seconds in the scheme of greater things matter little. In those thirty seconds Charles Bannister gathered his thoughts. When he spoke, as he was expected to, his thoughts were ordered and not hopeless.

'You are not, I sincerely hope, Henry, telling me that I have been under surveillance. Here in London? I know all about the Cambridge matter, but here? In London? Followed?'

'I am not.'

'Then what?'

'I fear Charles, that the subject of, ah, our interest is your dear friend Miss Cameron.'

'And you are suggesting what?'

Colvil in fact was not quite clear what he was suggesting. The report had, ostensibly, been sent across to him because of his interest in the Cameron file. Ostensibly. There were seven Intelligence officers working on Cameron, including the tails. It took a rota of five to guarantee twenty-four hour unobtrusive cover. Each one knew the background and which personalities and fringe personalities were involved. Bannister's appearance had been a puzzle. As Colvil was in charge of the file, each of the case officers believed he would have known of Bannister's involvement. None believed it could be anything other than Colvil's astute use of his brother-in-law as a channel of what was going on in the mind of the old academic.

So only Colvil was aware that he had not asked Bannister to make extraordinary visits, especially late at night, to the apartments of Juliet Cameron. For the moment, if Bannister had need of a secret, then it was to be safe with Colvil.

'Why did you not mention this, this morning?'

'My dear Charles, I did not know this morning. We are, with very few exceptions, quite inefficient.'

'I am not surprised.'

'Of course you are not, otherwise you would have been sensible enough to avoid such a visit, especially so late at night and especially for such a long period.'

'I had hoped that I would not be caught up in your blasted scheme.'

'Caught up? Or caught? Anyway, it is hardly my scheme. It is entirely the doing of the wretched academic. It was not we who betrayed but he. Had he not, then there would be no need for this, ah, arrangement. As to your own part, I'm afraid Charles, that is something quite different.'

Bannister's sense of dignity had yet to desert him.

'My part? My God Father James. This is not some charade. Blast it old man, you're not suggesting that there was anything, anything, well, untoward about my visit?'

Colvil blinked, screwed his monocle back into his

214

face and peered into his oyster tray. Head bent, his voice intoned neither judgement nor absolution.

'Charles, oh Charles. I am only able to explain the obvious. I leave the inexplicable to Rome. But you must understand that, considering the warning signs, it is very difficult to come to any other conclusion. A visit to a lady's rooms at such an hour and for so long . . . well there are those among my suspicious colleagues who will eventually, not now, but eventually, conclude that your visit to Miss, ah, Cameron, was what I understand the insurance trade calls "purely social, domestic and pleasure".'

Bannister was certainly not going to ignore the opportunity for a reasonable explanation. After all, this was not a colleague, nor was Henry talking to him in any official guise. Henry Colvil was his brother-in-law, Mary's brother. This was a professional and a family matter. Bannister went on the offensive.

'Henry there are some matters which you must understand. Whatever our feelings about Cameron's past, the fact remains that I have known him for many years and he has, for his own reasons, called on me for help. Part of his distress is the way in which he sees his daughter so clearly upset.'

He paused. Colvil was, if closely examined, still jolly, but for the moment, unapproachable. A small round English Buddha wishing life were less complicated and longing to return to his oysters.

'And you, Charles, are of some comfort. How commendable, or so it might be in other circumstances.'

'Henry, I have told you the circumstances. Cameron is upset, his daughter is upset, I know the reasons and I am trying to be as comforting as is possible although it now turns out that I'm being imprudent. Or rather, I have been. End of story old man.'

Colvil took up a fresh napkin from the pile on the whatnot at his elbow and tucked the crisp linen into his collar. For a second or two he contemplated the oysters, selected a shell, stroked a fresh lemon slice over the flesh and held it up in admiration. He smiled without humour at Bannister.

'It is not end of story Charles, far from it. You miss an important point. You say Cameron is agitated.'

'Of course he is.'

'Why is he?'

'Oh come on old man, that's obvious.'

'Is it?'

'Of course it is. You're about to have him exposed. Anyone in his circumstances would be agitated.'

'So they may. But how does he know he's about to be, um, exposed?'

Bannister looked perplexed.

'Well, I suppose . . .

'You suppose what Charles?'

'Well, he must know.'

'Mm. So you keep saying and so it would seem. But my point is Charles, who has told him? We most certainly have not. Someone has. Who?'

The oyster slithered down Colvil's gullet and he

sipped at the still chilled Chablis and dabbed his lips with the end of his napkin.

'I would dear heart, be grateful for your thoughts.'

Thirty-Four

Polly and Mary had decided, along with the rest of the over-eating population, that 'The Diet' started next Monday. Mary became quite gloomy when she saw advertisements for clothes she could no longer attempt to wear. That morning she had, with fairy-tale venom, cursed the mirror on the wall when it had condemned her to a generous size sixteen and the rail for the woman with the fuller figure. Polly, at twenty-two, was described by an aunt as a good and healthy child which was not much fun when you wanted to be pale and interesting.

It was after lunch, which neither had taken, and they were in Paxton's wondering about cottage cheese and lusting after Brie. Mary had just ordered two large tubs of taramasalata when Henry came in. Henry had come for his two fresh eggs.

'My dears, what princesses to find on such a glum day. If the rain raineth any moreth I shall emigrate to Sienna.'

His beam and bubblyness were catching and even a very staid and very middle-aged minor European aristocrat looked up from her suspicions of the bacons and smiled. Colvil caught her eye and gave a slight bow.

217

They had, after all, known each other in Vienna. But then had not everyone?

'Polly, you are looking so ravishing. How the young men must sigh after your company.'

'Uncle Hen, you're a fraud. But thank you.'

'So I am, but not to my niece I hope.'

Mary too had caught the mood and ordered rollmops to show so.

'You should see the latest. He has green braces and shares in BP to keep his hair in place.'

Colvil nodded. 'Ah young Nick, what a delightful fellow. So full of anecdote and a philosopher, or so I remember.'

Polly remembered the meeting at the Bannisters' country house when everyone treated Nick's arrival with polite indifference or suspicion, everyone except Henry who had soon discovered Nick Potts had read PPE, had got a first, had a father who had worked on the buses and a mother who had worked at anything that would pay the extra needed to supplement Nick's grant at Oxford. Colvil was an outrageous snob. He had enjoyed Nick's comfort. He had also asked an assistant to run the name N. P. Potts through the Department's computer. To Colvil's surprise there was nothing on it apart from his address, driving licence number and credit card and hire purchase details. Colvil was disappointed. He had expected Nick to be more interesting. But now he nodded his enthusiasm for the young man.

'Such a bright young man.'

'I would have said luminous.' Mary's sarcasm was ever guaranteed to annoy Polly.

'Can't you be nice about anyone? I never bitch at your friends.'

'I do.'

'That's what you call loyalty, I suppose.'

Paxton's was too small an establishment for anything but small talk. Neither Polly nor Mary was good at small talk, especially with each other. Mary believed they could tolerate each other's company for an afternoon at the most, and then under exceptional circumstances. The fact that they spent the best part of two hours together meant they were on the edge of their 'Best Say Goodbye Time'. By the time Mary had gone to the small desk to pay and Henry had collected his clutch of eggs, Polly had made her excuses. She would be in tonight but her sudden mood change suggested it would be best not to ask when. Mary did not.

Colvil and Mary walked slowly along Jermyn Street each with a thought and a question, neither sure how best to test the other for an answer. Mary, always the more straightforward member of the nursery, tried first. They were peering through a window of oriental rugs and Henry had made some reference to the patterns never being as haphazard as they sometimes appeared.

'Oh we're all like that Henry. Well, parents are anyway.'

Colvil nodded, the brim of his brown Coke lower than ever on his brow.

'Polly?'

'She's just part of it isn't she?'

'She's your daughter. So my dear, you cannot be anything else but imperfect, or so my friends tell me is the accepted pattern of parents and children.'

Mary smiled at the shudder her brother gave when he spoke of children. Henry Colvil detested children unless they were young enough to be friends. He believed that children smelled. When they were still mites they smelled atrociously, when they were toddlers and scalliwags they smelled of the doubtful places in which they had played and when they became teenagers their habits left them with alien and reprehensible odours. Polly, on the other hand, had always twisted him to suit her cause. He adored her and she him. Polly would normally tell her Uncle Hen her troubles. If Mary had not been there today, he would have known by now what bothered her. He wondered if Mary knew.

'Not really. It's a casserole of disappointments I suppose. She broke up with her boyfriend . . .'

'The bongo player?'

'The drummer? Yes. Then she thinks that no one really likes Nick.'

'And do they?'

'Yes, I think so. That's part of the problem. Because we don't all rush about and make a fuss, which she would hate anyway, she thinks we're being snobby.'

'Which you're not.'

'Probably. But if we made a fuss she would tell us that

we were making a fuss and that wouldn't be acceptable. Then . . .'

'Mm. Mm?'

Mary turned from the window and wondered if the Armenian could hear them through the glass. They rounded the corner and walked down the sloping side street towards St James's Square.

'Then I suppose I'm a bit grumpy lately. It's nothing special. Charles. He's a great deal on his mind. Number 10's being difficult. Dougal's playing silly devils, but then he does that every six months anyway and, well, it's time he had a break.'

'Our Scottish friend?'

'Dougal? No. The only break he needs is just behind his collar stud. No Charles.'

'But the dear boy loves to worry. He was born to manage crises. Along with the Latin prize he gathered a furrowed brow. And I must say, he wears it with such dignity.'

'I'm serious Henry.'

'Oh dear. Oh very dear. You think Charles has a particular worry for his brow?'

'Maybe.'

'Brothers have so many entries in diaries when sisters have been so coy. Maybe is a quite unsatisfying adverb.'

Mary laughed but with little humour.

'That, Henry, is because you're not a girlfriend. Someone I can thoroughly distrust.'

'Try me. I shall put on a bitchy voice and promise not to pick up the nearest telephone once you're gone and tell all those who would wish to rejoice in your secret.'

Her voice was as uncertain as his was waspish.

'I hope it is a secret, Henry.'

'And so do I. Secrets are so much more fun than dusty copperplate in common time and place. If you have a secret Mary, you must share it with me. At the very least I may be relied upon to wallow in its mystery.'

They passed the fish restaurant. The dark and dusty green with the old and latticed windows reminded Mary of the playhouse in the big garden of their childhood. It was there that brother and sister had plotted against visitors, the vicar's wife in particular and authority of all persuasions. It was there that they had fought out the trials of their own Olympians. It was in that old playhouse they had told each other their secrets and remembered each and every one to this day. A cab was dropping a not yet tired business man outside a discreet bar inside which his memories would be massaged by hardly clad hostesses. Another playhouse. Another man with another secret. Perhaps it was no secret. She looked at Henry and thought again of the playhouse.

'I think Charles is having an affair.'

Henry's step did not falter. Mary looked to see if he had heard. Colvil took her arm. He thought tea quite possible. Yes, he would neglect his eggs this day. She looked again.

'Henry? Did you hear what I said?'

'No my dear. No I most certainly did not.'

Yes, tea for two. Tea in the East Indies and Public Schools.

Thirty-Five

Juliet Cameron watched from the Back-benches. She sat alongside Wigton in the top tier, the green benches used by lollers and listeners with few cares of office and even fewer hopes. She watched Bannister in his seat on the Government Front Bench on the Speaker's right. Bannister, she thought, was one of those politicians who would be entirely out of place on the Back-benches. When his time in office was done he would find a seat below the gangway among the knights and then, she supposed, it would be little time before he would be found on the red benches of another place. She watched as he lay back, one ear to the speaker set in the head rail of the Bench and passing the occasional and cautious remark to Baxter at his side.

Wigton must have been paying more attention to her than to the debate.

'Think they own the whole beggaring world don't they luv?'

'Who?'

'Your friend. That's who. Mind you, between them and the Bank, dare say they do.'

'He's not *my* friend.'

'Well thank bloody goodness you've happened on that one for yourself. Everything all right now?'

Juliet did not reply. The Opposition spokesman was working himself into a lather over Government policy on police responsibilities. Even his own supporters, including Juliet and Denis Wigton were having difficulty in following his argument and even more in following his enthusiasm. Indeed they were in the Chamber only because they had told the Speaker's Office that they wished to speak and hoped to be called. Now, to escape Wigton's well-meant intrusiveness into her private life, Juliet Cameron went into that Gilbertian nodding which Back-benchers are given to when they want to impress their own Front Benches, mock the Opposition or, if they think cameras may be on them, catch the attention of their voters at home.

Wigton, however, was not impressed. He had also had a couple of extra White Shields that lunch time and it had been a very late lunch which had finished long after others were thinking of where to dine that evening. Juliet Cameron liked Wigton. His kindness in her early days in the House had been genuine and uncomplicated. Sober, Denis Wigton was a good friend. Less than sober, Denis Wigton was a pest.

'You see Jules, I hear things I do. I do. I hear things. You know?'

The conversation came from the corners of mouths. His slightly slurred and insistent. Hers, whispered, articulate and increasingly annoyed.

'Denis, for the millionth time, there is no friendship that is any more than that. Okay?'

'Your ma never tell you not to exaggerate?'

224

'And did yours never tell you to mind your own business?'

Wigton fell silent at this. He looked down at his clasped hands. They'd been good hands. The hands of a hard grafter. They were the hands of a clumsy fool. He did not look up as she brushed by him and almost hurried to the Lobby, barely pausing to nod respectfully at the Speaker. In the corridor she saw Bannister. When he'd left the Chamber she had not noticed. Didn't matter. There he was, in front of her.

'Hi.'

'Hello Jules. Have you eh . . .

'He's fine.'

'Oh that's good.'

It was not good. Her father was not fine. Bannister had started to move on. The corridor was a very public place. She did not want him to go.

'Actually Chang. He's not at all well.'

'I'm sorry.'

'Don't be. You're not a doctor. There's nothing you can do about it. Anyway, it's not that sort of unwell.'

Bannister felt uncomfortable. He nodded to a passing MP who was not at all suspicious about the meeting of the Chairman of his Party and an Opposition radical, but would be later when rumours of sorts slipped into the Kremlin.

'No really, I am sorry. Give him my regards will you?'

'You could. He'd like that.'

'I'm not sure I could.'

'I hear you're in Cambridge again.'

Bannister was quite startled. How did she know? Who had told her? Why had she found out?

'So I am. How did you know?'

'Pa told me. Aren't you speaking to the Union or something? It was on the screens. He asked if you'd come and see him.'

Bannister shook his head. He could easily do so. In some ways Henry and his friends would probably like that. He would not. He would not do entirely what they wished. Bannister had said he would, but he would not.

'I'm going to be very pressed for time.'

She heard what he was saying. She felt sad. Even confused.

'Well if you change your mind, come for hot chocolate.'

'In Cambridge? Where?'

The smile was warm.

'Home. You'll be very welcome.'

She had gone when Sharpe caught up with him. A message to ring the office. Rose was puffing and blowing at the other end of the internal telephone. The PM was in his room, would he pop along. No. The Private Secretary had not said what it was about. But then, according to Rose, the Private Secretary would have been more likely to have invited her to join his lodge than tell her what the Prime Minister wanted from Bannister.

The PM was in an agitated state when Charles arrived. He had long ago earned himself the title of

226

Bombardier from an old and gallant Member from the shires who tended to stamp about muttering that there were only six six-inch guns left in the Navy. He had, on one occasion at the In and Out, dined with a recently dropped Minister of State to whom he had said that, in his opinion, the Party could only rely on leaders who exhibited leadership.

'Not enough officers about. Too many damned NCOs.'

The ex-Minister had egged on the old boy. But, surely, anyone who became Prime Minister had the qualities of any level of leadership.

'Not this blighter, I tell you. He'd have made a corporal of the hut, a bombardier this one, I promise you. A bombardier. Good one mind you. Bombardier, all the same.'

By the morning, the miffed and former Minister had started to spread the nickname. By the end of the week, and two exceptionally damning sets of opinion polls, the name had stuck.

The Bombardier was now showing all the indecision for which he was disturbingly famous within the inner circle of colleagues. He had heard rumours. It was on these occasions that Bannister excelled.

'What sort of rumours?'

'The usual Charles. You know, some one fancying his chances for, well, this job.'

The PM tapped the arms of his chair. His eyes were kind. When the Bombardier smiled he usually meant it. When he did not, he usually convinced others that he did. Now, there was no smile. He meant Charles to understand his uncertainty.

'You see, Charles, it's not the job. It's not the leadership. You understand that don't you?'

'Of course I do old man. Of course I do. And you're right. We cannot afford to have anyone believe there's any doubt about Number 10. Mm?'

The Prime Minister nodded furiously. He liked Charles Bannister, sometimes. He just wished that he would not make him feel so, well, so classless. It wasn't that the PM wanted to be seen to be in any particular class. In public life when everything, or almost everything, was known about you, then there was no point in assuming an identity or a station that could be questioned, or worse, ridiculed. Being inferior was not what you were supposed to be when you were Prime Minister. Bannister was leaning against the bookcase.

'Tell me, what makes you think there is anything in this rumour which has not been in the others?'

'It's not what's in the rumour, it's who Charles. It's who.'

'And.'

'Well, it's Dougal.'

Bannister felt relieved. This was clearly one problem that had been taken from him.

'You mean Dougal plans to run against you. Surely not.'

'Of course not.'

Bannister's confusion was obvious. 'Mm?'

'No not Dougal. In fact it was Dougal who put me on to it.'

'I'm lost old man. I thought you were saying that the rumour is that Dougal wants to be PM.'

Bannister was not really that bright. The PM's smile was that of the fourth-form geography master pulling the slightly stupid yet likeable youngster through the mysteries of alluvium assessment.

'I was. It is. But don't you see, it was Dougal who told me about it. I'm surprised it wasn't you Charles. Or the Chief Whip. Dougal's got his ear to the ground you know.'

'I see.'

'This rumour's going the rounds that he's trying to get support to run against me for the leadership. Right.'

'Mm.'

'Well, as I've told you. Dougal picked up the rumour and came to warn me.'

'That he was going to run?'

'No Charles. You really are dim sometimes aren't you? No. Dougal came to tell me that there was a rumour and to watch my back because whoever was putting it about, well, up to no good, that's what Dougal said.'

'So whoever it is, it's not Dougal.'

The Bombardier chuckled at Charles's naïvety.

'Course it isn't. Course it isn't. Crickey Charles. I mean, I know he'd like the job, who wouldn't? But not yet. No, thank goodness for Dougal, he's one of the few people I can trust. You know that. You two have been friends for years haven't you?'

Bannister's bemused expression never quite surfaced.

'Oh yes, for years. I suppose I know Dougal better than most people.'

'That's right. Now Charles, have a word with him will you? I really would like to know who started that rumour.'

Thirty-Six

When Bannister got back to his room, Baxter was sipping a small whisky and Rose was fussing in the outer office and muttering about the cheek of some people helping themselves.

'Anyone would think he was on his daddy's yacht.'

Bannister smiled. The idea of Dougal's father having a yacht was bizarre. Old Baxter, as he had been known in the publishing business, had the reputation of being the meanest and the shrewdest in the world of books. It was his express desire, and the only one ignored, that Dougal should never get his hands on the Baxter publishing tiller. Yet Old Baxter need never have worried. During the years that Dougal had nursed the company to the modern ways of accounting for every penny spent and never publishing a book unless it would at least recover its costs, Baxters had made money. Even now, under his remote gaze, the company had avoided the take-overs rumoured for its future.

Dougal Baxter was a skilled operator and knew all about take-overs. As he went to his own room and was offered a glass of his own whisky, Bannister wondered exactly what was behind Dougal's latest take-over bid.

'Easy Charles. Easy. You've convinced him that it's not you who's after the job so I had to invent someone else.'

'You?'

'Of course not. I told him that was the rumour. He's very impressed with my integrity you know Charles. And why not? After all, at this rate I'm likely to be his nominated successor. Don't you think that's nice. He knows I want the job one day and he also knows that I'm his most loyal subject. What could be sweeter?'

'So when the pressure becomes too great, he actually stands down in favour of you?'

'Absolutely Charles. Don't you think that would be sensible?'

Bannister sipped the Glenmorangie and eyed Baxter for a quiet thirty seconds.

'Dougal, I thought I had made this very clear. The purpose of this Party is to maintain power. It is not to further the ambitions of you or anyone else for that matter.'

'Of course not, that comes with the package.'

'The package, Dougal, is reliant on the Party forming the Government. The last Government. This Government and the next Government. They way things stand, even with bad opinion polls and all the other things you and I know about, our best chance of maintaining power remains in our ability to make the Opposition look dangerous. They must be made to look as if they will threaten the amount of money people have.'

Baxter leaned back in the chair. He really was not interested in his friend's lecture, but he would let him continue because it was best that Bannister should build up his confidence as one who knew and then Baxter could knock him down sufficiently to catch him just before he hit the ground.

Bannister bruised easily these days. For a long time it had been the other way about and Baxter did not want him hobbling at the crucial moment. When the time came Baxter actually needed Bannister as his campaign manager, not for the Party Chairman's organizing ability but for his reputation as an old school, respectable, sensible, safe pair of Party hands. And so he listened while Bannister went on about loyalty, the need to pull together and the disruptive nature of Dougal's ambition. Baxter had heard it at least three times during the past week and a half. There was a temptation to conduct the final movement with the yellow pencil in his hand. He contained his amusement.

'My dear Charles, we don't have to find out who started this rumour. We can go one better than that. We can tell the Bombardier that we have dealt with it very quietly and there'll be no more nonsense.'

'And when he asks who it was?'

Dougal clasped his hands behind his back and recrossed his ankles on Charles Bannister's desk.

'We tell him that you and I dealt with the little

rascal and it's better the whole matter's forgotten and that the villain is so relieved that from now on he would die for him. Neat?'

Bannister turned to look from the window. For a moment he stared at the scene below, of people going about their business beneath the Palace of Westminster's lights, of an apparent normality which seemed to Charles so bizarre.

'I shall not take part in this charade. Nor shall I let you continue to make a mockery of the trust which, for the moment at least, you're supposed to enjoy.'

Dougal sighed the sigh of the long sufferer of a fool.

'There is no need to get on your high horse with me. Let me tell you . . .'

Whatever it was that Baxter was about to tell him never came out. Bannister's temper was on a short enough fuse.

'And another thing Dougal, I have been considering the implications of what you said about Juliet Cameron.'

This was different. Baxter swung his black Italian-shod feet from the corner of Bannister's desk.

'Come on Charles, you're not still worrying about that Chang thing are you? For Christ's sake, we're both grown men aren't we?'

'I told you at the time and I'm telling you once more. It was not true and whoever told you the silly pack of lies should be dealt with. I think you should tell me who it was.'

'Hey, calm down.'

Baxter sensed an anger he had not seen in Bannister. Surely Nick had been right. Nick was reliable. He kept a finger on what was going on and who was going on with it. The whole affair had obviously been boiling up in Bannister's breast. Baxter had not expected this.

'I will not calm down. It was scurrilous. You should know that and you should know also that the implications of the rumour could be devastating.'

Baxter shrugged, picked his glass from where it had left a damp ring on the leather and swigged the last drops of his whisky. He thought it not quite the time to suggest a another.

'I don't see that it should be. I don't suppose Mary would take much notice even if it did get back to her.'

There were moments when Dougal Baxter showed so clearly what Charles preferred to call his unbrightness. This could be one of the better ones.

'Mary? Look old man, I don't think you understand. I'm not concerned about Mary, she's far too intelligent to be taken in by a such an obvious piece of nonsense. I'm talking about us, the Party, the Government. Even you.'

Baxter was not very upright in his chair. Him?

'Me?'

'Of course Dougal. You. Hasn't it got into your thick head that we can take only so many rumours and so-called scandals? Hasn't it got through to you that if Number 10 started to fall apart then so would Government and it would be an election, not a convenient game of musical chairs. In the present mood Dougal, we'd lose. You've said as much yourself. If we lose, you stand no chance in your time of getting to Number 10 unless it were to give Pickfords a hand with the Bombardier's packing cases.'

Baxter's innate slyness meant that he had a fine nose for opportunity and that in turn meant he spotted a political lifeboat a little faster than most.

'But the Bombardier will bail out before we get to that point Charles.'

'Oh no. Not he. The Bombardier has everything to lose and all he has is Number 10. Apart from his ambition to play in goal for England, he's never wanted to do anything but be Prime Minister. That, incidentally Dougal, is where you and he differ, you've wanted to do *everything* else.'

'You really believe he would go to the country?'

'The Bombardier isn't even of a generation that uses such expressions. He has a generous nature. But when it comes to it, well frankly, I believe from talking to him that his generosity will be spellbinding. He'll sink the whole damn ship and be generous enough to take all hands with it.'

'My God. He'd be mad.'

'No Dougal, he'd have a seat in the Lords, which may on occasions of elections general amount to the same thing. So just be careful. If I were you, I'd put your informant in place – preferably a thousand miles from the House.'

Thirty-Seven

The meeting in the Athenaeum was quietly conducted. So quietly conducted that the meeting in the Athenaeum did not take place. The four men who took part were similarly dressed and presented an air of disdain for the mundane. Each had, over years in and around Whitehall, become used to power. They had been among the powerful since their days at Cambridge. They had been taught by those who imagined themselves to be, and perhaps quite rightly, the best in their field. They had been taught by those who understood arrogance and its injustice and who applauded the notion that those beyond the pale of the university need never be considered. And so each man had, at the foot of his mentor, learned the futility of humility, the weakness of apology and the pleasure of ruthlessness. All had been directed, quietly, sensibly and efficiently, towards Whitehall and Westminster. Each had decided for himself which road to take to power. None had chosen politics where power was for the main illusory and, where it did exist, transitory. Each detested democracy sufficiently to have no regrets in having chosen bureaucracy over politics.

The largest of the four fondled a good toothpick given him by his catamite. He has listened as the others talked. The matter was very simple, as all matters were when stock was taken, once ambition was clear.

They had wished Grishin to publish his memoir. At first Grishin had said that he would not. They had quietly encouraged him. He could expect, they had suggested, large sums from such a book. Others had published and others were now comfortable. But Grishin was comfortable. He had, as many in his trade had, made sensible investments with some of the funds given him by the KGB for his operational costs. The KGB had trained him in most deceptions and so he had deceived. Yes, thanks to the easy flow of KGB operational expenses, Grishin was comfortably off in three or four capitals of the world. So he had no need of the promises, not yet anyway. There would be, they had suggested, a chance for him to become famous. His story would make him something of a celebrity.

Grishin preferred not to be a celebrity. Although times had changed, his former masters in the KGB had long arms and even longer memories. For the time being, Grishin would wish to remain quite anonymous.

It had taken a little thought but they had managed to change his mind. They had explained that such a book would be a contribution to academic understanding of the post-war international relationship and his vanity had been massaged. They explained that a book showing the way in which London and not Washington had recognized his talents, his foresight and his understanding would be invaluable to his future. A book that showed his perception that it would be better to throw in his lot with the British rather than the Americans because the former, rather like himself, were interested only in the common good, well, that would be in everyone's interests. A book like that would for ever assure his place in London's affections and naturally its protection. Grishin had agreed.

It was at this point that they had mentioned a couple of names, people they had known about for some time. A little tidying to be done. He had not understood why. These were small people. One was dead. But eventually he accepted the very British point that bygones should never be bygones.

He had kept to himself the four other names of those in very high places. Perhaps one day he would be asked to place those on public record. He thought not. Meanwhile he was content to keep the names as insurance.

And they were content. The two insignificant names would lay to rest the notion that traitors remained uncovered. A public hanging was good for morale and reminded the chattering and even the ruling classes that scores were best left settled on the gallows. Exposing Cameron would satisfy those who believed a traitor had after all remained unmasked. Exposure would also protect the four men. It was important that those in power elsewhere believed that the unfinished business was now done.

But to be certain, they had decided that little should be easy. It was not the nature of the four, nor their calling, to present matters for easy decision. A Prime Minister should, for example, always be made to feel that a decision had been difficult but correct. In that way a Prime Minister's reputation with his supporters remained intact, even enhanced. Most importantly, his gratitude to the court of mandarins that presented him with such wise and impartial advice knew few bounds. Positions and power remained in the right hands, which was essential if the illusion of democracy were to be maintained and stability kept uncomplicated.

And so the four men had created a sensible confrontation. Controller, Secret Intelligence Service, had agreed to voice his objections and be the subject of speculation that he was interested in nothing more than a quiet end to his career and his knighthood. He did not really want a seat in the Lords but it would have been churlish to set it aside.

One of C's three deputies had been encouraged to provide the opposition within the Department and in turn encourage his brother-in-law to intercede with the Prime Minister on the side of right. The Prime Minister had, as expected, put off the decision and then, with wise counsel from others, had agreed to publication. What could have been simpler?

To complete the marquetry of deceit, one of them had arranged to give Cameron a warning of what was to come. Kind, anonymous letters. A hand from the past, unnerving the present, taking care of the future.

There is little like an agitated old don to inspire his Fellows to exercise their simple and loved instinct for spite and to tell those who come after information and sensation that yes indeed, during the weeks before the mask was snatched from him, Cameron had shown all the signs of a man living with an intolerable secret.

The trial, if it came to one, would be a great spectacle. Treachery would be rewarded and they, the four, could continue as if nothing had happened. But there was now a complication.

It would have been better for the plan and for the moment if Cameron's agitation were noticed only in college among his colleagues and those interested in his welfare. But Bannister's involvement had brought news of Cameron's state and the idea that someone might have tipped off the old professor was causing disquiet among Friends not privy to the overall plan.

And so, that evening, in the sensible comfort of the Athenaeum, the four had discussed what might be done. They had agreed. It would, thought the largest of the four, be sad about Bannister. He had always liked the fellow. An agreeable man. But there it was. It was best done quickly and he nodded his agreement and wondered about a small absinthe before dinner.

Thirty-Eight

Dougal Baxter had often thought it would be pleasant to smoke a cigarette after making love. He had never done so. He had never smoked. He had never seen the point. He had thought it foolish since the time a clinic wall-chart showed the result of smoking on lungs. He had seen a similar chart on the consequences of not brushing teeth and another on excessive alcohol. Baxter believed being a non-smoker and having an almost fanatical concern for gums and teeth was not bad out of three. The champagne was not cold but it was champagne and it did make sure that he did not doze. Dougal Baxter fell into the category of men who after making love choose to turn away, become ticklish, immediately fall into a deep slumber which for some inexplicable reason would be trumpeted by sudden snores.

He sipped at the wine and held out his glass. Kay Bennet tugged the champagne bottle from the ice bucket by the white leather sofa where she knelt and poured into the outstretched glass. They were celebrating nothing in particular that he would tell her, but Dougal had felt in a generous mood and anyway, after two or three glasses of champagne, Kay Bennet did all exotic manner of things which Dougal longed for from the time he paid what he regarded as the outrageous price at the off-licence store.

While he sipped the fresh wine, Dougal stroked her breast and played with the long nipple as if it might have been a cocktail nut. She ran her hand along his bare leg until he shifted, smiled and wagged his finger as a nursery teacher might correct a not so naughty toddler.

Baxter had had his way and for the moment did not wish to be distracted even when Kay rose and stood, legs damply apart and very close to his cushioned head. Baxter closed his eyes, not in anticipation but to concentrate on a small plan hatching in his mind. He had started to wonder about the idea during their foreplay and had seen its very possibilities shortly before reaching a particularly noisy climax. Kay often wondered at Dougal's stamina and control. What she never knew was that, like a well-trained whore, he often thought of the most inanimate details while making love. He had one image of the parliamentary bible, Erskine May, from which he would sometimes mentally quote long passages. It did nothing for Dougal's respect for parliamentary scholarship, but it did quite a lot for his sexual dignity by prolonging the period between penetration, which he enjoyed most of all, and orgasm, when, for reasons he had never understood, he more and more had to act out his appreciation. A therapist might have mentioned conventional techniques and increasingly long evenings of alcohol before bed, but then Douglas Baxter would no more have dreamed of consulting a therapist than a terrorist would have seriously sought absolution.

So Baxter rolled to his side, propping as he did his glass on the back of the sofa. Kay Bennet pouted, which was a waste of time because he did not notice. Instead, Dougal patted the white leather with his spare hand and she sank into the soft cushions and nestled against his still damp body. He put an arm about her shoulder and reached over to continue his almost absent-minded stroking of her still tense body.

'Listen my dear, I have a little idea which will amuse you.'

Kay Bennet thought it late for anything but the

242

animalistic amusement which she enjoyed each day. She moved and tucked further into Dougal's folded shape and rubbed herself against his groin. Baxter was a difficult man to distract once satisfied.

'Do we have to Dougal?'

'Of course.'

She reached for his glass and sipped before handing it back.

'Go on then. What now?'

'Now my dear, now is an idea. How well do you think Charles Bannister likes you?'

She was silent and he prompted her.

'Well?'

'I'm not sure. Why?'

'I think he likes you very much.'

Kay sat up, her silky hair naturally about her shoulders, her breasts now quite proud as she straightened her back and her shoulders in defiance.

Dougal was amused, for he had a plan.

That evening he had dined at the Travellers and was walking back towards the House along Pall Mall. Turning the corner into Waterloo Place he had met the Cabinet Secretary treading down the steps from the Athenaeum. Dougal could smell the whiff of aniseed and perhaps a small cigar. They had crossed The Mall together and had spoken of little and that of even less consequence until they were on the path by the park when the Cabinet Secretary had mentioned a matter of surveillance which may have come Dougal Baxter's way as Minister responsible for the Secret Service. That matter had not come Dougal's way although there had been hints. Dougal never doubted what the Cabinet Secretary had to say although he did often worry himself about those matters the bureaucrat never mentioned.

But on this evening Dougal had been surprised.

Now he had a plan, falling very easily into the oh so casual suggestion from the Cabinet Secretary, who, as he said, wished no part in any future discussion. Dougal had agreed. The Cabinet Secretary had parted with an observation that he felt so much more reassured that a delicate matter had been so sensibly placed in the safe custody of one such as Baxter. Dougal had smiled his agreement once more and had been rewarded with a murmured aside that one day, he, the Cabinet Secretary, hoped he could expect a closer working relationship. Dougal Baxter's ambitions for Number 10 had not been overlooked.

Baxter pulled Kay down until her chin was resting on the matted hair of his chest. He smiled into the defiant eyes. He really quite liked her.

'Charles does like you my dear. In fact you must not judge him by his stiff collars. He really is quite human.'

'Dougal, please. Don't talk like that. You make me feel cheap.'

He stroked her shoulders and she shuddered.

'Absolute nonsense. There's something I want you to do for me. Charles has a friend in Cambridge, his old tutor or something ridiculous. Have a chat to him about him will you?'

Kay was mystified. Have a chat about what?

'I can't simply say to him, "Oh hello Mr Bannister, Dougal tells me you've got a friend, why don't you tell me all about him." You crazy or something Dougal?'

'Come now Kay, let's be a little subtle. I want you to take over the draft of my Police Federation speech. Ask him to go through it in detail with you. I'll warn him that you're coming and I'll tell him that it's important. Now, he's going up to Cambridge in a couple of days so you can use that as an excuse. Tell him that it needs to be cleared before he goes. See? Easy-peazy.'

Kay got up and from the jumble of discarded clothes picked up her large sweater. She slipped it over her head and wriggled into it. The sensuous movement was not intended to excite. It gave him another idea.

'Don't go over in the morning. I'll tell him it will be ready by, say, nine, ten o'clock, tomorrow evening.'

'It'll be done by lunchtime.'

'Nine, ten o'clock will do fine. And, eh, Kay, wear something different, you know, something like that fun thing I bought you.'

'You're joking. There's hardly anything of it. I'll get thrown out of the House. What's this all about, Dougal?'

Dougal hugged a cushion in his nursery pleasure of his scheme.

'Charles has been a little, shall we say, tired, lately. His friendship with Miss Tartan Drawers is getting out of hand. I need to know what he thinks of her father.'

'What on earth for? And what's that got to do with this tutor guy?'

'Oh didn't I tell you? He's Cameron's father.'

Kay slid to the floor by the smoked-glass table and took a handmade and exotically packed cigarette from an ebony box. She lit the end, she drew deeply, her eyes closed and she passed it to Dougal.

'Go on?'

'I'm worried about him my dear. You see if I make a big thing of it, he'll just clam up. But if I knew a little more of when he goes up to Cambridge and if she's there when he goes, then . . .'

He smoked a little more and passed it back to her.

'Then you really know if he's fucking her. That it?'

Douglas chuckled. 'Mm. Something like that.'

'Does it matter?'

'Of course it does my dear. Of course it does. If Charles is being silly then it's better I know before someone tells me, officially that is. After all Kay, I am Home Secretary.'

'Aren't you supposed to be his friend?'

'Not supposed my dear. I am. I am. That's why I need to know. I do have Charles's interests at heart you know.'

She drew once more and passed it back to him. In a quiet dream Charles Bannister was more interesting than she had hoped.

Thirty-Nine

Morning had broken with a crash of crockery and tempers. Mary Bannister, at her usual morning task of scraping toast into the sink, had cursed the clockwork and clicking toaster which had performed its daily trick of producing bread damp and white on one side, charcoal black on the other. In an unguarded moment Mary had said it was time they bought another toaster. Charles had said it was an unnecessary expense and anyway the toaster had been a wedding present from an aunt. Mary's response over the years since the machine had reached its mechanical senility was always to laugh and continue what had really become something of a family joke. On good mornings it was an amusing start to the day. This was a bad morning.

'Well I'm going to buy one anyway.'

Bannister irritably rustled his newspaper.

'It's not the money Mary, it's the principle.'

Polly's intervention was both unnecessary and unwise.

'How can you have a principle over twenty-five pounds? That's all they cost.'

Bannister said nothing. Mary opened the pedal-bin and dropped the offending bread between its black plastic-lined jaws.

'Polly when will you learn? When your father talks about principles, it's nothing to do with money.'

Bannister grunted.

'Quite right.'

Mary stuck in her knife.

'Nothing at all to do with money, it's all to do with what your father believes is right.'

'Mary, sarcasm is quite unnecessary. All I'm saying is that there are some things in life which need not change.'

Polly looked bewildered.

'A toaster? A silly toaster? Is this all about a toaster? My God!'

Mary really wished that her daughter would keep out of morning. Polly's belief that everyone should behave sensibly, nicely and quietly only aggravated an atmosphere which had been tense for weeks on end.

'No darling, it is not about a silly old toaster, it's about people's nerves being on edge.'

'It is Mary, about a principle. I will not have you make trivia from an important issue.'

Polly was shaking her head.

'This is amazing. I can't believe I'm hearing this.'

'Polly.'

Mary's warning was urgent.

'No, seriously Mummy. What's everyone getting screwed up over a toaster for? The thing's never worked anyway.'

Bannister's raised voice surprised his daughter even more.

'There is nothing wrong with the toaster.'

'What d'you mean there's nothing wrong? Come on

Daddy. It's gross. Christ, if you get stressed about a toaster no wonder the economy's in the whatsit.'

Bannister looked surprised.

'In the what?'

Polly shrugged.

'Well, in the shit.'

'Polly!'

'Oh Mummy. For Christ's sake stop saying Polly. I know who I am.'

'I sometimes wonder.'

Bannister's voice was frighteningly quiet. He folded *The Times* and laid it quietly and precisely on the breakfast table. Polly slurped noisily at her morning bowl of hot chocolate which only annoyed her father more and Mary rolled her eyes and said she wished she had stayed in bed.

Bannister scraped back his chair and, without a further word, walked from the kitchen. A few moments later they heard the front door close behind him. Mary looked exasperated. Months before, she might have looked sad. She had got over that. She looked at Polly who was making a point of filling in the cryptic crossword. She would have liked to have annoyed her father even more by filling in the back-page puzzle which he always did last thing at night, but apart from putting in spoof answers, she knew there was no way she could. Mary tried a smile. It was not too successful and anyway Polly was studiously reading the questions.

'I'm sorry darling. My fault.'

'Don't be ridiculous. For Christ's sake, what's the

matter with him? Why don't you just throw the thing away?'

'It's not that easy.'

Polly got up, slammed down her felt-tip, yanked the plug from the work-surface wall and dumped the toaster in the waste bin. Mary eyed the bin, its lid not quite closed over the chromium bulk.

'You've just thrown away twenty-five years' hard labour.'

Polly was back at her hot chocolate.

'If someone would just tell me what's the matter with you two, maybe I'd know what you're talking about.'

'The life and times of a frustrated daughter. It'd be a good title for a book.'

Polly felt sorry for her mother, but not for her father. She loved them both and equally so, but she was really fed up with the rows and even worse the long silences. She put down her mug and rubbed at her eyes.

'This may not be the best time to tell you . . .'

'Oh dear.'

'Please Mummy, will you listen?'

Mary nodded. 'Sorry.'

'You don't have to be sorry, especially as you don't know what you're sorry about. That's your problem you know.'

'Oh that's it is it? I had wondered. I'm glad I know.'

Polly was not going to take on the bitterness in her

mother's voice. When she spoke, it was from behind hands covering her face.

'I'm getting a flat.'

'You're what?'

Polly took her hands away. Her cheeks and eyes were red from rubbing.

'Getting a flat.'

'But you can't.'

'Why not?'

Mary plugged in the percolator and switched on. It was something to do. Twenty years ago, or in a 1940s film, she would have lit and dragged heavily on a cigarette.

'Well, you live here.'

'I'm twenty-two.'

'You still live here. It's your home, well this and the farm.'

Polly's face was back in her hands. Her voice was muffled.

'It's still my home. I just, well, it would be nice to get out. You know, be independent.'

'Will you be by yourself?'

Polly, elbows on the table, looked through her fingers.

'What's that mean?'

'What I say. Will you be by yourself?'

'You mean am I moving in with Nick?'

Mary took an earthenware mug from the cupboard.

'Actually Polly, there's really no reason to tell me what I mean. I actually know what I mean. My little brain can manage that. I asked if you were going to be by yourself. In my day it was called flat-share. What it is in yours I'm sure I don't know.'

'In your day it was called shacking up.'

Mary slammed down the mug. She turned. Her expression said enough was getting close to being enough.

'Polly, I asked a simple question. In case you've forgotten, I'm your mother. I do have a right to know what you're doing.'

Even as she spoke, Mary knew that whatever the mystery of the Bannister household, she no longer had any right to know anything. She wished she had not spoken. Polly said exactly what Mary was thinking.

'When you feel you have to tell someone you have a right to know, it means you don't.'

Mary took no notice of the urgent percolator. She hardly saw Polly flounce from the kitchen. But she felt very, very old. She raised her head to the ceiling and said so.

'And then dear God, and then there was one.'

Forty

Bannister took his misery to the House. He walked into his room with a nod and hardly a word. Rose produced his first coffee of the morning.

'Mr Colvil called. Would you bell him he said.'

'I'm sure he didn't.'

Rose looked up from her notebook. 'Didn't what?'

'Ask me to,' he paused, 'bell him. Not a Colvil expression.'

He wished that he had not said that. But he wanted to hit someone and after twenty years or whatever it was, Rose was a reliable punchbag.

'Sorry.'

She sensed something was wrong. Yet again. She did not really care what it was. She did not like to see him so glum. The grumpy Bannister she could handle. The glum version worried her.

'Okey doke. Tell you what. You want to telephone him yourself or shall I give him a bell and put him through.'

There was a split second between sarcasm and friendship.

'Rose, Rose, Rose. What would I do without you? Mm?'

'Get your own coffee. Make your own telephone calls, then get someone with longer legs and shorter skirts.'

'Well, in the meanwhile, it'll have to be you. Did he say what he wanted?'

'Mr Colvil just gurgles.'

Her smile slipped as she went back to her page of messages.

'And Miss Cameron called. Said would you call. Something about the Cambridge visit? Said you would know? And Mr Baxter was on about his speech.'

'What speech?'

Rose shrugged, her bobbled cardigan hunched, and she peered again at her spiral notebook and her perfect shorthand.

'Search me. Wasn't it Police Federation?'

Bannister nodded, more to himself than to Rose.

'I remember now, I asked to get an idea of what he was talking about.'

'Could be. Anyway he said he'd pop over with it after dinner.'

'Where? Here?'

Rose nodded. The pebbled spectacles slipped further down her sharp nose.

'Right. Don't forget you're supposed to be dining in tonight. Chief Whip.'

Just a few months ago, he would not have needed Rose to remind him. He was losing grip. He sat further back and more upright.

'Absolutely. That'll be fine.'

He was pleased Dougal was being sensible and hoped the speech ran along the lines everyone expected. He could not imagine for one moment that Dougal would want the annual confrontation. In his present mood, he probably would hope to placate them. A standing ovation would be so unusual for any Home Secretary that he would imagine the headlines were his for the taking. As Dougal never went for anything but a standing ovation and the biggest headlines, Charles Bannister was concerned that his friend would be promising too much in his determination to be in a position to pounce from the top of every opinion poll at the very moment the Prime Minister stumbled. Yes, he was pleased Dougal had offered to go through the speech.

Later, crossing Palace Yard, he saw Juliet Cameron. He had not forgotten to telephone. He simply wanted to keep some distance. The Cambridge visit was unfortunate. She looked tired. The night before, her first back with her father, had been traumatic. At first he complained about the noise of her arriving motorbike. Then he had called it dangerous and what would happen when he needed her and she was trapped beneath some huge lorry. Later, her concern showing, she had once again found him wandering about at night and when she went into his study to see him, he had accused her of spying.

'He told me he didn't need me there.'

'Of course he does Jules. Of course he does.'

She was close to tears. Stupidly, he thought she seemed lovelier in this state. Vulnerable he supposed and instinctively he knew he was being foolish when he heard himself promise to help.

'Look, why don't you tell him you've had a word with me and that I'll try to get over after the meeting. How will that do?'

'Oh please Chang. You should see him. I don't know what it is, but it's almost as if he's dying.'

'Of course he isn't. Tell me exactly what he's doing.'

She went over the night-time prowlings in the study and the sorting of papers. Cameron was not eating and was spending long hours sitting with the light out in his rooms in college. The Master had enquired, almost too delicately, if it might not be better for Cameron to find a sanctuary in one of the local nursing homes. That had done nothing more than upset Juliet even further.

'They couldn't care less about him. They just want his rooms.'

She looked into his eyes as if searching for something more than a promise.

'You will come won't you? I don't know anyone else I can trust. It's not medical. It's something else.'

Bannister scraped his foot and looked up.

'Has he, has he had any strange telephone calls or letters?'

Her puzzled expression was genuine. She shook her head. 'I don't think so. Should he have?'

'No. No. Just a thought. Older people react differently to events which you or I find mundane. An aggressive telephone salesman or something. There are many such people. Blasted pests of course, but, well, just a thought.'

'No. It's nothing like that. He could handle that sort of thing. You will come won't you?'

He looked across her shoulder. He could see the sturdy stride of Wigton making ground towards them. Bannister did not need Wigton's northern hopsack. He started to move away.

'I promise. I'll do my best. Bye.'

She watched him and hoped she could trust his promise. Juliet was still watching as she turned and Denis Wigton was up to her. She jumped. Wigton's shaggy brows came down over his eyes as he stared after Bannister.

'Still fraternizing with the enemy I see.'

She did not say a word. Instead she walked straight on and headed for the Members' Entrance. George Sharpe was standing inside the door and held it for her. She did not hear what he said, but she was starting to feel Westminster closing in on her. The House was taking over her life. Juliet had a decision to make.

Bannister by then was sitting in the back of a London taxi talking to his brother-in-law.

The vehicle was often hailed, yet it never stopped. It belonged to Colvil and was driven by His Man. Colvil had never learned to drive. He thought it a very silly pastime. A small firm in North London had fitted smoked glass to the passenger compartment. While it was being done the interior was improved and a special telephone set installed in the side panel. Colvil had then sent His Man on a course, first to learn to drive because he could not, then to learn to drive about London, a city about which he knew almost nothing. The cab had been a sensible investment. It was always available, comfortable, easy to enter and almost entirely financed by the Travel and Duty office of the Department. Colvil sat well back in the hide seats, hands resting on his stomach beneath the tartan travel rug.

'You see Charles, our feeling is that although the daughter is not implicated, it is better that you, well, keep a decent distance from the young lady.'

'But she's in the House. I can hardly turn the other

way every time she appears in the corridor or in the Lobby. Mm?'

'Of course you can't dear boy. Of course you must not. But should there be moments when, let us say, you find yourself engaged in some social occasion, then you should not.'

'If I am, how can I not?'

'You must disengage.'

'Henry, one has to engage before it is possible to disengage.'

'Then you must do as I say and disengage.'

Charles stared through the side window and, not for the first time in the past ten days, envied the ordinariness outside. He envied the simple drudgery of five-thirty and the six-fifteen from Charing Cross to Orpington or whatever it did. He envied the uncomplicated lives he imagined other people led and he forgot for a moment in his self-pity that he had no idea whatsoever how other people led their lives.

Henry too looked from the window. His look was of one expecting to be cheered from the kerb. He wondered if he would avoid the temptation to respond with the slow hand motion taught so carefully in royal nurseries and rehearsed in open landau and perfected from a balcony overlooking The Mall. As he gazed, he wondered at his brother-in-law's silence and the curious hints rather than guidance of his Herod. He waited for Charles to turn before speaking.

'Your little visit to the, ah, the ah fens, make this matter somewhat complicated.'

Charles closed his eyes and yawned.

'Is there anything simple in this? I am to give you any information on Cameron's state, but I am not to see his daughter so that I might ask. I'm encouraged to call on him in order to give you a firsthand account but I'm not to call on him because his daughter may be there. Frankly old man, whatever it is I am supposed to do is, well, it's clear as mud.'

Colvil twitched the end of his nose.

'We . . .'

'We?'

'I, Charles, I, would suggest that when you have been about your business at Cambridge, you do indeed visit the Cameron of Cameron, but that you do so in college and not at his home.'

'How do I know he'll be there?'

'He shall be dining in hall tomorrow night. You might mention that you are dining too.'

'But I'm not.'

Colvil had never cared to speak his mind or simply. It was always something of an embarrassment to say to others what he meant. His chosen profession had allowed him to develop a thought pattern which rarely came to a full stop but faded on ellipses.

'But you are Charles. You are. I believe you have a somewhat late and therefore apologetic invitation to dine in hall with the Master after your pellucid excursion among the Party's youth.'

Bannister shifted and turned to face Colvil who was

now fussing with his rug and pretending not to notice his brother-in-law's growing rage.

'Listen old man, how do you know I'm getting an invitation? Mm?'

'Well dear heart, it seems that the Master has but recently noticed that you're to be in Cambridge, so he naturally felt that you should be present in college. It would be less than courteous not to give you, such a distinguished old member, the chance of putting up for the night.'

'My God Father James. And you fixed this?'

Colvil disliked scenes. He stared at the gloomy London late evening. They had completed their circumnavigation of the two royal parks and were coming up to the St Stephen's entrance of both Houses of Parliament.

'Yes Charles. One did. Now, we shall set you down by the Jewel Tower and you may contemplate so much that might have been.'

Forty-One

That night Bannister dined, as arranged, with the Chief Whip. It was a regular arrangement. The Chief Whip had his own table in the Members' dining-room. It was comfortably near the door and he sat with his back to the wall and his frown on the rest of the room. The Prime Minister, making a rare appearance, was dining further along, where he normally dined and by the mix at his table he was assuring the right of the Party that he had not lost his nerve.

At the far end, where they always sat, Opposition Members huddled and muttered against their own Front Bench, something which they did often, more often than attacking the Government. Charles Bannister thought it curious how, even at dinner, MPs divided on Party lines.

Two promising Back-benchers were joining them. One was in need of praise for the way in which he readily toed the voting line. He could always be relied on to go into the right lobby on the right occasion and, without urging, to encourage reluctant colleagues. Surprising how much a consommé and a too long dead piece of fish could act as a pat on the back. The MP was clearly looking for a job in the Whips' Office, which he rightly saw as a stepping-stone to higher things. Tonight the Chief Whip would tell him that a lesser Minister was about to offer him a job as his PPS. The Parliamentary Private Secretary was unpaid and acted as a Minister's eyes and ears in the Commons. It was a good way for an ambitious MP to get Departmental experience and be noticed. Later the MP would go home, rather pleased, to his wife who was just a little more ambitious than he and he would think of something to say when the notice appeared in his local paper.

The other Back-bencher was not such a push-over. Indeed he had started to drift down leg side. The Chief Whip was a member of the MCC and often used cricketing metaphors. The wavering MP needed a talking to and he would get it in the gentlest way. If he did not respond then the Chief Whip would set his parliamentary pit bulls to work. The Whips' Office was quite capable of, and quite happy to dig up dirt on its own Members and use it either directly or through an MP's agent or constituency chairman.

But before the Back-benchers arrived, the Chief Whip was far more interested in one of his more senior colleagues.

'What the fuck's Dougal up to?'

'Is he up to anything?'

'Course he is Charles. The PM tells me Dougal told him that someone's putting it about that Dougal's after Number 10.'

'And?'

'And the clown believes him. I've had the devil's own job convincing the Bombardier that there's nothing in it. He actually believes Dougal's keeping him on an inside track. Then he has the gall to tell me I'm supposed to be doing that. Come on Charles, you know him, what the fuck's he up to.'

'Nothing. Oh, I imagine he was, but not any more. I've had a word with him.'

'Put him straight?'

'Of course.'

'Good man. But you might have told me.'

'Nonsense. You've got far too much on your plate. I know, don't forget I was doing your job for three long years.'

'You're sure Dougal will behave himself?'

'Leave him to me old man. If it gets out of hand, you'll be the first to know.'

The Chief Whip looked dubious.

'I hope from you. I get immensely irritable when the private line goes and that little turd comes on with his "Oh dear me, Dougal dropped by and he tells me we seem to have ourselves a problem".'

Charles was about to tell him that he too had had similar bleatings from the Bombardier when the first of the minnows swam in from the Back-benches. The four dined unremarkably and without resolving any of the problems but quite successfully pretending that they had. Bannister was glad to make his excuses and leave when he did.

In his room the list of late notes from Rose included the invitation to dine from the Master. According to the note, the Master had checked times with the Party student society and with a little juggling and no hanging about, there would be time for sherry before dinner. It was after ten and too late to telephone the lodge and anyway Bannister had half a mind to say thank-you but no thank-you. He had a sense of being manipulated which was quite unnerving. Normally it was Bannister who set up events and the people about them.

Ever since his days in the Whips' Office, Bannister had enjoyed king-making. He now feared that he was being used in a far more involved and elaborate manner than simply being a sounding board or even a conduit for the fall-out from Cameron's nervousness. He sat in his large swivel-chair, fingers in a pyramid beneath his chin and, for fifteen minutes, contemplated what was happening.

Cameron was about to be exposed. There was nothing he could do about that. Cameron was agitated. Bannister did not know for certain why this was happening and, in truth, nor did Henry's lot, otherwise they wouldn't want someone to come up with independent analysis. Or did they? Did they simply want Bannister to get alongside the old man and tell them indirectly if they were making a good fist or not? It was an attractive idea, but again, he did not know. Then there was Jules.

Bannister swung his chair through ninety degrees until he was facing the wall and another portrait of his admiral hero. What would the great man have done? His dark blue cap at a jaunty angle, his reputation made, he could have done anything he wished. But would he have? No. He would not have been, what had Henry said, 'engaged' in the first place. On the other hand, he might just have called for the famous naval signal, 'engage the enemy more closely'. But she was not the enemy. To Henry and The Friends she was. But to Charles?

He turned back to his desk, doodling like some Victorian general pondering the consequences of committing his hussars at first light and against hopeless odds. Why shouldn't he? He tap-dialled Juliet Cameron's number and got her answering service. He said no messages and thought about calling the flat but then remembered she would have gone to her father's house. There was no point in disturbing the household, so instead he called back the answering service, very formally confirmed the arrangements to see Professor Cameron tomorrow and then left a message with the college porter to present his compliments to the Master and say that Mr Bannister would be dining the coming evening. There had been no need to do either of those things. Rose could have sorted it in the morning, but he felt in need of decisions. Decision-making had been taken from him during the past few days. That was going to change.

He telephoned Mary to say he was on his way. He let it ring for twenty or thirty seconds. There was no reply. Blast! He took his heavy coat from the corner stand and left. By the door into Palace Yard he chatted for a few moments with George Sharpe while a taxi did not come. The light on the parliamentary railings flashed but no taxi appeared. Sharpe volunteered the information that Miss Cameron had driven out on her Kawasaki just two minutes earlier and when Bannister had said what had that to do with him, Sharpe had said nothing at all. The inference in Sharpe's tone made Bannister annoyed.

Rather than show his tetchiness Bannister decided to ignore the call for a cab. With barely a good-night to the expressionless Sharpe, Bannister dug his hands deeply into his coat pockets and headed for the iron gateway leading onto Parliament Square. He had nodded to the two policemen and was crossing the square by the church when he heard his name. It was Kay Bennet.

She was hurrying and almost tripping in a long dark velvet cloak complete with hood which was now thrown back like some tragic heroine.

'I'm sorry. Dougal had to go and he asked me to bring this over. I was just on my way. I buzzed through but there was no answer. He wanted you to see it before I put the final figures in.'

'Tonight?'

She nodded. With it came the smile and the half-open mouth.

'Yes. He wants it first thing, so I said I would. Do you mind?'

She handed him a dark blue folder. It was Dougal Baxter's Police Federation speech. Bannister had forgotten all about it. He looked at it and then at Kay Bennet. She seemed to be distressed.

'Is it important? Tonight I mean?'

She bobbed her head, her silky hair folded into the cloak's collar, lifting this way and that.

'Really, it is. Lots of policy stuff. I promised that I'd do it tonight and leave it on his desk for first thing.'

Bannister wanted to get home. He could still taste the fish. He felt irritable. But clearly Kay Bennet was under some pressure. She kept saying that Dougal was very sorry that he had to go elsewhere but would he be so kind as to look at it? As Bannister had more or less insisted that Baxter toe his line, then he could hardly refuse. But now?

'All right then. I suppose we'd best go back to the House.'

He looked across at the neo-Gothic building, still with most of its lights burning. He would rather not. There was always the Party headquarters. That was just ten minutes walk. Kay Bennet was nodding again.

'Fine.'

It was not fine. He did not want to go back. He felt irritable, but again it was not her fault. He looked at the folder. It was quite thick.

'There's an awful lot of it. What's he written, a novel?'

She chuckled. It really was quite warm in her throat.

'No way. It's huge type and every little bit is a different paragraph. Apparently they've pulled the plug on his idiot board so he's got to read it from the script instead of those transparent things.'

It was Bannister's turn to smile. The Federation really did have it in for Baxter or, he suspected, anyone else who happened to be Home Secretary that year. By claiming that the transparent screens were not working, they imprisoned Dougal Baxter in the old mould of reading his speech from a script and the hope that he could look up every few seconds to try to sound natural. The Federation knew that Ministers now liked to speak into the screens, one either side of the rostrum, and that would give the television audience the impression that it was all ad lib and brilliantly pre-sented. The Federation was not allowing any Home Secretary Brownie points on his own terms.

'Very well. Let's walk back to the Front Office. This shouldn't take five minutes.'

Kay Bennet took the folder back.

'Look don't you worry. I'll drop it in first thing in the morning. See it then. As long as he's got it by ten, he should be okay. Night. Sorry to hold you up.'

She started away.

Bannister was surprised. He took a couple of strides and touched the arm of her cloak.

'Wait a minute, where are you going?'

She had put up her hood against the damp London wind, chilled from the Thames. He could not quite see her expression in the shadow of the street lamp and the folds of her cloak.

'Home. It's just round the corner, remember? I'll tart up the grammar and spelling tonight. I've got the desktop there.'

'I see. It's very late.'

'It's always late with Dougal. But you don't need me to tell you that. I was just off to a party when he dropped this in and asked me to bring it over. As I said, sorry to barge into your evening.'

She really was quite plausible. Dougal would have been proud albeit apprehensive. Almost too convincing. Bannister was embarrassed. The most obvious thing to do was to take it back to her desktop, just five minutes walk away. He did not care to suggest so, especially at that time of night. He did not have to. It came from Kay Bennet.

'You could send someone over to the flat in about thirty minutes and pick it up.'

'That's all it would take?'

'Absolutely Mr Bannister. I've almost finished the final draft and I can run a spellcheck and paragraph ranging through it in ten minutes then spend ten on the keyboard. Okay?'

'Why don't I come? Now? If you don't mind that is?'

Kay Bennet had thought Bannister would never ask.

They walked back to her apartment. The lift was now fixed and within ten minutes of their meeting she was leading Bannister into the flat. She handed back the folder and offered him a drink. He said a very small whisky and no ice and she said fine and undid the silk ties on the cloak. It was long, dark green and velvet and so full that there was no need to hold it about herself. She turned her back to him as he helped her with it. For a moment he did not move, then recovered and found himself standing there with the cloak while she floated to the bar. The dress was not what he had expected. There was very little of it and it was deep and softly burgundy. She turned and handed him a large tumbler with whisky in it and took the cloak. When she came back from the bedroom, he was standing in the same spot not having started the whisky nor the speech.

'Won't you sit down?'

Her voice had changed. More assertive. On her own territory.

Bannister sat at one end of the sofa and Kay Bennet

at the other. She sipped white wine from another long thin glass, let her shoes fall to the floor and snuggled into the white leather and its plumped cushions. The more she wriggled the less of the dress there appeared to be. Bannister buried his head in Dougal's speech.

Bannister read with far more attention than he would normally give even one of his own speeches, never mind Dougal's. The speech was good. It was full of policy-fillers, most of which Bannister knew about. He was almost absorbed, not because of the prose but because he did not entirely trust Dougal not to bury a political howler deep in the text. At one point Kay took his glass as he sat making neat marks with his gold propelling pencil. She liked that. He did not for one moment imagine the second glass to be larger, nor the whisky deeper. He did not imagine it at all.

Bannister had almost finished the speech and the second whisky. He looked up. She was reading a magazine. He watched her. Her legs were very long. She knew he was watching. He was supposed to. She let him for a few seconds more and put down the magazine. She got up and took his glass. He said he would not have another and she put the glass on the bar and came back empty handed. Bannister felt better.

'What d'you think. Good?'

'Yes. Not bad at all.'

She looked pleased and said so.

'Thanks.'

Bannister got up.

'You wrote it?'

270

'Research by Potts and Bennet. Original words by Bennet. Run titles.'

Bannister nodded his approval. It was quite usual for a good private office to provide a Minister with a speech. Certainly anyone in Cabinet had little time to put together an important policy paper, although it was very likely that a Secretary of State would wish to write the final draft and finished article. In Dougal's case, Kay was his scribe. She knew what he wanted and he would soon tell her if there were anything else. So far her political antennae had been well-tuned and the results successful.

For Dougal, being successful meant getting the right headlines and no hassle from Number 10. Kay had thus far kept him clean and clear. She bent to pick up the speech. The dress was as low at the top as it was short at the bottom and Bannister, embarrassed in case Kay should look up, stared busily at the other side of the room only to come eyeball to navel with the unframed nude.

'Would you like a coffee before you go?'

Bannister looked from the painting to Kay and to her eyes. They were slightly mocking. Humorous? Maybe. He could see the similarity. He could see the body move just as hers moved beneath the thin silk. The breasts with unbruised halos were as he imagined hers to be. But it was what the artist had seen, had known were in the eyes. It was the eyes. The eyes have it. The eyes have it. He could hear the intoning Speaker risen from the throne in full wig and buckles.

271

The ayes have it. The ayes have it. That was Bannister's world. Not here. Not this life-size painting that made him want to look again and again. Not this woman with her strange scent of oils. It was a world which he did not understand.

He must have said yes because Kay had gone and he could hear the familiar rattle and clunk of the universal coffee machine and even the smell above all the other smells in his mind. He was tired. His was not self-control and yet Bannister's whole life and been based on self-control. He moved towards the kitchen. Kay was standing side-on to him, unaware of Bannister as she watched the clear bowl slowly filling with black, strong liquid. She was smoking. It looked old, picked up from some gutter. It had a scent he did not recognize and which mixed exotically with the aroma of ground Chaga. He stared, fascinated as she, slowly, side to side, caressed her breasts, free beneath that same silk. He wanted to look away. He could not. She turned, standing legs slightly apart, content, inhaling.

'Does this bother you?'

Bannister did not understand. He had entered the hallway of another world. Not his world. He said nothing, picked up his heavy, sensible overcoat and left.

Forty-Two

The day began in silence and ended with nothing said.

Bannister had been withdrawn when he arrived home the previous night. Mary was in bed. She was reading her stars. She had tried everything else to hand including *Country Life* (which she only read for the house advertisements); *Private Eye*, for any reference to Charles (which there was not); *The Times*, for the letters and for the puzzle (which she had yet again failed to complete because she could not be bothered to get up and fetch *The Oxford Dictionary of Quotations*) and the London *Standard* which she read for stars and sport (because tennis in Australia made her forget the bitter rain that day, which she loathed). Her stars suggested that a major decision would be followed by a disappointment for one she loved. She was about to go to the bookcase after all, when Charles arrived home. He kissed her on the forehead as if she were a fast-failing aunt and he was about to leave.

'Good day on the Rialto darling?'

Bannister looked at his wife and silently praised their normality.

'You know I'm in Cambridge tomorrow?'

'No Charles, I've not yet caught up with today. Start again. Good day on the Rialto? Or do I mean in?'

Bannister knew she meant both. His mind was quite numb.

' "O, what a goodly outside falsehood hath!" Mm?'

'I beg your pardon.'

'It's the bit before isn't it. You know *Merchant of Venice*. Before someone says in the Rialto you have rated me, or something. Mm?'

Mary beamed and grabbed her *Times* from his side of the bed.

'Charles! How clever. Oh welcome home. That's it, nine letters, "falsehood".'

But he wasn't listening. He still had strange scents and feelings which disturbed him. He supposed it was something to do with deception on one's own terms, or whatever the writer had said. He went into the bathroom, stripped, turned the shower to its sharpest and tried to scrub himself clean.

By the morning Mary had caught his mood of silence. Whatever worried him, Charles would not let her in. Breakfast was never much more than monosyllabic. That morning, they might have been in retreat. Polly had not come home. Charles did not notice she was not at breakfast. When he rose to go, Mary said she would walk with him across the park. The rain had stopped, the morning had cleared, she needed air. He did not object and opened the door and closed it with a courteousness normally reserved for strangers.

The park was not a place to stroll. Those who used it for a short cut, did so with gloved fingers gripping unnecessary briefcases, with heads bent for the winter against expected gusts and shoes thickly soled and already scuffed by dank leaves and hidden stones. The

Bannisters walked slowly but unspeaking until they reached the Horse Guards side and Mary prepared to turn back while her husband went on.

'Polly says she's moving out. Has she told you?'

'Mm?'

'Moving out Charles. Leaving home.'

He looked down at her face. He thought it a kind, trusting face. He was not quite sure when he'd last noticed, if at all.

'She's what?'

'Polly darling. Your daughter. She's getting a flat of her own.'

'Oh.'

They walked on a little and then Charles stopped. Turned.

'Where?'

'I think Pimlico.'

'Who is paying?'

Mary shook her head. She wasn't sure. She said as much. Bannister nodded slowly as if that was what he had expected, which it was not. He had not expected anything.

'I see.'

'You see what Charles?'

'I'll see, eh, I'll see what I can do. I'll have a word with her.'

'You don't mind?'

'Having a word? No why should I?'

'No. You don't mind she's moving out? She may be going to live with someone.'

Bannister looked again at his wife's upturned face. His nodding head was more a slow bounce of dawning. He started to go.

'We all do that don't we.'

He did not say goodbye. He simply went. His figure now hunched and he deep in thoughts he could not hear.

The car took him to Cambridge by eleven and handed him over to the well-oiled machine of constituency glad-handing. Bannister, thoughtful and unseeing as the car sped up and along the motorway and then into the city, switched to automatic as soon as he stepped out and pressed the first CBE-seeking Party hand of the day. He made three speeches and was given two lunches and made a joke about both at tea. At the students' meeting he spoke without notes and wisely and thoughtfully and surprisingly sensitively about the Party and the need for morality not as a standard but as something to be understood and then accepted, rejected, attacked or fought for. They wished that he would stay and the younger dons who had come out of curiosity went home, or some to their high tables, and remarked to those who asked how he had been that Bannister was a deeper, more interesting man than they had expected.

In his own college Bannister drank the Master's sherry and sat once again, though this time with less fuss, in hall and this time with a much frailer looking Cameron. Cameron spoke hardly a word during dinner. By his glass was an envelope. It was brown and foolscap.

Cameron kept touching it, perhaps daring it to move. He'd brought it with him from his rooms. At one point he had appeared to offer it to Charles, then changed his mind. Then quickly, he stuffed it inside his jacket, but throughout the rest of the evening his hand would slip beneath his gown to touch his breast pocket in case it had gone.

Dining was a noisy affair although little was said. As once before, Cameron snuffled at his food, spilling some, choking a little on some, tasting nothing. He guzzled his wine, but unlike once before, the butler made fewer visits to his side and by pudding, Cameron's glass stood empty.

Later, they sat, several of them in a semi-circle while claret was given and fruit sliced. Cameron made a couple of attempts to crack nuts but failed and silently gnawed at a charcoal biscuit. Once or twice the Master raised his eyebrows at Bannister. Once or twice someone would try to engage the old boy in conversation. They failed. But when they had turned away to others, Cameron would look up from under white eyebrows, accusingly and without hope.

It was nine before they reached his rooms. Cameron said he would stay that night. Bannister encouraged him to sit and for them to talk, but the conversation was slow and soon fell behind the monotonous tick of the grandfather clock.

'Jules, eh, Juliet said you had not been sleeping much.'

Cameron sighed and started to roll the silk tabs on his gown.

'She's a fool. Imagines things.'

The voice was crackled as if a grit of that morning's porridge had lodged awkwardly. Bannister shook his head. He hoped comfortingly.

'She cares about you. She says you're worried about something.'

'Am I?'

'She thinks so.'

Cameron had rolled one silk as far as it would go. He let it fall. He wanted to get up and shift but could not.

'And you? What about you? You come to spy?'

Bannister was patient. He smiled softly, careful not to mock.

'Of course not. I came, if you remember, because you said you would wish to see me. Well, well here I am.'

Cameron lay further back in his chair and stared at the ceiling. For perhaps a minute, perhaps longer, nothing was said. Bannister found relief in his own patience and wished the silence to go on. When Cameron broke the spell, Bannister was off guard and totally unprepared for what the old man would say.

'So what's the matter with you Charles. Eh? What's the matter then?'

Bannister's surprise was genuine. His confusion made it appear false.

'Nothing at all. Usual worries of Government. But you know all about that don't you?'

Cameron eyed him. It was a long and sideways look. It was a look which searched for a speck of trust in a man's face and found none. He started to gurgle and searched for a handkerchief. He struggled with an inner pocket somewhere and his gown slipped to the crook of his elbow, his discreet velvet markings of scholarship lost in the folds as he pulled a dirty, once white, piece of linen from beneath his cardigan.

'You know about integrity Charles? Do you?'

'I hope so.'

Cameron gurgled again, his throat rasping beneath his words. He spat into his handkerchief, wiped his damp lips and stuffed the rag into his cuff where it would come to no harm.

'Do you now.'

He was watching Bannister. Bannister nodded. Yes he did. Cameron opened his mouth to speak, seemed to gasp for a little more breath, did so, and then spoke once more.

'Integrity is a demand others make on you. You have a choice. Once you've made that choice, if you go back on it then, then, then, you have betrayed others and worse still . . . what?'

Bannister left the silence to itself before he answered.

'One has betrayed oneself.'

Cameron rocked his head up and down. He could have been a drunk proving a point about world confusion. He was not a drunk. He was not drunk.

'Which is worse?'

The younger man remembered such similar conver-

279

sations in these very rooms all those years ago. Then he had learned that there were no answers, only other questions.

'That implies one is better. Can that be?'

For a moment, Cameron smiled. For a moment satisfied with his pupil.

'It cannot.'

There was a longer silence. The clock ticked off the seconds and then the minutes. Cameron's head was on his chest. Only the near-yellow fingers with the too long nails playing with the silk tabs showed he did not sleep. Bannister tried once more.

'Is there anything that you would wish to tell me?'

'Should there be?'

'We often have things to tell each other.'

'Do we Charles? And you, you have something to tell me?'

Bannister's voice was very quiet. The final consonant final.

'I believe not sir.'

The clock whirred as if to chime and did not. Cameron did not look up. His voice was deep, quiet, from his chest.

'I will not detain you Charles. I will not detain you.'

Bannister stood. He believed him.

Forty-Three

The house was in darkness. Bannister had left the taxi further along the road, not sure of the address and the house too obscure at that time of night. He thought of knocking but was embarrassed to do so. The decision was taken from him. An upstairs light appeared, followed by curtains being closed. He pushed the white marble-sized bell.

Jules was in her heavy dressing-gown. She had bathed and was about to go to bed. They went through to the same room as before and she threw a few woodchips from the log basket on the embers and puffed with the bellows. Bannister said yes to a seat and no to whisky. He was not at all sure why he had come. He had nothing he could tell Cameron's daughter. She knew how ill he was. She knew as much as she could be told. Bannister was not about to tell her of the past, of Henry Colvil's Department, of his own role. But he felt the need to tell her something, to warn her of the horrid times that would come. Now they sat quietly, wondering about the short dancing flames as if some pagan truth would help lighten the moment.

'What did you think?'

'I was shocked. He seems to have deteriorated so quickly. It's only a couple of days, but he was almost another person.'

She nodded, hearing what she knew but wanting him to tell her.

'I don't know what it is. It's not something I can see or feel. He doesn't have lumps or pains in his arms or anything that I can understand.'

Bannister took her hand, then the other. How close could he get without saying what he knew he must not?

'Jules, I think you should stay here, with your father.'

'I am.'

'No. I don't mean just at night. I think you should be here all the time. Not come down to London at all. Not for a few days anyway.'

Her look was urgent. She searched his eyes for answers to questions she'd not asked.

'You know something and you won't tell me. Why?'

Bannister wanted to let go of her hands and walk about the room. He did not want to answer trapped by her trust. Her hands tightened on his. His voice was almost a whisper.

'There are some things that I cannot tell you. But you must trust me Jules, trust me. It's better that you stay here. Don't come to the House. Stay with him. He needs you.'

'He's really ill isn't he? He's told you.'

Bannister shook his head, his head bent, his eyes away from hers.

'Not that sort of illness.'

'Oh my God, it's not . . .'

'It's not what?'

282

Her eyes were closed.

'Something terrible. Cancer or . . .'

'No, no. Nothing like that. You've seen him. He's depressed, he simply needs you here.'

Juliet moved closer and put her arms around him, her head on his chest. He could feel her warmth and smell the dried scent of her washed hair.

'You must stay. You can call me if you need me, but you must stay.'

She tightened her arms. He could feel her quietly sobbing. He held her until she slept and then until she awoke. They said little in the early morning. She drove him to the station and in the parked Ford across the way from the house, coincidence being what it is, the same man as before made a note in his log and, later, a brief call on his radio.

Forty-Four

He met them, the Cabinet Secretary and Henry Colvil, in the park. It was gone nine o'clock, but not much beyond it. It was damp and gloomy and matched Bannister's mood. As they walked he told them almost word for word, scene by scene, of his evening with Cameron. He tried to tell them that he had tested Cameron's trust, but had failed. He fell silent as nothing was left for him to say, but then remembered the envelope.

'He had an envelope with him. He seemed nervous about it.'

Henry Colvil, his cane at the trail, glanced at the Cabinet Secretary and then at Bannister.

'One must assume that we know nothing of its contents.'

Bannister shook his head.

'Absolutely. I'm sorry.'

The Cabinet Secretary stared ahead waiting to ask the question if Colvil should not. Colvil did.

'Was it marked in any manner? An address? A name?'

'I don't know. When I saw it, it was face down on the table.'

'And what happened to it my dear. Do we know?'

'He put it in his pocket. I'm afraid that was the last I saw of it. I'm not sure it was important.'

'Was to Cameron, Bannister. Was to Cameron.'

The Cabinet Secretary's voice was sombre. Bannister wished that he had not mentioned the envelope. He disliked inconclusive discussions. No one but Cameron knew anything of the envelope. He had not seen an address, even a stamp. He did not even know if Cameron had received the envelope or was to send it or even if it were intended as a letter. He stopped.

'Look, I've told you everything I can. I'm sorry I didn't get what you wanted but quite frankly, I'm not really up in these affairs. Mm.'

The other two were, for the moment, silent. The Cabinet Secretary was staring at the sky, hands behind his back again, half-seated on his umbrella. Colvil tapped at the damp path with his cane.

'You're sure there is nothing more to say? Nothing you would wish to tell us rather than . . .'

Colvil looked up to Charles's gaunt face. His eyes full of hurt. Colvil would have liked to ease Bannister's pain but that act of friendship was for his confessor, not for his brother-in-law. Bannister looked from one to the other.

'Nothing more.'

He turned, left them and made back in the direction of the House where Big Ben chimed the quarter hour.

Colvil and the Cabinet Secretary walked on, turned right to The Mall and St James's. The Cabinet Secretary breathed through his nose, noisily at times, especially when he was coming to a conclusion. This was one of those times.

'I suppose Colvil, we'd best get on with this one. Yes?'

Colvil thought so and said so. He would put the necessary arrangements in hand before the half hour was gone.

Forty-Five

It was five minutes after ten o'clock. The chapel clock was always right. The two men passed the porters' lodge without asking directions. People did throughout the day. The college grounds were open to the public and were often used as a thoroughfare between one part of Cambridge and another. But the head porter had been around for a long time. He had once been a policeman. He knew the difference of purpose and step, of silence and conversation. These two were official.

He watched until they had disappeared from his view through the window and then strolled to the lodge door. They did not cross Fellows' Lawn, but skirted on the flint stones and flags. They ignored the first entrance to the building on the right and the second. He was about to wonder if they were going through the arch and onto the pathway leading to the courts and lanes beyond, when they turned and trotted briskly up the steps, through the open doorway and onto the staircase. The head porter glanced up at the windows, bare and empty except for one. The floor lamp was burning in the window of old Professor Cameron's set. Perhaps he was expecting them. He was the only one in on that staircase, the head porter knew that. He knew everything. Perhaps they weren't strangers to the professor. They were to the college. The head porter knew that. What bothered him was that they knew their way. That was odd. So he watched on, for a while anyway, and then went back in, but keeping half an eye on Front Court. Distracted by a busy lodge and a lazy assistant, the head porter did not notice the two men leave, not by the way they had entered but through the arch to the courts and the back lanes beyond.

Forty-Six

It was shortly before one o'clock. Baxter had just come from the Millbank studios. His speech the previous day to the Police Federation had been something of a success. Cleverly, he had put a junior Minister on the windward side the evening before. When it was clear there were few waves, Baxter had made it known that he would be available for interviews after nine o'clock. He had made the excuse that he was deep in discussion about some ways of countering latest European Community inroads into the British penal system and could not possibly be disturbed until shortly before ten. It meant that current affairs and news editors had been hunting his attention. Baxter had guaranteed what would have probably happened anyway, two days of publicity for his ideas. Few of them were new, but the packaging was and that, for the moment, was what mattered most.

The lunchtime interviews down, Baxter was in triumphal mood and in the House. He had been looking for Bannister since early in the morning. Secretaries of State rarely went to the Commons unless there were set piece engagements such as Statements to the House, Prime Minister's Questions, questions to their own Department or the Budget or a Division. Baxter's visits were more frequent than almost all his Cabinet colleagues other than the Chief Whip whose workplace was the Palace of Westminster. Baxter believed that when the chance came for him to go for Number 10 then, above all things, he would need the support of the rank and file Members. He had learned that in politics it was necessary to have power bases. Not one but three or four. None in conflict with the others. When the time came, the Party managers would know that Dougal Baxter was the alternate candidate. He never wanted to be the front runner.

Baxter had worked out from his own observation of modern political history that the bitterness and vitriol of a leadership contest meant that the number one candidate needed a broad back. In Dougal's opinion that meant it was easy to be stabbed. So Dougal was always to be seen about the Tea Room, the Pougin, the Harcourt, but never the bars. Dougal would never make the mistake of buying a Member a drink, not because he was mean, which he was, but because if he bought an MP a drink it would mean that he had not bought for another also, and therefore, to Dougal's way of thinking, he had given opportunity for a petty grudge. A Prime Ministerial hopeful would fall on petty grudges.

But on this morning, Baxter was not canvassing. He was looking for Kay Bennet who had business in the Vote Office and then for Bannister. He found Kay coming along the Committee Corridor.

'Well? You didn't call my dear.'

She was modestly dressed. Something from Liberty.

'I'm not your dear.'

'Oh my, a little too much of the juju? I hope it didn't lead to anything silly?'

'You weren't about.'

'My speech you know. It went down quite well.'

'I write good speeches. It should have done. Anyway, I did call. I left a message.'

'Oh that.'

'Oh that was all it was worth. He didn't say anything.'

'He must have done. I'm not stupid you know.'

Kay Bennet walked past him and headed for the main staircase. It was a very public place for a scene and she knew she was safe. A policeman was standing at the top end talking to a messenger, they both smiled, but from a distance. She was walking quickly and her legs were much longer than Baxter's. He spoke in a mutter that was not too far from a snarl. Dougal Baxter never forgave anyone who usurped his dignity.

'Come on Kay. What did he say about her?'

They had turned and were descending the stone staircase.

'Nothing.'

'He must have said something.'

'He didn't. N-I-X. Nix. Okay?'

She stopped suddenly on the edge of the staircase where it twisted to the ground floor. Baxter did not slip, but it was close. She fixed him with a look of disdain.

'Next time Dougal. Do your own snooping.'

'It was not snooping. Anyway, you didn't get anywhere?'

There was sufficient sneer in his tone, but not enough to say he was confident. She bit deeply.

'I screwed him.'

'What!'

'You heard. I screwed him.'

She did not bother to keep her voice down. Baxter looked about nervously. There was no one behind. She was not stupid.

'I don't believe you.'

'Yes you do.'

Kay Bennet walked on and through the swing doors to the Central Lobby. Baxter stood, watched the doors close and then turned in search of Charles Bannister.

Rose told him there was a meeting going on. He detested Rose. She never failed to annoy him. She peered at him through her lenses, sniffed, and gave the impression that he was so insignificant that, overnight, she had forgotten who he was.

'Was he expecting you to come in?'

Passing Home Secretaries were not usually treated as feed reps on a morning when the milking parlour had been condemned by the health inspector.

'Mr Bannister does not have to expect me.'

He brushed by her warning and went in. And stopped.

The Prime Minister smiled, but only just and Bannister most certainly did not. The Bombardier welcomed him.

'Ah Dougal, come in, we were just discussing something which might interest you.'

Baxter closed the door. Most of the wind had spilled from his bombast and he sat in the corner chair.

'I didn't mean to interrupt.'

'I hate to think what you might do if you did.'

Bannister was tetchy. Baxter looked at him. He was tired. His eyes were red rimmed and he seemed hunched. The silence was almost embarrassing. The PM smiled at both.

'Nice speech Dougal. I must say I wonder how you expect to deliver but it was a change to get some headlines written by sympathetic sub-editors rather than bounty hunters. Don't you think?'

Of course he did. He said, 'Actually I had expected to show it you first, but I didn't finish working on it until about three in the morning. Charles saw it of course.'

The Bombardier sensed the tension and was amused.

'At three in the morning?'

Bannister in his innocence, shook his head.

'Not me I'm afraid. I was in bed.'

Baxter looked up. It was a sharp look, trying to read anything at all into Bannister's remark.

'You said I'd be, eh, interested?'

The PM looked at Bannister than at Dougal.

'Absolutely. Absolutely. Charles has just convinced me that we should stop this man Grishin. Not have his book. I know you'll think, oh dear, here we go again, decision one hundred and something, but there it is. No book.'

Baxter's surprise included his mouth staying open for a fraction too long.

'But I thought it was all agreed?'

Bannister coughed. He felt unwell. He coughed again, this time into his pocket handkerchief.

'We have, old man, just disagreed it.'

'Yes. Charles thinks that, on reflection mind you, he thinks we have nothing to gain from it and that we should hold back until we need it. Friend Grishin will be allowed to finish it, in fact I believe he has almost, but we will sit on it. What do you think?'

Baxter did not think at all. He had every reason to want the defector's book published. He had made a promise to the Director General of the Security Service that her Department would appear throughout the book and favourably so, especially since her time as DG.

Baxter did not like the idea of delayed publication. He suspected that Bannister's motive was the protection of Cameron and that the book would never see the light of day. He smiled at the Prime Minister.

'I think you're absolutely right. I was going to make a similar suggestion myself but I thought it was too late to do so.'

The PM got up and patted Dougal on the shoulder as he headed for the door.

'Never too late Dougal. Never too late. You of all people should know that.'

The door closed. Bannister was looking at his admiral.

'What the hell's going on Charles. Why wasn't I told about this?'

'You weren't to be found and anyway, I'm not sure it's any direct concern of yours.'

'You'll not protect him you know.'

'Protect who?'

'Come off it Charles, don't come the innocent with me. Little Miss Tartan Drawers isn't worth it.'

Bannister closed his eyes and counted very slowly.

'I'm very sorry old man, but would you mind leaving? I have some very important matters to attend to. Family matters.'

Dougal was standing by his desk.

'Cameron's a traitor. Having a daughter with big tits doesn't make any difference. He's still a traitor.'

Bannister swung in his chair to face Baxter.

'There are times old man, when you manage, without any sign of effort, to disgust me. I have to tell you Dougal, this is one of them.'

He closed his eyes again and waited, then heard the door close. Two minutes later there was a soft tap and it opened again. Rose put down his coffee, with two shortbreads.

'Problems?'

'An understatement Rose. A glorious understatement. Mr Baxter is, well . . .'

'Up to his old tricks?'

'And a couple of new ones.'

Bannister sipped at his coffee and eyed, but left, the shortbreads.

'And old Professor Cameron? How's he?'

The straightness of the question startled him.

'What makes you ask?'

'Well you seeing him and all that. I suppose you did didn't you? Last night I mean.'

'Yes. Just for a few moments. No, he's not too well.'

He hurried on, taking another sip for cover.

'And on top of it all, Polly's moving away. She claims she's getting a flat. God knows why.'

Rose beamed, or as best she could.

'Oh that's smashing. Really it is. I bet she's pleased.'

Bannister grimaced at the very thought.

'I'm not sure I am. I'll end up paying. You watch.'

'Course you will. And you won't mind. She'll be bright as ninepence in it. Where's it going to be?'

The telephone interrupted an action replay of the conversation in the park with Mary. It was for him. Henry Colvil. Rose was about to leave, but something made Bannister wave her to stay. He listened to Colvil for a few moments. The message was precise. Almost professionally curt. At the end of it Bannister said nothing, simply put down the receiver. He sat for a moment, maybe two. When he did speak it was a soft whisper of disbelief.

'My God Father James.'

What colour had been left had quite drained from Bannister's face. Rose put her hand on his arm which rested not a hand's reach from the silent telephone.

'You all right? Mr Bannister? You all right?'

His head turned slowly towards her, his eyes disbelieving.

'He's dead.'

'Who?'

'What?'

'Who? Who's dead?'

Bannister's gaze had not shifted. How could he be?

'Cameron of course.'

Her hand went to her mouth yet there was no melodrama in her concern.

'Oh my God no.'

Bannister nodded in confidence.

'He is, he's committed suicide.'

Forty-Seven

When he got there it was late afternoon. A policeman stood by the entrance to the drive and at first was reluctant to let him in. He asked him to wait and went to the front door. He spoke to whoever was inside and a couple of minutes later waved Bannister and his car through. Juliet Cameron was in the only room he had ever seen in the rambling Edwardian house. The curtains were drawn for it was already dusk and would soon be dark and the room was barely lit. The hearth was dead and a small curved reflector electric fire stood in place of the sweet smouldering logs of last night. Its two coiled strings of light gave little comfort to a room that was already in mourning.

She avoided his outstretched hands and made a gesture to an armchair though she made no attempt to sit herself. She looked as he might have expected her to look. Her hair was wispy and piled, the long skirt and matching jumper somewhat hastily and indifferently put together. Her eyes were cried out and to Bannister she was vulnerable and he wanted to take her in his arms. He sensed that he could not and thought that he understood.

'How are you?'

She looked at him, not believing the question.

'How am I? How am I supposed to be? Anyway what does that matter?'

'It matters. Of course it matters.'

She walked to the mantelpiece and searched behind some postcards and college invitations. She took a packet of cigarettes. It surprised him. When she lit one, it was with little style, clumsily, inhaling too much. They had, he imagined, been her father's. She put them back on the mantelpiece and took from the clock an envelope. A brown, slightly scuffed, foolscap envelope. She tapped it on her hand, almost losing a grip on the cigarette. Her voice was cold. Rehearsed.

'You knew didn't you? Why, for God's sake, didn't you tell me?'

She passed the envelope to him. It was unopened. It had his name on it.

'What's this?'

'He gave it to me. This morning. I went to see him in his rooms after I dropped you at the station. He gave it to me. He said to give it to you.'

Bannister did not open the envelope. Juliet did not ask him to. He put it in an inside pocket. She was trying to inhale and coughed. She threw the cigarette in the fireplace and watched it smoulder with an acrid ashtray odour. She turned again.

'You did know, didn't you?'

'Jules please. I did know what?'

'That this would happen.'

Bannister had never felt so miserable. How could he, even now, tell her what he did know. But now, he did not know, could never have believed that it would end this way.

'I swear I did not.'

She did not believe him.

'That's why you told me to stay wasn't it? Because you knew.'

He shook his head slowly, in agony, from side to side. His voice was low. Hopeless.

'Jules, I swear, I swear, I swear. I did not know.'

'Don't Jules me. You knew all right and you knew they were coming. Come on, just for once, be honest.'

Bannister looked really puzzled. She believed his look. He skipped back a sentence.

'Who was coming? Where? Who are they?'

'The two of them. Your heavies.'

'Jules, honestly, I don't know what you're talking about. Tell me.'

'Two men came this morning. Shortly after I left. They were with him for about half an hour.'

'Who were they?'

'You tell me.'

'Don't the police know?'

She turned away once more and tried another cigarette. This time the smoking was in earnest.

'They won't say a damn thing. But they were there. The head porter went up to see if he was all right and the door was locked.'

She drew heavily on the untipped cigarette and felt dizzy. She did not throw this one away.

'Go on.'

'He opened it with a master key.'

'And?'

'And? What d'you want, a countdown? An A to Z of his last seconds?'

'I wanted to know that's all.'

'You damned well did know didn't you?'

'I swear I didn't.'

'Then who told you?'

'What?'

'That he was dead. The whole thing's been kept quiet until this afternoon. But you must have known as soon as it happened. Who the hell told you?'

She rushed at him, tears streaming down her lovely cheeks and struck out at him. She hit him as hard as she could and then collapsed on the sofa, her body heaving with her misery. And he did not bleed.

He touched her shoulder wanting to hold her as he

had last night. She stiffened away. Her voice was harsh. It was a voice he had never before heard.

'Go. Just go. Just leave me. Just go back to your friends and tell them they've won.'

Forty-Eight

Bannister was back in his car and heading along the Hills Road into the city. He wanted to talk to the Master. He wanted to find out about the two men. He did not reach the city. The telephone burbled. It as Rose. He listened, made a couple of comments, looked at his watch and put down the telephone and told his driver to head back to London instead. The Prime Minister wanted him immediately. What sort of immediately he had asked Rose. The very immediately sort of immediately she had replied. She sounded very solemn. Bannister felt he was going to get the answers anyway.

It was eight o'clock before he reached Downing Street. Bannister was shown up to the private sitting-room in the flat. The Prime Minister was still smiling and for a brief moment Bannister wondered if he knew how to look serious without appearing stupid. The Cabinet Secretary was on the sofa and, much to Bannister's surprise, Henry Colvil was there. He sat primly, feet close together and delicately shod on the only upright seat in the room. The Bombardier did not offer Bannister a drink. The other two men were not

299

drinking. He suggested the sofa and wasted no time in formalities.

'A bad business Charles, a very bad business.'

Bannister sensed something which disturbed him. It was the informality of the meeting and, in particular, Henry's presence. If this were a matter of high Intelligence, where were the heads of the two Services? Why Henry Colvil and not CSIS? Or why not CSIS as well as Henry? He was about to ask, when the PM continued over his thoughts.

'This is an informal meeting Charles, because there are some very special circumstances.'

Colvil shifted his feet and the Cabinet Secretary, head back, stared at the ceiling. The PM thought this pause sufficient and continued.

'I gather you've been to Cambridge.'

Bannister's caution was obvious, his response carefully worded.

'Cameron, as you know, was once my tutor and so I immediately felt it my duty to call on his daughter, to see if there were anything I could do.'

'That's nice Charles, really nice.'

The smile was quite genuine. It slipped.

'And could you?'

Bannister lowered his head. He wore his guilt without shame. His voice was firm, but not matter of fact.

'No. She did not require my help.'

'What a pity. It's really nice to help friends in these sorts of situations.'

The Bombardier looked about him for agreement.

Colvil smiled sympathetically. The Cabinet Secretary was still looking at the ceiling. Suddenly the Prime Minister stood up. Bannister started to, but stayed when the PM stretched out his hand.

'No stay where you are Charles. I've got a couple of things to attend to downstairs. Anyway, or any road up, as old Wigton keeps saying to me, any road up, it's perhaps best if I'm not here for the rest of the conversation. But I tell you what, I'd be grateful if you'd just pop into the Cabinet Room before you go. Couple of things I'd like to clear up before the morning. Okay?'

And with that, his two-buttoned blue suit still buttoned and uncreased, the Bombardier was gone and the door quietly closed behind him.

The Cabinet Secretary's head came down from its heavenwards gazing and Henry Colvil got up and peered at a not very nice Corot owned by the State and then more approvingly at a very good Linfield water-colour, a recent and personal purchase by the Prime Minister's wife. The Cabinet Secretary observed Bannister for a few seconds and was about to say something when Bannister burst in anger.

'My God Father James you two. What the hell's gone on?'

The Cabinet Secretary nodded to Henry who had turned, somewhat startled by his brother-in-law's outburst. The Cabinet Secretary nodded once more.

'Colvil? Would you please?'

Henry took a deep breath and returned to his seat across the room. He placed his hands in his lap and gripped one thumb with the other and drew another breath.

'I'm afraid Charles we have sad tidings brought us and difficult duties to perform.'

'Oh do get on with it Henry. We know the poor man's dead. I want to know why.'

'Because he took his life dear heart. Quite conclusively.'

'You mean your heavies did so.'

The Cabinet Secretary grunted.

'What you mean? His heavies?'

'Shortly before the porter found Cameron, a couple of thugs from the Vauxhall embankment branch of Exit paid him a visit. According to his daughter, they were there for about half an hour. Within an hour at the most, he'd killed himself.'

Colvil was fidgeting with his fingers. He really was not enjoying this.

'Not so Charles. They actually, ah, found your friend. He was, to paraphrase an unfortunate expression, dead on their arrival.'

'That's not what I heard.'

'Alas, your informant was misinformed.'

'I see.'

The Cabinet Secretary was back on the ceiling. His voice was that of a man thinking aloud.

'I fear you do not see all.'

Bannister stood, his hands on his hips beneath his jacket, his back to both men. His sigh was long and painful.

302

'You're right, I don't. But frankly, what I do see I do not like one little bit.'

He turned and looked first at the Secretary, then at his brother-in-law. There was no response. He tried once more.

'Cameron committed suicide. Is there any doubt about that?'

The Cabinet Secretary shook his head. Charles went on in his best and assured courtroom manner.

'Right. Well let us assume, for the purpose of this discussion, that he did. The next question must be why. I saw him last night and clearly he was in some terrible state. But not necessarily in such a state that he would willingly, willingly, take his own life. So gentlemen, why did he?'

Bannister went back to his seat.

The Secretary looked at Colvil. Colvil looked at the Secretary. The Secretary looked at Bannister.

'You could tell us.'

'Me? I'm asking you.'

'So you are. We believe, the Prime Minister believes, that you have the answer to your own question.'

Bannister was on his feet again. He turned, turned once more and sat down. His agitation disturbed Henry whose voice was gentle, patient and sorrowful when he spoke.

'You see dear heart, it would appear that your involvement is beyond that of friend and former student.'

'What the hell are you talking about?

Colvil found the atmosphere and matter distasteful. He said so.

'Charles this is difficult, especially because of our relationship. But I am afraid that I am here because of our relationship. This, for the moment, is a private matter and with your co-operation we shall be able to keep it so.'

Bannister started to ask a question, perhaps voice his confusion. The Cabinet Secretary raised a forbidding hand.

'Just a moment. Hear what Colvil has to say.'

He waved in Henry's direction without looking at him. Henry pressed the insides of his shoes together and sat very upright, his hands once more across his round stomach.

'Charles my dear, this is the picture now presented. You have known all along about Viktor Grishin's book, yes?'

Bannister nodded, he did not see what could be unfolded in this curious bazaar of secrecy and suspicion peddled by the Secretary and Colvil. The latter gave a small cough and continued.

'You knew that Cameron was known to be an enemy of the State, a person who had on many occasions attempted, sometimes successfully, to turn otherwise loyal subjects of His Majesty and on four or five occasions, loyal subjects of the present monarch. Yes?'

Another nod.

'And my dear, you were privy to the most important

piece of Intelligence. You knew that Cameron was about to be exposed.'

'We all did.'

'So we did Charles, but none other than yourself had direct contact with Cameron in spite of my warnings that these meetings would be quite unwise.'

'Meetings which you later encouraged.'

The Cabinet Secretary grunted.

'Mistake.'

Colvil was looking at his hands. He looked up and straight into his brother-in-law's drawn and strained eyes.

'It would appear, Charles, that you were the only person who was in a position to know what was about to happen, who had direct contact with him and who, and my dear it pains me to say this, was so emotionally involved with, ah, his, ah, his daughter that you found it beyond your conscience to keep this national secret.'

Bannister's eyes were bleeding his emotion and confusion before them. His voice was a stammer of the confidence and outrage of a few moments earlier.

'My God Father James Henry, what on earth are you suggesting?'

Colvil looked back at his hands. He did not answer. The Cabinet Secretary did.

'You warned him that he was about to be arrested.'

Bannister's head was back, not in studied concentration but in agony.

'Are you both off your chumps?'

The Secretary continued and the knife slipped beneath Bannister's ribs.

'Or you told his daughter, who in turn told her father.'

Bannister thumped the side of the chair with his fist.

'I will not have this. What nonsense is this? What in blast's name is going on? How and why should I have told Juliet Cameron anything at all?'

The Cabinet Secretary twisted the knife, but not all the way. That was for later.

'You stayed last night with her.'

The Party Chairman did not physically slump in the chair. His mind did. He spoke quietly with no reason to convince two friends, now interrogators, now accusers.

'I stayed because she was upset. I stayed bcause she wanted to talk. She is a friend. I stay with my friends.'

He did not look to his brother-in-law. Colvil did not look up from his hands. The Cabinet Secretary had no pity, he wished there to be no chance of compromise. His speech was from the chancel steps.

'We know exactly what time you arriv-ed. We know exactly what time you left. And before you raise points of order, may I say we know exactly the other times of your goings and comings, including those of your visits to Miss Bennet. You give some impression that perhaps there is no health in you.'

Bannister clapped his hands to his sides.

'All right. This really has gone far enough. I think the Prime Minister should be here.'

'That Bannister would be less than wise. The Prime Minister is aware of all the details and the implications.'

It came out as implic-ae-si-ons. The Cabinet Secretary was in full ecclesiastical flow.

'He will, as he indicated, wish to have words before you leave. We do rather hope the matter may be concluded with the least fuss. But I am afraid there is one other item to be ticked from our agenda tonight.'

The other man sat down again. He would hear them out and then talk to the Bombardier and remove himself from this Kafkaesque nightmare.

'Go on.'

Colvil looked away. The Secretary gave the final twist to his blade of accusations.

'As you know, one of our concerns was the unfinished business of that period.'

Bannister's raised eyebrow was genuine. 'What period?' The Secretary indulged him. 'The period when Cameron was particularly active. He recruited a number of people who went on to higher things. Hence our concerns. We have, of course cleared the names of the majority on his dirty little list. One or two escap-ed. Maybe three or four.'

Bannister stared.

'So?'

Colvil picked up the thread and with sad heart wound it about Bannister's.

'You see Charles, we have believed there must be greater motive for your decision to warn Cameron.'

'But I did not.'

Colvil continued, his ears truly closed to Bannister's cries for belief.

'You once suggested that all we had to do was check his supervision list. It was an almost impossible task. But we did, eventually, and we eliminated everyone, except one.'

'Who?'

Colvil was back with his hands.

'I'm afraid, dear heart, you.'

Bannister was silent. He fixed his eyes on the ridiculous pattern made by scuffings on the newly laid carpet. He remembered again days playing with lead soldiers and model cars in the library of a great uncle where all the patterns of Axminster represented streets and forts. He could not will himself to such innocence.

'You honestly believe that Cameron turned me? Do you?'

The silence of the other two would be unbroken unless provoked.

'Henry? Do you?'

Colvil looked up. He saw before him naïvety but no traitor.

'No, Charles, I do not. But I am afraid the evidence is damning enough. There is no John the Baptist.'

Forty-Nine

The Prime Minister was at his centre seat in the Cabinet Room. He was going through his boxes. He liked his boxes. He saw things in one collection which others saw only in fragments. That was what being Prime Minister was about. The power of knowing. He wanted to stay being Prime Minister. He tapped the chair to his right. It was the Cabinet Secretary's but they were alone.

'Now Charles, what are we going to do?'

'You do understand that this is all nonsense don't you?'

'Not nonsense Charles. Maybe all the ends are not properly tied but at least we've got a knot haven't we?'

Bannister was in a daze. He had lost his mark of the mandarin. He needed another answer. Needed to know.

'What do you believe?'

'Is that important?'

'Of course it is. I am not and I have never been disloyal.'

The Prime Minister's face became the face of a solemn pastor. The face of the Pastor Davidson all the years ago warning the young lad that missing but one Sunday at chapel was the first relaxed grip on his faith and that it would not do.

'Never disloyal? You have been disloyal to Mary'

'But . . .'

'But nothing Charles. If you can be disloyal to someone whom you love and whom you took before God, then anything is possible. You do see my point don't you?'

Bannister looked away. He saw the Prime Minister's point, but how could he argue that it was nothing to do with what they were going through. He sighed. Resignedly.

'What would you have me do?'

The PM leaned forward. He patted Bannister on the knee.

'That's the ticket. Action. That's what we need. Now what we must avoid is this thing blowing up into something that'll disturb us. Right?'

'Yes.'

'Good. In the past there's sometimes been criticism when we haven't acted quickly enough. Well, we're not going to have that happen this time are we?'

Bannister was expressionless.

'Go on.'

'Well, I think, Charles, that the stress you're under is not good for you. It's not good for Mary and of course . . .'

'It's not good for Government.'

'Right. So, well I know it's a bit of a joke in some ways, but, well, I think it would be better if you decided to spend more time with Mary and Polly. Take it easy and things.'

Bannister shifted in his chair. Looked around the Cabinet Room, at the boxes, at the power.

'There is no question of this going any further?'

'Of course not. You have given me your word Charles. That is enough for me.'

'And it would not be good for the Party if it went further especially in public.'

The Prime Minister's pastoral mask was back in place.

'You're a wise old bird Charles. Very wise. Very wise. After all, that's why we're all here isn't it?'

'To keep the Party in power.'

'No Charles, no. We're all here because the Party *is* in power. Now off you go, write me a nice letter and we'll fix a party or something to say thank you and things and, who knows, when all this has gone away, I'm sure you'll be back in here. You'd like that wouldn't you?'

Charles Bannister got up. Wanted so much to explain sense. Could not. There was no one to listen. Incongruously he found himself murmuring his thanks and went to the door. He looked back, probably because he was about to say something, even in encouragement to the Bombardier. But he did not.

The Prime Minister was back at his papers. Another agenda.

Fifty

Bannister sat in the rear of the Jaguar. It had been
waiting. His driver had held open the back passenger
door at the policeman's nod moments before Charles
Bannister stepped from Number 10. They drove
through the barrier at the end of Downing Street and
he hardly noticed the curious peerings of a straggle of
late night and muffled tourists wondering if this were
the Prime Minister. None recognized him and the
policeman smiled at the driver rather than her passenger.

Instead of turning left into the House, the Jaguar
swept on and by. It was best to go home. Bannister
glanced up at the Jewel Tower and vaguely remembered
Colvil's dull reference. There were many memories.
Things left in his mind for explanation. Like the envelope. The envelope? He had forgotten it. But not the
look of anguish on Juliet Cameron's face. He reached
to his inside pocket. Still there. It was brown, foolscap.
Scuffed at the edges. He saw it now as he had seen it
before where it rested face down at high table. Now
he read the spiky fist of the dead man. Charles Bannister MA QC MP.

Bannister ran his index finger beneath the flap and
removed a single sheet of college notepaper. The same
handwriting. No date. No greeting. No farewell.

Just four names.

A Selected List of Fiction Available from Mandarin

While every effort is made to keep prices low, it is sometimes necessary to increase prices at short notice. Mandarin Paperbacks reserves the right to show new retail prices on covers which may differ from those previously advertised in the text or elsewhere.

The prices shown below were correct at the time of going to press.

☐	7493 1352 8	**The Queen and I**	Sue Townsend	£4.99
☐	7493 0540 1	**The Liar**	Stephen Fry	£4.99
☐	7493 1132 0	**Arrivals and Departures**	Lesley Thomas	£4.99
☐	7493 0381 6	**Loves and Journeys of Revolving Jones**	Leslie Thomas	£4.99
☐	7493 0942 3	**Silence of the Lambs**	Thomas Harris	£4.99
☐	7493 0946 6	**The Godfather**	Mario Puzo	£4.99
☐	7493 1561 X	**Fear of Flying**	Erica Jong	£4.99
☐	7493 1221 1	**The Power of One**	Bryce Courtney	£4.99
☐	7493 0576 2	**Tandia**	Bryce Courtney	£5.99
☐	7493 0563 0	**Kill the Lights**	Simon Williams	£4.99
☐	7493 1319 6	**Air and Angels**	Susan Hill	£4.99
☐	7493 1477 X	**The Name of the Rose**	Umberto Eco	£4.99
☐	7493 0896 6	**The Stand-in**	Deborah Moggach	£4.99
☐	7493 0581 9	**Daddy's Girls**	Zoe Fairbairns	£4.99

All these books are available at your bookshop or newsagent, or can be ordered direct from the address below. Just tick the titles you want and fill in the form below.

Cash Sales Department, PO Box 5, Rushden, Northants NN10 6YX.
Fax: 0933 410321 : Phone 0933 410511.

Please send cheque, payable to 'Reed Book Services Ltd.', or postal order for purchase price quoted and allow the following for postage and packing:

£1.00 for the first book, 50p for the second; **FREE POSTAGE AND PACKING FOR THREE BOOKS OR MORE PER ORDER.**

NAME (Block letters) ....

ADDRESS ....

....

☐ I enclose my remittance for ....

☐ I wish to pay by Access/Visa Card Number ☐☐☐☐☐☐☐☐☐☐☐☐☐☐☐☐

Expiry Date ☐☐☐☐

Signature ....

Please quote our reference: MAND